AT THE EDGE OF THE FOREST

Other Works by Dennis L. McKiernan

The Black Foxes Series
Shadowtrap (formerly titled *Caverns of Socrates*)
Shadowprey (coming soon)

The Faery Series
Once Upon a Winter's Night
Once Upon a Summer Day
Once Upon an Autumn Eve
Once Upon a Spring Morn
Once Upon a Dreadful Time

The Mithgar Series
The Dragonstone
Voyage of the Fox Rider

HEL'S CRUCIBLE DUOLOGY
Book 1: *Into the Forge*
Book 2: *Into the Fire*

Dragondoom
Stolen Crown (coming soon)
Tales of Mithgar (a story collection)
The Vulgmaster (a graphic novel)
The Iron Tower (omnibus edition)
The Silver Call (omnibus edition)
The Eye of the Hunter
Silver Wolf, Black Falcon
City of Jade
Red Slippers: More Tales of Mithgar (a story collection)

AT THE EDGE OF THE FOREST

A NOVEL BY

DENNIS L. MCKIERNAN

THORNWALL PRESS
TUCSON

Thornwall Press
2115 N Wentworth Rd
Tucson, AZ 85749-9741

First print edition, November 2012

To my very own thunderbolt
MLee

Acknowledgments

My deepest thanks to Justin Raley for his advice on pistols, especially on the handling and operation of the Smith and Wesson M&P .40.

And to the Tanque Wordies, whose feedback was most valuable in the crafting of this tale.

And to my wife, who is my first reader, and who kept me in this twenty-first century throughout the work.

And a special thanks to Michael Stackpole, fellow author and good friend who helped me with the ins and outs of e-book formatting.

Too, I would like to extend that special thanks to Frankie Robertson (also a fellow author and good friend) for pointing the way to the uploading of e-books onto Amazon, Barnes and Noble, and other sites.

"There are more things in Heaven and Earth, Horatio,
than are dreamt of in your philosophy."

Hamlet: Act I, Scene V
William Shakespeare

AT THE EDGE OF THE FOREST

1

"Dammit, dammit, dammit," muttered Raven, struggling to stay upright, the leather soles of her loafers slipping and sliding on the tall, wet grass of the steep slope as she made her way upward. "Sissy, Sissy, why do you have to live way out here beyond the edge of nowhere? And why can't you have a driveway like a normal person? Not that it would have done me much good."

As a foot skidded again, Raven gritted through clenched teeth, "Take off your shoes, you idiot." She paused in her struggle and looked around for a place to sit, finding nothing but the knee-high, water-slick thick green growth gleaming in the few shafts of sunlight that had managed to pierce through rifts in the clouds. Sighing, the slender woman tried to balance on her right foot as she reached for the left, and—whoops!—suddenly she found herself sliding facedown back toward the muddy two-track where her Porsche had been abandoned.

Clawing at the grass, she ground to a stop with her skirt rucked up around her waist, and her entire front side—face, arms, blouse, skirt, panties, and legs—drenched.

Raven rolled onto her back, the movement causing her to slide downslope another foot or so, as she shouted, "Elizabeth Ryelle Conway, I'm going to strangle you!" Her threat flew out across the wide meadow below and came rebounding from the tree-covered slope beyond: *strangle you . . . angle you . . . you. . . .*

Raven laughed as her other side soaked up the wet. "In for a penny, in for a pound."

She pushed a now-damp stray lock of her namesake raven-black hair out of her eyes and sat up and pulled off her shoes. She got to her feet, her bare-soled footing somewhat secure as she carefully straightened her sodden clothing and then cautiously turned about. "Now where's my purse?" After a moment: "Ah."

With wary steps, she fetched the large bag and looped the strap over her head to her opposite shoulder, then looked upslope at the isolated dwelling—a modest, one-storey log house with a steeply pitched roof sitting on a patch of level ground at the edge of the forest rising beyond, the peak of the house not as tall as the looming elms behind. "Cathleens Haven," it was called, named after some long-ago ancestral grandmother who had built it back in the day, with squared-off logs notched to fit and the flooring inside pegged to the joists below, just as were pinned the joists and rafters above. In fact, there was not a nail anywhere in the structure—just oak pegs.

Raven frowned and once again looked for the path that she knew was somewhere on this blasted slope, but the tall wet growth concealed it. Her gaze settled upon the nearby small rivulet of water dashing down the hillside. "Maybe I should walk up the stream. Surely it's not as slick as the grass. And it's not as if it'll get me any wetter, even if I fall on my face again."

She edged over to the brooklet and stepped in—*Oh, chill!*—and found the pebbled footing narrow but firm. Up she trudged, now and again coming to small ledges or runs of small ledges, where the flow babbled across and down. "Singing your way to the sea, eh?" asked Raven, receiving but a burble in reply. Up these steps she went, the shelves no hindrance to her long shapely legs.

Finally she reached the level patch of ground and turned toward the house and strode past a pool fed by the stream flowing from an outcropping some hundred or so feet farther upslope and just barely inside the woods. Her mother had once said the house had been built up here because of that unfailing spring, and in the quiet Raven could hear the small fall of water that served as a shower, should she want one.

It had been some seventeen years since she last was here. She had been ten at the time, and Sissy eight. Back then, Grandmother Meredith owned the house, back when she still had all her mental faculties. Raven and Sissy had delighted in hearing her tell stories of the forest and the land and of this place—some scary, others comical . . . or sad—and Raven and Sissy would laugh or cry or fearfully hold on to each other. It was Grandmother Meredith more than any other soul who had caused Raven to follow a path that had ultimately led her to become a writer. Sissy, on the other hand, was an artist—watercolors mostly; she loved their transparency—which fit her reclusive lifestyle. Poor

Sissy, she and her mysterious illness, one that finally had sent her to live away from civilization.

Raven glanced to her left, where the beginnings of the pathway started its meander down the hill. "Ah, there you are, you sneaky snake. It's all your fault you know. Why couldn't you just stay out in the open?"

Nearing the house, with its broad covered porch running across the front and down each side, "Sissy!" shouted Raven. "It's Rave. I've come to strangle you."

Raven stepped up onto the veranda and past the rocking chairs and to the door.

She knocked.

No answer.

She knocked again.

Still no answer.

Raven lifted the wooden latch and pushed open the door and called out to her sister. "Elizabeth? Sissy? Are you here? I need some clothes. Mine got all wet on your blasted grass slope."

Raven stepped inside; the place was just as she remembered: the great room with its stone fireplace, brass andirons and fireplace tools and rocker and sofa and side chair and an oriental rug off to the right, and the small kitchen with its pantry and counter and cabinets and sink and wood-fired bronze cook-stove with its copper flu to the left, along with the oak table and chairs. Straight ahead, a short hallway led toward the back and the other three rooms. And just to the right of the hallway, a short ladder led up to a loft for storage and sleeping space for overflow guests, not that there had been any in the past few years. Raven sighed, for candles and lanterns sat here and there, meaning that the place, as expected, still had no electricity. It was like stepping back in time a hundred years.

"Sissy?"

Still no reply.

What if something has happened?

Swiftly, Raven moved down the hall to the big bedroom. But for the bed, chest, bureau, wardrobe, and small vanity, it was empty, though Sissy's comb and brush and silver compact lay on the dressing table.

The little bedroom had been turned into a studio, with Sissy's table and sketch pads and pigments and brushes and such. But Sissy wasn't there.

She wasn't in the tub room, either, though her toothbrush was in the glass on the sink counter, along with a comb and a partly used bottle of the kind of shampoo Sissy favored: Drama Clean.

Raven stepped out the back door. An insect of some sort lazily buzzed past, now that the rain was gone.

Raven looked at the small tool shed, with its cords of wood stacked alongside. *Oh, God forbid.* She rushed to the door and jerked it open, but it was empty of her sister, and only axes and wedges and augers and spades and rakes and hoes and buckets and other such tools met her gaze, tools out of another age, tools of dark rugged bronze and gold gleaming brass, verdigris-tinged copper, and dull gray tin, some with smooth wooden handles of hickory and ash and oak. Grandmother Meredith always said this land needed such tools, and she worked her gardens and split her wood and maintained her living with them.

Tools, but no Sissy.

Sighing in relief and closing the door and moving

back, Raven looked up the hillside toward the edge of the woods. *The Deep Dark Forest, we used to call it, and when we played in there we stayed close to the edge.*

An occasional bird flitted from branch to branch, but there was no sign of Sissy.

You are probably up there looking for mushrooms, or greens, or for something to mix with your pigments.

Raven turned and went back inside and fetched a towel from the tub room. She paused momentarily to look at the simple copper tub as she contemplated taking a bath. "Ah, but that would mean lugging hot water from the stove in the kitchen. Of course I could take a cold shower up at the falls, but . . ." Raven moved to the bedroom and stripped out of her clothes and dried herself. Then she rummaged through the wardrobe and settled on a light summer dress. *The blue will go with my eyes.*

She hung her wet garments on the line out back as the sun continued to break through the overcast.

Now to raid the pantry.

Time passed, and Raven went down the now-found pathway and to the Porsche, stuck in the ditch where she had skidded off the lane. *Poor baby. Maybe tomorrow, or perhaps the day after, the ground will be dry enough for me to drive you out.* She fetched her athletic bag, packed with her kit and a few clothes and a pair of Skechers, and headed back up to the cabin.

When evening drew on, munching another PowerBar, she lit a candle in its glass and stepped to the front porch. *Sissy, Sissy, where are you? Didn't you get my letter?*

"Sissy!" she called, and then again: "Sissy!"

But for the crickets and the echoes of her own voice, only silence greeted her.

2

Raven tossed and turned throughout the night, the laced rope webbing under the feather mattress creaking with every move. *Lost? No, not Sissy. But what if she's lying injured somewhere in the woods? What if some monster has taken her to do who knows what? Serial killers. Serial rapists. Maybe like that father and son—where was it? Montana?—mountain men out to get themselves a woman to wive the son. There's an uncommon phrase: to wive. Ah, the writer's mind. Then again Sissy might be off at a gallery. Maybe there's a show. She's certainly famous enough. No, no. Not a gallery. Sissy can't be anywhere but here. The DNA tests . . .*

Ridden with anxiety, still Raven managed restless fits of sleep interrupted with moments of lucidity. And as she shifted and the support ropes groaned below: *Well this is a nest that can't keep a secret. It'll shout to the world if anyone makes love in its feathery folds. Did Sissy and I ever hear it, when we were up in the loft? Straighten up, Raven. Get your thoughts back to finding Sissy.*

Raven rolled onto her back. *As unlikely as it might be, if Sissy went somewhere other than the woods, chances are she would have taken her purse.*

Raven got out of bed and lit a candle and began rifling through the drawers, all the time feeling guilty, feeling like a burglar invading someone's privacy. At last, buried deep in the chest at the foot of the bed, there it was. She pulled the drawstring top open. *Empty, as I thought it would be. She never . . . she can't go anywhere. Oh, God, how so very lonely she must be.*

Eyes brimming, Raven put everything back the way it was, then blew out the candle and slipped once more into bed.

First thing tomorrow. Tomorrow. First thing tomorrow, Sissy, I'll find you.

Raven fell back to sleep, only to later emerge with worry and then fall asleep again . . . and again . . . and again. . . .

Dawn finally came, and Raven groaned out of bed and shuffled to the kitchen and glanced at the stove, one that long ago had come all the way from Europe. *I can't keep eating PowerBars. Time to cook something.* She found wood shavings and kindling and matches and soon had a good blaze going in the bronze wood-fired range. She rummaged about in the pantry and got out the powdered milk and powdered eggs—*yuck!*—and cut a pair of slices off the cured bacon slab. She discovered a home-baked loaf of bread, a few days old. *Sissy was here to do this.* Soon the bacon was sizzling in the copper skillet, and the coffee was brewing, made with spring water and Folgers. Raven looked at the plastic container of coffee and then at the pantry, and she wondered who brought groceries to Sissy. *It's not like she can run to town and do her own shopping. She can't abide it—oh, perhaps for a very short while, but not for any extended time. Besides, she doesn't even have a car, and Benton is nine miles away. And the nearest neighbor?* Raven frowned, trying to remember. Bacon popped, and she shook her head and gave up.

Ah, my gourmet breakfast: reconstituted milk, reconstituted eggs, pan-toasted bread, and salt-cured bacon. Oh well, at least it'll be filling.

The coffee, though, she savored.

She saved the bacon grease in a small glass jar with a plastic lid and washed the skillet and plate and silver utensils in the sink, one that once upon a time had been Dutch tole, but too many dishes over too many years had left most of it raw tin. The kitchen itself had running water; thanks to the spring and copper plumbing, it was about the only "modern" luxury in the place. That and a flush toilet in the tub room. *All because some grandmother way back when wanted to stop carrying buckets. And a more recent grandmother got tired of trips to the outhouse in the dead of winter and put in a leach field on the slope and in the meadow beyond. No wonder the grass is so tall and green. But other luxuries? No electricity. No central air. No land line. And . . .*

Raven opened her handbag and fished around for her cell phone. She turned it on. . . . *And no signal. Crap! More bars in more places, my ass. Where else but at Sissy's in the whole good ol' You Ess of Aye would there be no damn signal? I should have known. No phone. No Internet. No e-mail.*

Enough of your carping, Raven. Get with the program.

Dressed in jeans and a tee, and wearing her

Skechers, Raven walked out to the shed and took up one of the spare axe handles. *Hmm . . . Not much of a bo stick, but as my sensei once said, 'take what you can and use it.'* She set off upslope toward the forest. There was only one regular path up to the woods—the one that led to the source of the spring. Just inside the tree line loomed the stone outcropping. Up on the side was the collecting basin, there where the copper plumbing pipes were buried in the wall and ran underground, all below the frost line. The basin itself almost never froze, the flow ever running. A small waterfall tumbled out from an overflow channel. *Cold showers. Lord, how cold.* Raven followed the steep path up to the top of the outcrop. There she paused and surveyed the woodland and sighed. *Hopeless? I mean, here you stand at the edge of the forest—and it's, what? forty, fifty miles by forty, fifty—and you expect to find your sister in sixteen hundred to twenty-five hundred square miles, when she might not even be in there? Yeah, Raven, but maybe she is and she might be close to home.*

She took a firm grip on her axe handle. *Okay, mountain men, rapists, killers, here I come.*

And she stepped into the woods.

Raven carefully swept back and forth, looking for tracks, overturned stones, broken branches, mashed-down undergrowth—she was, after all, a writer, and in her suspense novels she had researched these things. But academic knowledge was no substitute for the real thing, and she grew increasingly frustrated and desperate, when she couldn't turn up a single piece of evidence that Sissy had ever been in here. *The rain. The goddamned rain. Washed everything away. But even had it not rained . . .*

Now and then she would stop and call out, "Sissy!" and listen for a response. But all she heard were buzzing insects and chirping birds and the scuttling of small furtive animals through the undergrowth and the sharp barking of squirrels overhead.

The forest itself smelled like greenery and overturned wet dead leaves and—*Oh, look. Mushrooms. Morels*—Raven picked several of the spongelike fungi and slipped them into—*Rats! No sack, no purse, nothing to*—she pulled up the hem of her tee and rolled the mushrooms into the cloth, then stuffed the "corners" of the roll back under her belt.

On she went, sweeping back and forth, calling for Sissy, receiving no answers. And as she crossed a small glade, suddenly she knew that someone or something or some *thing* was watching her.

Oh, crap!

Gripping her axe-handle bo stick and trying to disguise the fact that she was aware of eyes on her, slowly she moved as if searching for tracks, snatching sidelong glances around, all the while praying that her martial arts training would be enough to take on whatever she might face.

Nothing. . . .
Nothing. . . .
Nothing. . . .

There! In the brush! Her heart leapt into her throat, even as a doe burst away from her, crashing through the undergrowth. And then it was gone.

Oh, thank God, it was just a deer and not a mountain man, rapist, serial killer, or worse. Still trembling, she looked at the club in her hand and muttered, "We need a bigger boat." Then laughed.

On she searched and called, yet she could not shake the feeling that she was being watched. *More deer? A wolf? A bear? —Oh, don't let it be a bear.* But she did not see who or what it might be, if anything other than nerves.

She continued till the sun stood overhead. *This is hopeless. I need more help.* She smiled. *I need a bigger boat.*

She worked her way back toward the house, and as she neared the edge of the woodland, she heard a car horn sounding a signal: three beeps; three beeps; three beeps.

What the hell? Sissy? I'm gonna strangle you! Right after I give you a hug.

She burst from the forest and ran toward the house.

3

Raven ran past the south face of the house and to the edge of the slope leading down to the meadow. *A red pickup truck. Someone coming up, carrying grocery bags. A man. Gray-haired.*

Raven shifted her axe-handle to a defensive position.

She could see the man was perhaps in his early sixties. He was whistling a soft tune as he trudged up the path, his gaze on the footway. As he neared the top, he looked up and paused. "No need for that big club, miss . . . miss." He frowned, and then said, "Raven?"

Raven plucked at a memory and asked, "Who are—?

"It's me, Aikens. Robert Aikens. I used to—"

"—Work for Grandmother Meredith," finished Raven, lowering the club.

Aikens, a lean man, standing perhaps five eight or nine, continued on up the path and onto the flat, saying, "I thought I recognized that black, black hair and those blue, blue eyes. Sapphires, I used to call them."

Raven smiled. "I remember, Mr. Aikens. What are you—? I mean, it's obvious what you are doing, but—"

"The Trust hired me to look after Miss Elizabeth," said Robert, strolling toward the house, "her being out here and all alone in her, well, you know, in her condition. She gives me a list, and I do whatever shopping is necessary, including fetching groceries and the mail. I deal with the house when it needs fixin' and other general handyman stuff . . . layin' in wood and such. —Oh, and I take her art into Benton and see that it gets to her agent."

They walked onto the front porch and Raven opened the door and stepped aside to allow Aikens to pass.

"Miss Elizabeth?" he called as he moved toward the kitchen table.

"Oh, Mr. Aikens," said Raven, leaning her axe handle against a chair. "She's not here and I can't find her."

"Probably up in the woods, lookin' for—"

"No, I don't think so. Otherwise she'd be home by now." Raven unrolled the fold in her tee and put the handful of morels on the counter.

Aikens set down the groceries, and turned and looked at Raven. "How long has she been gone?"

"All I know is she wasn't in the house when I arrived—just before lunchtime yesterday. Like you, I thought she might be up in the forest, looking for mushrooms perhaps. She didn't come home last night, and I searched all this morning, but the woods are so vast, and I couldn't cover but a tiny"—Raven shook her head, tears brimming—"I called and called, but she didn't . . . didn't . . . " Raven's words sank to silence.

"That doesn't sound too good," said Aikens, frowning.

Raven took a deep breath and brushed at her eyes. "When did you last see her?"

"Let me think. Just four days back. She looked fine. We had tea and a nice long chat, like we do most every time I come."

He hitched up his pants, and Raven saw Aikens was wearing a rope for a belt.

Oh, crap. I'm an idiot. I brought my purse into the house, with its lipstick and compact and nail clippers and keys and my damned cell phone, and ball-point pens and— ah, me, I was running on autopilot!

"I'll have to go into Benton and report this," said Robert. "Maybe get some help, though I don't know of any who might come, the woods being what they are."

"I need to go with you," said Raven. "I'll call her agent. Dr. Jameson, too, since he called me. One of them might know where she is."

"That's unlikely," said Robert, "her being out here with no phone and all. But, yes, we'll run right in. There's a bit more groceries to bring up, and the mail. Then we'll go."

Raven grabbed her purse and down they went to the pickup. She threw the bag into the cab, and then helped carry groceries. And as Robert dropped the mail onto the table, she saw her own letter to Sissy in the pile.

Swiftly, they unloaded the sacks, putting the goods—beans, flour, potatoes, another slab of cured bacon, boxes of cereal and mixes and such, onto the pantry shelves.

As they turned to go, Raven said, "Wait. Let's make certain we don't overlook something in the letters that could possibly give us a clue as to where she might be," and she began shuffling through the stack, setting aside offers of car insurance and low mortgages and the like.

"Here's one from Gray Thompson, her agent."

Aikens pulled a drawer and handed Raven a silver paring knife.

She sliced open the envelope and extracted the letter inside. "Hmm . . . It's an offer of $120,000 from a private collector for the oil painting *Michael Defending Mary*."

Robert whistled. "Whew. I liked that one, too, but $120,000?"

"Mmm . . ." replied Raven, abstractedly, still reading through the letter. She then refolded it and put it back in the envelope. "Rats. Nothing in there to help us."

She opened two more of the personal letters—one from an art admirer; another from a gallery in California, asking her to come out for a show—neither of which was of any aid.

"Oh," said Robert, "speaking of your Dr. Jameson, Miss Elizabeth did get a letter last week from him. Something about you taking a test, too."

Raven nodded. "He's doing a complete DNA workup on me as well. He wants to make certain whether or not I have the same problem as Sissy."

"Wonderful thing, science" said Robert. "I've been mailing in those weekly cheek swabs and drop-of-blood patches for her. I sure hope they can help Miss Elizabeth."

"Wait a moment," said Raven, "here's one for me. From the Trust. I wonder what this is all about." Raven opened the envelope only to find another envelope inside. "Looks like an invitation. Who would . . . ?" Raven opened the second envelope. "Hmm . . . It's from Cousin Millicent. She's getting married. Photo of her and her beloved." She glanced at the image—a stocky dark-haired man and a tall thin brown-haired woman—and then handed the announcement and picture to Robert. As he gave them a cursory once-over and then stuffed them back in the envelope, Raven shuffled through the rest of the mail. Mostly flyers and a few magazines that someone, probably Robert, had pulled all the staples from. "Well, that's it. There's nothing in the mail to show where Sissy might be."

"Let's go then," said Aikens.

As they got back to the truck, Robert drew the rope belt from his pants and in its place he slipped a leather one with a big shiny buckle. He retrieved a pocket knife and his billfold and a handful of change, and then hopped in the truck and turned the keys dangling from the ignition.

They both buckled in and Aikens K-turned and headed back down the two-track dividing the wide grassy meadow and toward Benton. As they drove by Raven's abandoned car, "That your Porch?"

"Porch?"

Aikens laughed and said, "Car. I like to call 'em that. So, is that your Porch?"

Oh, Porsche. Raven smiled. "Yeah. I goosed it when I shouldn't have."

"Well, we'll drag it out of there when we come back," said Robert.

They rode a moment without speaking, then Raven asked, "How was Sissy when last you saw her?"

"Fine. Just fine. That girl, I swear, in the two years she's been here, she's been getting lovelier by the day. If I were thirty, forty years younger, I'd've come courting.

Hell, even twenty years younger."

Raven laughed. "She always was the beauty in the family, with her ash-blond hair and grey eyes."

Robert nodded, and after a moment said, "Well, she's done gone plumb—what's the word?—ethereal, yeah, that's it: ethereal."

Raven sighed and said, "It was hard to keep a boyfriend when she was around. I threatened to strangle her so many times, it became a family joke. But I'd give up a year's worth of dates—not that I've had that many—if we could just find her."

"Actually, Miss Raven, were I a young man to come courting and if I were to find the two of you here, well, I tell you, it'd be difficult to make a choice." Redness crept up Robert's throat and suffused his face.

"Why, thank you, Mr. Aikens," said Raven, smiling. "That's the nicest thing anyone has said to me in a while."

"You got no boyfriend?"

"I had one, but he found a stripper more to his liking."

"Dang fool," muttered Aikens.

Aikens' pickup slewed round a curve in the lane to turn southwesterly. The land on the left containing Hunters Wood continued to rise until the uplift became a high, sheer bluff that ran to the horizon and beyond. The meadow continued to widen, now more than a mile across between the grassy slopes that led up the forest on both sides. Now and then a small thicket grew in the broad reach below, but in the main only grass covered the bowl of the valley; it was as if the woodland confined itself to the heights on both sides above. Some five miles south of Cathleens Haven they exited the valley and were no longer on Trust land. They turned left onto a narrow asphalt road and again ran southward toward Benton, a small farming town of some five thousand souls, catering to the orchard-grove industry, apples mostly, though peaches were making inroads.

"There's the sheriff's substation just ahead on the left," said Aikens, "where we can report Miss Elizabeth missing."

"Is there Wi-Fi in town?"

"Yup. At the one and only Starbucks. We might be little but we ain't too backwards."

"Damn, I should have thought to bring my laptop. It's back in the, um, 'Porch.'"

They both laughed, and then sobered, as Aikens pulled into the parking lot at the substation.

Inside, they met Deputy Mills, and reported Sissy missing.

Mills, a short man in his forties, balding and somewhat paunchy, swiveled in his chair and said, "Hmm. Her. She's an odd one, your sister. Yelled at me to stay down at the foot of the slope, when I dropped by for a visit and to give her the number to call should she need to, being way out there like she is."

"She has a medical condition," said Raven.

"Besides," said Aikens, "she has no phone."

"Not even a cell?" asked Mills.

"There's no blasted service out there," said Raven.

"You sure she hasn't just run away?" asked Mills.

"She isn't some disgruntled teenager," said Raven.

"You don't have to be a teen to run away," said

Mills. "Just 'disgruntled,' to use your word. Plenty folks run away, and without a phone and bein' sick and all, well, she might have just taken it in her head to—"

"How could she?" asked Raven. "No phone, no car, an affliction. I mean, she can't even ride more than a few minutes without becoming deathly ill. Just getting to Cathleens Haven was a terrible ordeal for her. And before you ask, she doesn't have a horse."

"Yeah, well, even so—" began Mills, but Raven cut him off.

"My sister is a world-renowned artist. If I have to, I'll go to Governor Alston, and—"

Mills threw out a hand. "Whoa, little missy. Don't get your panties tied in a knot. I'll go out and see what I can do."

Raven, seething over "little missy" and "panties in a knot," bit her tongue to keep from cursing at this five-foot-two Chauvinist pot-bellied pig.

"You'll need men," said Aikens.

Raven added, "And dogs."

"Hunters Wood?" snorted Mills. "Dogs won't go in there. Most men neither."

Raven was astonished. "What?"

"I said—"

"I heard you," snapped Raven. "What's the matter with you people. My sister is missing and—"

Mills shook his head. "There's just something about those woods. Strange things have happened. It's like they're jinxed or something. Dogs, men, women, it don't matter—"

Raven had a momentary flashback to this morning when she sensed someone or something watching her as she looked for Sissy. But she mentally shoved that thought aside and said, "My sister and I used to play in the forest. And Grandmother Meredith and my mother picked mushrooms and herbs and greens and wild onions in the woods. I searched in there myself today. And if an old woman and her daughter and granddaughters can go in—"

"Well then you must lead charmed lives," said Mills.

"Charmed lives my ass," said Raven. But before she could say more, Mills stopped her.

"Look, Miss Conway, I'll round up some men, and we'll see what we can see, but I don't promise anything. I mean, those woods are practically endless. They're what, two, three thousand square miles of forest? Someone lost in there, well . . ."

"My sister's not lost," said Raven. "She has an infallible sense of direction."

"Maybe not if she's ill," said Mills. "Otherwise she'd be home."

"Are you discounting the fact that some monster might have grabbed her—a serial rapist or killer or worse?"

Mills jerked back as if slapped, or as if this were something he hadn't considered. "Here? In Benton? Hell, we haven't had nothing more than a fistfight in I don't know how long. Sure, there's Halloween to contend with, and Homecoming pranks. And a few migrant troubles, but it's not pickin' time yet. But a serial killer or such; ain't gonna happen."

"Listen you—" Raven stopped and took a deep breath, as if counting to ten. "Have it your way. Just get some men and come to Cathleens Haven. I'll help."

"Me, too," said Robert.

"First thing in the morning," said Mills.

"There's daylight left today," said Raven.

"But at the moment I have no men, and if you want a sizable search party, well, then . . ."

"All right, Deputy. All right." Raven spun on her heel and slammed out the door.

"She's a firecracker, that one," said Mills.

As he followed Raven, Aikens turned and said, "She's also the acting head of Hunters Trust."

"What?" asked Mills, startled. "Holy shit." The deputy jumped to his feet and grabbed his hat and rushed out after.

4

"What'd you tell him?" asked Raven, as she watched Deputy Mills rush to his car and speed off.

"Oh, just that you were the acting head of Hunters Trust," said Aikens, grinning wickedly.

"Ah, that. Robert, I have virtually nothing to do with the Trust. It's mostly administered by Allenby. Me, I sign a paper now and again, but little else."

"Mills doesn't know that," said Aikens, another wicked smile crossing his features.

Raven laughed. "Whatever works." Then her mood shifted. "Ah, God, I feel like I should be out there hunting for Sissy, not in here chivvying a deputy sheriff to get off his behind and help."

"You know those woods are endless, Miss Raven," said Robert, "and we'll need an army to search even the forest near the house."

"Yes, I know . . . I know." Raven took a deep breath and slowly let it out, and looked across the street at a McDonalds. "I'm not really hungry, but I also know I need to keep my energy up. It's been seventeen years since I was last here; Big Macs are all right, but is there a place in this mighty metropolis where we can get a decent steak and a glass of good wine?"

Aikens grinned. "Well, the vast town of Benton runs more to burgers and beer, but Fred's has a fairly good steak, and I know she keeps a couple of bottles of cabernet on hand."

"Fred is a woman?"

"Yeah."

"And . . . ?"

"How about I let her explain it," said Robert, grinning. "Her place is just outside of town, not that it's very far."

"Then let's have at it, Mr. Aikens. I'll call Sissy's agent on the way."

As they got in the truck Raven flipped open her cell phone and keyed it on. As soon as it found a signal, it sounded a run of beeps. "Missed Calls. My agent, and Mr. Allenby, and Cousin Millicent. But first I'm going to call Sissy's agent."

Raven punched in Gray Thompson's private number.

After a moment. "Gray, this is Raven Conway. . . ."

"Yes, I'm fine. . . ."

"Look, Gray, I hate to interrupt, but Sissy's missing and I was wondering—"

"That's right, missing. . . ."

"We don't know. . . ."

"Look, I was wondering if you—"

"No, no, there's no need to come. I've notified the sheriff and there'll be a search tomorrow morning. . . ."

"He has to round up a search party, that's why. . . ."

"I know, but this is a small town and—"

"FBI? Not yet. Tomorrow for certain if we don't find her after we—"

"Yes, yes, I'll let you know. . . ."

"That's right. . . ."

"All right. All right. Look, I've got other calls to make. . . ."

"You, too, Grey. Bye-bye."

She snapped her phone shut and muttered, "Damn."

Aikens said, "I take it he didn't know anything?"

Raven nodded glumly.

"We knew it was a long shot," said Robert.

"Yeah, we knew, but still I was hoping."

Robert swung the pickup into a small lot at a converted farmhouse. A sign hanging from eyehooks on the porch declared, "Fred's." Somehow, that simple sign lightened Raven's mood.

"I'll listen to the voice mail after we eat, and make any calls after that."

As they got out and started for the door to Fred's, Raven asked, "Is there a library with Internet terminals in town? I want to look at something, and, drat it, I didn't bring my laptop."

"As a matter of fact, there is," said Robert. "Kids without computers go there to study, but since school's out for the summer, you might actually be able to wrangle a little time."

"Fredericka Johanna Olsen, honey, but everybody calls me Fred. It was either Fred or John or Jo, and since my brother already was the Joe in the family, I chose Fred." The tall, robust, heavy-boned woman laughed, her wide smile filled with large teeth. She had pale blond hair and pale blue eyes and looked to be in her fifties. "Swedish father, German mother: Papa gave me his last name, but Mama insisted on bestowing me with the first two."

She poured Raven a glass of cabernet from a bottle of Markham Reserve.

Aikens had a beer, a Negra Modelo, a Mexican brew. Raven had noted the Tecate logo on one of the windows and one for Corona on another, and she guessed that Fred stocked these imports for when the migrant pickers came.

Raven and Robert each ordered a New York strip, baked potato, and a garden salad.

"And how would you like that done, sweetie?"

"Medium rare," said Raven.

Fred turned to Aikens. "And you, baby cakes?"

"Just warm it up."

"The steak, or me?"

Raven nearly snarfed her wine.

Robert turned a shade red.

Fred laughed and went toward the kitchen.

Raven smiled at Aikens. "She seems nice. You two have a thing?"

Robert ducked his head and shyly said, "Yeah."

"Good for you," said Raven, grinning.

"We've been seeing each other for some time now."

Raven looked around. Something niggled at the edge of her mind, but she couldn't quite catch it. There was just one other customer, and he was at one of the tables in a separate room of the farmhouse. Whatever lunch crowd there might have been was now gone, and Raven could hear the muted clank of dishes being washed somewhere remote, as well as kitchen sounds.

Fred returned, bearing two garden salads and a bottle of ranch dressing for Robert and two cruets for Raven—

vinegar and oil. She paused and said, "You probably don't remember, but your mama used to bring you and your sister here for ice cream."

Raven said, "That's it! I knew this place somehow looked familiar."

Fred laughed. "Having a déjà vu moment?"

"Exactly so."

"You two were pretty little things, and you've grown up to be pretty as well. And I'm sorry to hear about your sister, Elizabeth, sick as she is and all."

"She's not really sick," said Robert. "More like allergic to modern civilization. But in truth, she's quite healthy, now that she's here at Cathleen's, and, uh—" Aikens' words jerked to a halt.

Fred frowned at him, and Raven said, "She's missing."

"What?"

"Sissy is missing."

"What happened?"

"We don't know," said Raven, fighting to keep her mood positive, fighting back tears.

She quickly sketched out the events of the past two days, and when she was done, Fred said, "Pah! Deputy Mills ain't worth the tin in his badge. When the supper crowd comes, I'll ask some of the men to be there first thing in the morning to help."

"Oh, that would be wonderful," said Raven, hope flaring in her chest.

"You're right," said Raven. "Fred grills a mean steak."

"Yup," agreed Aikens. "Bakes a mean potato, too."

They were walking into the Andrew Carnegie Library of Benton—one of the many Andrew Carnegie libraries scattered across the nation, all of them named after the steel baron philanthropist of the late eighteen, early nineteen hundreds.

Soon Raven was sitting before a terminal.

"What are we here for?" asked Robert.

"If we're going to search the woods near Cathleens Haven, then I want to get some satellite photos of the forest in the vicinity of the house and some maps of the terrain."

Raven powered up the terminal and clicked on the browser icon. When it came up, she keyed in maps.google.com. A moment later, "What th—?"

"What is it, Miss Raven?" asked Aikens.

"There's no satellite view of Hunters Wood. The whole area: it's scrambled."

5

"Scrambled?" asked Aikens.

"Blurred out," said Raven, "as if it is a secure location. Here, let me try this." She clicked on "terrain" and gritted, "Rats, that's blocked, too." She shifted to map view, and roads appeared, but the forest was merely a blank, with no roads, not even two-tracks, going through. "All of Hunters Trust land is blocked: not only the forest but Cathleens Haven, too."

Aikens rubbed his jaw. "Who can do that?"

"The government is all I know. They ask Google and Yahoo and others to blur and blank critical areas."

"Hunters Trust is a critical area?"

Raven turned up her hands. "I suppose. And since the house is on Trust land . . . Do you know anything at all about this?"

"Not even a clue," said Robert. "Let me see if Mildred knows." Aikens stepped away and spoke to the librarian. When he returned, he said, "Mildred says it's always been that way. Kids try to Google the place and get the same results."

"Maybe Allenby will know why," said Raven.

She sighed and shut down the terminal. "So much for that idea."

Raven sat a moment in thought, then she looked at Aikens and said, "Robert, while I make some calls, I'd like you drive to the drugstore and pick up whatever first aid gear you can think of."

Robert cocked an eyebrow, and Raven said, "When we find Sissy, we don't know what we might need—bandages, splints, disinfectant, and the like. Oh, and get a litter, too, just in case we need one, though I hope to God we don't. You know Sissy's sensitivities, so take care to avoid them. Charge them to the Trust."

Aikens, nodded and said, "That's good thinking."

Raven smiled. "I'll be on a bench out front."

"There're better ones across the street in the park," said Robert. "Wooden, not concrete like here."

"All right," said Raven. She stood and they went outside. As Aikens headed for his pickup and Raven started for the park, Aikens stopped and said, "Oh, and I'll run to Miller's Garage and get a chain."

"Chain?"

"Yeah. To pull your Porch out of the ditch."

"Ah," said Raven, and she crossed the street and into the park in the city square.

She took a bench by the lion fountain, water tumbling from its mouth. Tears brimmed in remembrance, for as children, she and Sissy had waded in the pool and had climbed onto the back of the stone-still beast. Taking a deep breath, she composed herself, and then punched in Dr. Jameson's number.

Carol answered and Raven identified herself. "Oh, Miss Conway. I was just about to call. Dr. Jameson wishes to speak with you. If you'll hold a moment, I'll see—"

"Before you do, Carol, let me ask you: have you heard from Elizabeth? A letter . . . or a call from a friend of hers?"

"Why, no. But maybe the doctor has. Is there anything wrong?"

"Well, I can't seem to find her at her house, and—"

"But we've been getting her swabs and patches," said Carol.

"When did you get the last one?" Raven glanced in the direction that Aikens had driven and felt guilty for asking.

"It came just this morning," said Carol. Raven could hear computer keys clicking. "Let me see. Oh, here. It's dated the twenty-first."

The day Robert had last seen her. It still doesn't clear him, but— Oh, come on, Raven, get your suspense writer's mind out of that track. Robert just isn't the type. He's worked for the family for most of his life. He blushes when he makes even the slightest compliment. And he is shy about being with Fred, but it's clear he loves her.

Raven jerked her mind back to the business at hand and said, "You say you were just about to call me?"

"Yes. Dr. Jameson wants to speak with you. I'll see if he is free."

Moments later Jameson's confident baritone came on line. "Raven?"

"Dr. Jameson."

"How are you, and what's this about Elizabeth?"

"I'm fine, and I can't seem to find her."

"Is she lost?"

Quickly, Raven filled Jameson in on the events of

the past two days. Then she asked, "Does this have anything to do with Sissy's DNA?"

"I don't see how it could, but then again I don't actually know what effect the changes I'm tracking might lead to."

"And my DNA?"

"That's why I was calling. I have your results. Unlike your sister, at the moment you do not have any mitochondrial drift, whereas Elizabeth's appears to be accelerating. And your own primary DNA looks solid, also unlike hers, which seems to have some of the so-called junk DNA changing. There might be a small shift in your own, but I won't know until we take time-related samples. I'll need you to send me cheek swabs and blood patches in about six months. Can you do that?"

"I will," said Raven. "Anything else?"

"Yes. Your telomeres, like Elizabeth's, appear to be able to completely regenerate. But I'll need to track them over time as well, to make certain."

"Telomeres? I seem to recall something, but—"

"They are the terminal chromosomes at the ends of DNA strands. Think of them as caps. Normally, each time a cell divides during regeneration, a little bit of the cap is lost. But in your case and Elizabeth's, it looks as if nothing whatsoever is lost, and that bodes well for longevity, but not so well for susceptibility to cancer. But in reviewing your family's medical history, there's a complete lack of occurrences of cancer. It's not anything I would worry about, were I you."

Easy for you to say. "I won't, Doctor. Is that it?"

"Not quite," said Jameson. "I'm not sure how to tell you this, so I'll come straight out: although you and

Elizabeth have the same mother, you do not have the same father."

"What?" Raven was stunned.

"You do not have the same father," repeated Jameson.

"I heard what you said, but I just, I don't, I—"

Jameson remained quiet.

Finally, Raven said, "Are you certain? I mean, if Sissy's DNA is changing—"

"No, that's not the case," said Jameson. "I have the results of the samples taken three years ago and at that time there was no noticeable change in her primary DNA, though the mitochondrial drift had begun. I am sorry if this has come as a shock, but there is no question: you two have different fathers. Same mother, different fathers."

Mother, what did you do? —Crap, Raven, you know what she did, just not why . . . or who.

"I'm going to have to take this in, Doctor."

"I understand," Jameson replied.

Raven watched as two teen boys skateboarded past. "Is there anything else?"

"I'll have Carol send you a reminder when we need those swabs and patches," said Jameson. "There's always a chance that your own drift might be latent. But if I were you I wouldn't be concerned."

Again, easy for you to say.

"Oh," added Jameson. "Let me know when you find Elizabeth. I'd rather keep on top of these changes we are seeing in her. Hers is a unique case."

Is that all she is to you: a unique case, and am I your control subject?

"And so I need you to send me samples. We might even have you come to the facility for a complete workup."

"I will send you the swabs and patches, Doctor. Now if you'll excuse me."

"Take care, Raven. And I hope you find Elizabeth soon."

Raven clicked her phone shut. *Changes he's seeing in her? What changes has he seen, other than in her DNA? What is he not telling me? Crap! I should have asked. "She's been getting lovelier by the day." That's what Robert said. Is she changing physically, too?* Raven sighed. *There's no way to know till we find her. And my mother, what happened and why? I'm going to have to talk to Grandmother Meredith and see what she knows . . . that is, if she remembers anything at all.*

Raven flipped open her phone and hit a call-memory number.

"Traynor and Traynor," answered Billi, her voice carrying a British accent.

"Billi, this is Raven. Is Eli in?"

Billi slipped back into her normal southern Alabama voice. "Oh, hey, Raven. Yeah, he's in."

Moments later, "Raven. I've been trying to get you. The publication party is all set, and your book tour is—"

"Eli, hold on. There might be a hitch it the plans. Elizabeth is missing."

Raven spent the next few minutes bringing Elias Traynor up to speed.

"Oh, my," said Eli. "I hope she's all right. And listen, sweetie, I'll handle everything at this end. I mean, the rollout for *Candlelight* isn't for three months. And

Gamin is more than a year away; that is, they haven't even finished the script revisions, much less started casting. And I—oh, shit, Raven, here I am talking business, and Elizabeth is missing. Is there anything I can do to help?"

"No, Eli, but thanks for asking. Look, I'll keep you informed, but if push comes to shove, my sister takes priority over editors, publishers, booksellers, fans, producers and directors, and anyone else who might come along."

"I understand, Raven, and I'll handle them. Now, go out there and find Sissy, okay?"

"Okay," said Raven, and she snapped her phone shut.

Raven sat a moment, and the boys on skateboards returned and circled the perimeter of the lion's pool, the wheels click-clacking over the sidewalk seams. After one complete loop, they headed back in the direction they had first come.

One more call, and I'm through for the day. Cousin Millicent can wait.

As she punched in the number, Robert's truck appeared, coming down the street toward the park, an auto wrecker—Miller's Towing—followed.

"Allenby, Allenby, and Cartwright," said Sarah.

"Sarah, this is Raven. I believe George is trying to reach me."

"Ah, yes, Miss Conway, just a moment, please."

Aikens honked, and Raven held up a hand, her index finger upraised. Then she pointed at the phone at her ear.

"Raven," said George Allenby, another baritone.

"George, you called."

"Ah, yes. It's just to tell you that you are now the official head of Hunters Trust. Seven years have passed, you see, and now your mother, Avelaine, is declared—"

"—Legally dead," Raven finished for him.

"Er, yes."

Memories flooded Raven's mind. *Your mother's plane is missing, Miss Conway, Miss Conway. . . .*

Twenty-year-old Raven had gasped in dismay. Eighteen-year-old Elizabeth had burst into tears.

Being the eldest, Miss Raven, you will become the acting head of Hunters Trust, when you turn twenty-one next year. In the interim, it will be administered by Allenby, Allenby, and Cartwright, by George Allenby, specifically. Your sister, Elizabeth, will succeed should anything—God forbid—happen to you. Should your mother be found alive, she will, of course, resume her rightful place as Trustee.

Raven and Elizabeth had continued hoping, but as the years passed, that hope seemed further away. Even so, faith had remained that one day Mother would return. And Raven had refused to take a significant part in the running of the Trust, wanting no part in it, for that would be to admit the unthinkable. "Mother will come back," she and Sissy assured one another. But now the legal acceptance of Avelaine's death dealt one more blow to that slim likelihood. Raven's seven years of denial had finally come home to roost.

Raven groaned. "First Mother and now Sissy."

"What? What did you say, Raven?" asked Allenby.

"Sissy is missing."

"Elizabeth? Your sister?"

"Yes."

For the seventh time that day, Raven explained, and when she finished . . .

"I'll send helicopters and people to help with the search, but first I'll notify the FBI," said Allenby. "If she's been kidnapped, the sooner we involve them, the better the chance we have to save her life."

As if she'd been kicked in the gut, Allenby's words slammed into Raven. *Oh, God. He's right. I write about these things, but they should not happen to—*

"George, do you really think that Sissy's been kidnapped?"

"Raven, like your mother and her mother and the mothers before her, you control a vast fortune, now," said Allenby, as if that explained all. "Watch out for yourself as well. I'll send some security."

"I did not think of—"

"I know you didn't, but if Elizabeth is missing—"

"I understand," said Raven, glancing at Robert waiting in his truck. "I have someone with me now."

"Good. Make certain that you are never alone. Have you kept up your martial arts training? You know, I had both you and Elizabeth engage in self-defense courses for just this sort of thing."

"Yes, though not as intensely as I should."

"Well, practice those techniques. We don't want you to disappear, too. And stay in contact."

"All right, I will. But there's no cell phone signal at Cathleens Haven, could you—?"

Allenby said, "Taylor will be bringing some papers for you to sign tomorrow. I'll add a satellite phone to the package. Will that do?"

"Yes. That'll do. Thank you, George."

"Have you any questions, Raven?"

"No. No ques— Oh, wait. I tried to Google a satellite photo of Hunters Wood. It's blurred out. All the Trust land is blocked. And so is the terrain map. Do you know why?"

"We pay a lot of money to keep it that way," said Allenby.

"Pay? Why?"

"It's a term of the Trust." Allenby's voice took on a cadence of a document: "There shall be neither survey nor exploration of Hunters Wood. And but for emergencies, it shall always remain private from the public, excepting the women of the lineage of Cathleen Hunter." Allenby added, "We take that to include satellite photos, though perhaps agencies of governments around the world take no note of it. Still, we try.

"What about the United States Government?" asked Raven.

"We think no one will violate the continuation of the President's private Executive Order Seventeen. After all, the Trust is a major campaign contributor to the candidates most likely to win, and they in return grant us this favor."

"Do you mean the President of the United States signed an executive order pertaining to Hunters Wood?"

"I do."

Wow! Raven frowned and then said, "Is there a history of the Trust, something I can use to familiarize myself with the whys and wherefores of all the particulars of the Trust documents themselves being worded the way they are?"

"I'll have Taylor bring a copy of what we have. Anything else?"

"Not that I can think of, George. —Oh, wait! Did you know that Sissy and I do not have the same father?"

"What?"

"Dr. Jameson ran my DNA, too. He says that we have the same mother, but not the same father."

"No, I did not know that. But who your father was is of no consequence in the governance of the Trust. It's matrilineal."

"Do you know who she might have been seeing in either my case or Sissy's?"

"No, I don't. All I know is that Kevin Conway was your mother's husband when you were born as well as when your sister was. As to whether he is your biological father, or Elizabeth's for that matter, I cannot say. Perhaps your grandmother knows."

"Grandmother Meredith."

"Yes. She is the only surviving grandparent on both sides, and she was living at Cathleens Haven during that time."

Oh, my, and here Grandmother Meredith is not always lucid.

"If you wish to pursue this, Raven, we can try to find a relative of Kevin Conway and take a DNA sample and compare it to yours and Elizabeth's DNA."

Do I really want to know?

"But as far as I remember, Kevin didn't have any brothers or sisters," said Allenby.

"Let me think about that, George," said Raven.

"All right. But if you decide to do so, let me know."

"I will, and thank you."

"By the way, Raven, did you get Millicent's wedding invitation?"

"Yes, I did. But why did it come through the Trust?"

"You were due to leave Germany, and none of us knew of your plans. So, Millicent asked me to forward it to you when I discovered where you were headed. After your call from Seattle last week, I sent it to your ultimate destination: Cathleens Haven"

"Mystery explained, then," said Raven.

"Not much of a mystery," said George. "Regardless, is there anything else, Raven?"

"No, I believe that's it. But should I think of something, I'll call."

"Well, then, you be very careful, Raven. Keep those you trust around you. By tomorrow, you won't have to worry."

"Thank you."

Raven clicked her phone shut and stood and walked to Robert's pickup.

If I were writing this as a story, Aikens would be a prime suspect. He had and has trusted access to the house, and he has the means, and, if money is the object, the motive. Hell, even if money is not the object—"She's been getting lovelier by the day"—he still could have hidden Sissy away somewhere, to do who knows what to her. He could even still have been sending in the cheek swabs and the blood patches. He could have read my letter and known I was coming, and just "happened" to have shown up bringing groceries. Is there anything wrong with this picture? Yes, dammit, there is. We've known him to be true to the family. He's genuinely worried about Sissy. And he's honest and open and old-

fashioned shy, and it's clear that Fred is his woman.
Raven climbed into the passenger side.
"Any news?" asked Aikens.

6

"Mi-mito . . . mito what?"

"Drift," said Raven. "Mitochondrial drift. Mitochondria has a kind of cellular DNA that only comes from a mother to her children."

"Male and female, both?"

"Yep."

"Nothing from the father?"

"Nope."

"Huah. I'll take your word for that. But what's this about a drift?"

"Jameson really doesn't know why her primary DNA and mitochondrial DNA is changing, just that it is. He thinks it is at the root of Sissy's sensitivities."

"Oh."

They rode without speaking for a moment, and then Aikens asked, "Can he fix her? Fix the DNA, that is?"

"I don't know. Stop the drift? Reverse it? Maybe, maybe not."

Again they rode in silence, but finally Raven said, "I see you brought Miller's Towing."

"Yeah, Jack said we'd probably ruin your Porch if we throw the chain around the wrong part and jerk on it with Betsy."

"Betsy?"

Aikens reached forward and patted the dash. "Betsy. Named her after an older woman I once knew when I was a teen. She initiated me into, well, you know." Aikens flushed, his face turning quite red.

"So, you knew her in the biblical sense," said Raven, smiling.

Robert merely nodded. But after a moment he said, "I've had several Betsys throughout the years—trucks I mean, not women. Fords, mostly, 'cause when I was a tad, I read or someone claimed Dillinger—or someone—said he liked Fords to rob banks because they had pep, and the Betsy I knew—the woman, I mean— well she had—"

"Pep?" said Raven.

"Yup."

Raven laughed, but added, "I believe it was Clyde Barrows of the Bonnie and Clyde fame who praised Fords; I think he said that they had all other cars 'skinned.' Of course, Clyde stole most of his Fords, V8s if I remember my research. I hope you aren't following in his footsteps."

"Oh, no, not me, Miss Raven. I never stole a penny or even a stick of chewing gum in my life, much less a truck."

They turned onto the two-track toward Cathleens Haven, Miller's Towing right behind.

When Jack Miller winched the Porsche from the ditch: "Uh-oh." He pointed at a large, jagged rock, and a dangling wheel. "You've definitely broken something in your suspension system."

Raven groaned. "Oh, crap!"

Jack got down on the ground and looked under the front end. "Looks like a busted lower control arm, Miss Conway. I'll haul her in and give her a good looking over and see what else might be wrong."

"Damn! Stranded," said Raven.

"Betsy and I will make certain that don't happen, Miss Raven," said Robert. "I'll run out here every day, and if you need something, we'll go get it."

"I got no parts for Porsches," said Jack, "but I can send to the city for what might be needed, or even tow it there in worst case."

"Thank you, Jack," said Raven.

Jack hoisted the vehicle, and then slowly headed back to town. As his tail-lights disappeared, Robert and Raven carried the aluminum-framed litter and first-aid supplies up to the house. Robert had also brought two bags of ice, and he threw them into a very old-fashioned wooden ice box, with its brass handle and hinges and tin-box interior. "They won't last long, so enjoy them while you can. I'll start bringing blocks next week, when the ice-house opens. They don't crank it up till just ahead of picking; there's no need before then. Anyway, you'll be able to keep eggs and such."

"Oh, that'll be nice, Robert," said Raven. "And now that we have cubes, how about I make us some lemonade?"

"Why, thank you, ma'am. I do believe that would be just the thing."

A few minutes later, with cool glasses in hand, she plopped down on the couch and Aikens took a chair.

"I feel like a yo-yo," said Raven.

"Jerked around, eh?"

"Yes. But the good news is, we'll have help tomorrow. Allenby is sending some people to aid with the search." *Oh, my, why did I let that out? If Robert is somehow mixed up in this— Shut up, Raven. Just shut up about Robert. He's not some mild and meek monster.*

Aikens nodded and said, "I just hope Deputy Mills can round up a passel, too."

They sat without speaking for a while. And then Robert said, "I do think she's all right. Maybe lost, but all right."

"Oh, no, she's not lost, Robert. I mean, Sissy has had an infallible sense of direction for as long as I can remember. It's as if she has a compass in her head, rather like she can sense the magnetic— Oh, wait. Ever since she started having trouble, power lines have really thrown her off, as if they are interfering with her sense of—" Raven looked about. "Ah, me, maybe *that's* why she's gotten healthy ever since she came here; there is no electricity in this place. It sounds stupid, I know, but maybe electricity somehow makes her sick. I'll have to tell this to Dr. Jameson and see what he says."

Robert nodded. "You could be right, Miss Raven. But does that explain the mito, er, mito—"

"Mitochondrial drift? I have no idea. Probably not, since Jameson said the drift has continued since she has been here. On the other hand, maybe the drift is what is causing her sensitivity to electricity . . . or as you said to Fred, her allergy to modern civilization."

Aikens shook his head. "Well, I don't know what it is about electricity that would bother her, and it doesn't explain why she might be lost. I mean, there ain't a power line within miles of this place, and certainly none running through Hunters Wood or anywhere on Trust land."

Raven frowned. "I don't know what it might be about electricity either, but I have some friends who might be able to tell us. When I get my car back, I'll drive to a point where I get a cell-phone signal and ask them."

"Shoot, I'll take you to do that, but first I think we have to find Miss Elizabeth," said Aikens. "I hate to think of her out there lost and all alone."

Tears welled in Raven's eyes. "Me, too."

Promising to be back early tomorrow and bringing searchers with him, Aikens left at the onset of dusk, and Raven stood on the veranda and watched his lights disappear to the south. Although Allenby had said to have some friends stay with her, she still couldn't trust anyone, not even Robert, and she felt guilty for thinking that he might have something to do with Sissy's disappearance. Even so . . .

Besides, help is on the way. So I'll only be alone tonight. But right now I'm bushed and grubby. Time for a shower.

Carrying her axe handle and a small basket filled with soap and a bottle of shampoo and a washcloth, and wearing one of Sissy's thin robes, Raven trudged up to the overflow waterfall. She slipped out of her Skechers and doffed her robe and set them on the large boulder beside the basket. Then she grabbed up the soap and washcloth and, taking a deep breath, she stepped onto the slab under the flow. *Lordy, oh lordy, Miss Raven, is this ever cold.* Raven jumped out and laughed, envisioning Butterfly McQueen saying, "I don't know nothin' 'bout birthin' babies," and adding, "and nothin' about takin' icy-cold showers."

As she stepped in again, *This would cool the ardor of anyone.*

She backed out and soaped herself up and set aside the washcloth and plunged back in to rinse off. Finally, out she jumped to take up the shampoo, but she suddenly felt as if someone were watching her . . . again . . . just like this morning. Her first instinct was to grab her robe, but instead she took up the axe handle bo stick and peered into the darkening woodland, Raven could see no one, nothing, no *thing.*

"Sissy?" she called. "Sissy?"

No one answered.

"Sissy, is that you?"

The splash of the waterfall overrode any faint sounds that might be coming from the forest.

But if Sissy called out, I would hear it.

For long, tense moments she watched and listened.

Maybe it's just my imagination.

Finally, she shouted into the darkness, "Whoever you are, take a good look."

Then she snatched up the shampoo and quickly lathered and rinsed her hair, all the while watching the woodland, except for ducking briefly back into the fall.

Without drying off, she grabbed up her things and went downhill and into the tub room. There she dried off, and slipped into her panties and a sleeping tee. And carrying the axe handle and a comb, she moved to the front porch and sat down in one of the rockers and combed her long, wet raven-black hair, waiting for it to dry.

Long moments passed and long moments more, as the weary day washed over her.

She fell asleep in the chair.

Wha—? What's that? Raven floundered awake—"Ow!"—with a crick in her neck.

A nearly full moon shown down on the meadow below, its bright light washing away the stars and illuminating the field with clarity.

I heard something; I know I did.

Yet only the songs of crickets and chorus of small peeping frogs penetrated the night.

But then pealed a high-pitched *Aroo! Aroo!*

A foxhound horn? What the heck? Is someone hunting in the woods?

Raven stood and stepped to the railing. *It sounded as if it were somewhere off to the right.*

Aroo! Aroo! It drew closer.

Suddenly a large stag with a great rack of antlers burst from the woodland and fled downhill and across the meadow. *Oh, how magnificent!*

Raven's heart raced with the buck.

Moments later a thunder of hooves hammered after the running deer.

Hunters on horses? But I don't see any. Where the hell are they? Raven shaded her eyes from the moonlight, but still she saw no horses or riders.

The stag, its raised white tail a beacon, fled onward, to vanish into the trees beyond.

The hoof beats followed.

Aroo! Aroo! The horn belled again.

The sounds slowly faded as the stag and its unseen pursuers raced into the west, up the far side of the valley and over the crest and beyond . . . until they finally fell to silence, a faint horn cry the last.

Sweet mother, what have I just seen and heard, or rather not seen, but heard? Ghosts? Spirits? Phantoms? And what does this have to do with Hunters Wood?

7

Raven stood in the moonlight and listened for long moments, but the running stag and pounding hoof beats and crying horn had vanished. Finally, she gave up and went to bed and attempted sleep, but it eluded her. Her thoughts were a tangle of doubts and speculations and conjectures and questions regarding her mother and Sissy and ghosts and Dr. Jameson's words and Allenby's warning and the possibility that Robert Aikens might be a kidnapper or worse. And something skated along the edge of her mind, but she couldn't quite catch it. She finally got to her feet and fired up the wood stove and made herself a cup of chamomile tea and drank it down and dragged back to bed, but even that didn't help. And it was nearly dawn when she finally, blissfully fell into complete sleep. But less than a full hour passed before a distant but growing *wop-wop-wop* of helicopter rotors split the silence of Cathleens Haven and dragged Raven awake. And as choppers came up the valley, for the second day in a row Raven groaned out of bed and plodded wearily to a front window.

She got there in time to see three military craft settle down in the meadow, and armed soldiers in combat fatigues begin pouring out.

Holy crap! An invasion.

Something caught her peripheral vision, and looking leftward she saw a black van roaring up the lane.

Mother of mercy! What has Allenby done?

Raven spun on her heel and raced toward the bedroom. Quickly she shucked her sleeping tee and hooked into a bra and slid into a pair of jeans. She pulled on a black shirt advertising Guinness and stepped sideways to the vanity. *Oh, man, my hair is a disaster.* She tried pulling a comb through and managed to loosen a few tangles, but gave up and grabbed a scrunchie and collected the mess into a ponytail.

As she made a quick stab at her teeth with a toothbrush, someone—*bam, bam!*—pounded on the door.

"Just a sec!" she yelled, as she found her Skechers.

Bam-bam!

"I said just a sec!"

She slipped into her shoes, and hurried toward the door and flung it open.

"Ma'am," said the soldier looming in the entrance.

God, he must be six ten.

The beret-wearing, arms-toting sergeant moved aside just as a captain, smaller by comparison to the sergeant though still a good six feet or so, stepped onto the porch. "Miss Conway?"

"Yes?"

"I'm Captain Raleigh Garret."

"Captain Garret," said Raven, closing the door behind and moving out to the veranda railing to see this horde descending upon Cathleens Haven.

By this time the black van had reached the foot of

the slope below, and three men in dark suits and ties got out. They were detained by soldiers, but flashed IDs. Farther down the lane and just coming into view sped a sheriff's car, its light bar flashing, followed by a number of pickups—eight or ten altogether, Aikens' Betsy among them. And trailing behind coursed a red Jeep with its top down.

Weapons in hand, the soldiers moved to bar the two-track lane.

The men in suits started up the pathway.

"General Manville sent us to help with the search."

Raven's attention was jerked back to the veranda. "I'm sorry, Captain Garret. What did you say?"

"General Manville sent us to help with the search for your sister and to protect you until security gets here." He gestured toward the lane where the soldiers waited to intercept the oncoming trucks. "I have thirty men to cover the ground and three Blackhawk S-70A's for air recon."

"Are you Army?"

"Yes, ma'am. Rangers." The captain rattled off a string of numbers and names, citing Army, Corps, Division, Brigade, and Battalion, ending with Third Ranger Company out of Fort Bradford."

Raven frowned. "Isn't Fort Bradford decommissioned?"

"Yes, ma'am."

"But still you're stationed there?"

"Yes ma'am."

"There's a story here, right?"

"Yes, ma'am." He did not elucidate.

"Does it have anything to do with Hunters Wood?"

"Hunters Wood?"

Raven gestured at the forest behind the house.

"Ah, no, ma'am."

By this time, the pickup-truck cavalcade had reached the soldiers, and Deputy Mills was out of his car and arguing with one of the Rangers.

"Sergeant Randall," said the captain.

"Sir?"

"See what that's all about."

"Yes, sir."

Raven said, "That's the local deputy, stationed in Benton. He's brought men to search for Sissy, um, my sister, Elizabeth, that is."

"Sergeant, let them through and have the deputy to come up here. Then go down and make those ragtag civilians a part of the party under my command."

The sergeant grinned. "Yes, sir." He touched his ear and spoke softly, and for the first time Raven saw he had an earpiece and a small wirelike mike running along his jaw. The sergeant then strode from the porch and toward the head of the path. He stopped the trio in suits, and spoke with them. One by one, they presented him their IDs.

Raven saw Aikens, accompanied by a soldier, moving to the man in the red Jeep. The man got out and showed the soldier and then Aikens some identification. A moment later, the man from the Jeep grabbed a duffel bag from the back seat, and he and Aikens started toward the pathway up the slope. Deputy Mills joined them.

The captain paused and listened. Raven now saw that he was also wearing an earpiece and mike. After a moment he said, "Let them through, Sergeant." And Sergeant Randall handed back the IDs to the three dark-suited men, and they came on toward the house as Randall started down the path.

As the trio of men came up the steps and onto the veranda, the one in the lead held up his ID and announced to the captain, "FBI." He turned toward Raven. "Miss Conway?"

Raven inclined her head.

"I'm Special Agent Marks. And with me are Agents Rose, and Billingsly."

Raven nodded and said, "Will there be a test after?"

"Test?"

"To see if I remember your names among all the others in this mob falling upon this house."

Marks smiled fleetingly and then said, "Director Kelly asked us to come and look into the disappearance of your sister, Elizabeth Ryelle Conway."

"The director of the FBI sent you? The director himself?"

"Yes, ma'am. Do I have your sister's name right?"

"Yes, you do."

"And just for the record, you are Raven Caitlin Conway. Is that correct?"

"It is."

"And is your sister still missing?"

"She is."

Mills and Aikens and the stranger with them reached the porch just as Agent Marks said, "We're with the BAU, and—"

"The BAU?" blurted Raven, tears springing to her eyes, her heart suddenly hammering away in her chest.

"My God, is there a serial killer involved?" She felt like screaming and running and running until she fell down. But instead she swayed on her feet. Dropping his duffel, the man from the Jeep quickly stepped forward and braced her by putting an arm about her, even as Agent Marks held up his hands, palms out, in denial. "I didn't mean to frighten you, Miss Conway. The truth is, we don't know what the situation might be. It's just that we were the closest team when the call came."

Captain Garret frowned. "BAU?"

"Behavioral Analysis Unit," replied the man supporting Raven. "Profilers."

Deputy Mills said, "Oh, my," and stared at the agents.

In that moment another helicopter came over the ridge to the west, this one a sleek corporate unit and with a logo on the side: HT.

"Who's that?" demanded Captain Garret, and he keyed his mike and barked, "Stand ready, but hold fire."

"What the hell?" asked Mills. "Army, FBI, now what?"

The men in the field below turned toward the incoming chopper, some going to one knee, others remaining upright, all their weapons now trained on the copter, a Bell 430.

"Captain," said the man still holding Raven, "call your men off. It's a friendly."

"And you are?"

"Nicholas Rogan. I've been hired by Hunters Trust to protect Miss Conway, and that chopper is from Hunters Trust."

Again Garret keyed his mike and said, "Stand down.

Stand down."

Retractable wheels appeared on the helicopter, and it settled in the meadow.

"I'm all right," said Raven, and Rogan released her. She stepped away and looked at him and unexpectedly caught her breath. Some thirty years old, he had deep brown hair, nearly black, that set off his dark brown eyes. He was athletic and trim, with a swimmer's body, and stood a half a head taller than Raven's own five seven. With his high cheek bones and slightly canted eyes he looked Eurasian—Caucasian mixed with Japanese or Chinese. He was dressed in denims—jacket, shirt, and pants. Under the Levi jacket, Raven could see part of a rig for a shoulder holster.

Rogan saw her scrutiny and he pulled out his ID and handed it to her. It simply said: Blackledge Security, Nicholas Rogan, CEO.

Captain Garret and then Agent Marks also looked at the ID and passed it to Deputy Mills, who handed it back to Raven.

As she returned it to Rogan, he smiled at her and said, "I might have some more of my men come, but right now, what you see is what you get."

The blades stopped turning on the corporate chopper, and a door slid open to let a long-legged blonde step down. An attendant handed her a briefcase. She strode across the meadow and toward the house, to the appreciative gazes of the Rangers and locals alike.

Agent Marks said, "Miss Conway, we'd like to set up a command post here in the house, if you don't mind."

"My thoughts as well," said Captain Garret.

"Yeah, me too," blurted Mills, belatedly.

Robert Aikens moved to the side of Raven and said, "Miss Raven, with all these guns and the gear they're likely to bring, if Miss Elizabeth comes anywhere near, why, it'll make her sick to death."

Raven nodded and said, "You're right, Robert." She turned to the captain and agents and gestured downslope and said, "If you want to set up a command post, do it down there."

Both the captain and special agent looked at Raven questioningly, but it was Rogan who answered: "We need to keep this out of common knowledge, but Elizabeth Conway has a medical condition: she cannot abide cars, machinery, electronics, or almost any sort of modern gear. That's why she's out here, away from it all. Miss Conway and Mr. Aikens are right: we'll have to keep all that stuff at the foot of the slope or in the field beyond."

Captain Garret said, "Understood," and Agent Marks said, "As you wish," but Deputy Mills said, "Well, hell," and snorted in disgust and spun on his heel and stalked down and away.

"We'll need to get whatever information you have, Miss Conway," said Marks, watching the deputy head for the path.

"That's damn little," said Raven.

"Oh?"

"Yes. Here's the sum and substance of it: I arrived here the day before yesterday around lunchtime. "Sissy, my sister, Elizabeth, that is, was not here. She did not return that night. All morning the next day—yesterday—I searched in the forest, calling her name without receiving an answer.

"Robert showed up—Mr. Aikens, I mean—at about noon, bringing groceries. Then he and I went into town to inform Deputy Mills and round up a search party. I made some phone calls: to Sissy's agent, her Doctor, my agent, and a lawyer at Hunters Trust. None of them knew anything of Elizabeth's disappearance.

"Robert and I returned, and spent the rest of the day here, but Sissy never came. Nor did she come in the night. Then you arrived. That's it."

One of the other agents—Rose or Billingsly, Raven didn't remember which was which—said, "So she could have been here while you and Mr. Aikens were in town, right?"

"Maybe, but if that were so, why didn't she stay?"

"Are you and she getting along?" asked the other agent.

"Of course."

"When was the last time you saw her?"

"Um, three years ago, just before she moved here."

"Three years, huh?" said Agent Marks, as if casting doubt on Raven's claim that she and Sissy got along.

Before Raven could respond, "That's what she said, gentlemen," said Rogan.

"Do you have a picture of her?" asked Marks.

"Just the one in my billfold," said Raven.

"I have flyers down in my jeep," said Rogan. "The pictures are from four years ago, but let me ask you this: just how many women do you think you'll find lost in this forest? My guess is at most you'll find one, and that will be Elizabeth. And before you bring it up, I know you'll need the flyers just in case she's *not* in Hunters

Wood."

Agent Marks said, "We'll use them to run a canvass of all the hospitals and medical facilities within fifty miles, perhaps a hundred. We'll also transmit them to various law enforcement agencies. One of them might have a Jane Doe. She might be suffering from amnesia."

"You won't find Sissy in a hospital or wandering the streets of a town," said Raven. "Prolonged exposure to modern civilization would kill her."

The long-legged blonde emerged at the head of the pathway and strode to the veranda and up.

"Why, hello, Nick," she said, flashing him a megawatt smile.

"Taylor," said Rogan, noncommittally. Then he turned to the others and said, "Miss Conway, gentlemen, this is Taylor Raines, of the firm of Allenby, Allenby, and Cartwright, managers of Hunters Trust, their one and only client. Taylor handles, um, special assignments."

"I'm a troubleshooter," said Taylor, again flashing that megawatt smile. "But in this case, the trouble now seems well in hand."

Raven, with her no makeup and her tangle of a ponytail and her lack of sleep, and dressed in Skechers and jeans and a shirt advertising beer, felt like an ugly duckling compared to this beautiful swan. In her middle thirties, Taylor was svelte and beautiful, and her ash-blond hair seemed her natural shade. Her makeup was flawless, since there appeared to be no makeup whatsoever on her clear-eyed face with its dark lashes in perfect contrast to her ice-blue gaze. Her hands were graceful, with long fingers and perfectly done nails. And her legs went from the floor all the way up, or so Raven had written about one of her own heroines. And she was dressed elegantly, from her Gucci flat pumps to the neckline of her Cavalli blouse, with a bit of cleavage showing, just enough to entice a man. Raven wished Sissy were here: she'd show up this platinum hussy. And the fact that Taylor seemed to have had a past with Rogan had given Raven an unexpected flash of envy, or perhaps outright cat-claw jealousy.

But then Taylor turned to Raven and held out her hand, saying, "I'm pleased to meet you at last, Miss Conway, and I love your books, especially the ones with Melody Hawk."

Damn! Raven took her hand, and found the grip firm and said, "Thank you, Miss Raines. It's always nice to meet someone who actually reads what I write."

"Oh, please call me Taylor, and I have a question to ask: are you going to write a sequel to *Rising Crescent*? I loved that story."

Oh, damn, damn, and double damn. I'm beginning to like this girl. "Perhaps one day," said Raven.

"Well I hope it's one day soon. Your hero reminds me a bit of Nikky, here."

Again Raven felt a momentary flash of jealousy. *Crap! Maybe that's it. Rogan does look somewhat like my own mental image of Jake Stone.*

Taylor held out the briefcase to Raven. "In here are two papers you need to sign, as well as the documents you requested. There's also the satphone that George Allenby wants you to have, along with a charger that'll fit in the PC socket of your Porsche."

"My Porsche is in the garage at the moment," said

Raven, "but thanks."

"When it needs a recharge, you can plug it into my Jeep," said Rogan.

Raven nodded and smiled.

Captain Garret said, "Look, we're burning daylight, and I'd like to get started. Mr. Rogan, if you could please show my men a few of those flyers of Miss Elizabeth Conway, I would appreciate it. And Agent Marks, if you'll come with me, we'll see about setting up that command post."

Nick looked at Raven.

"I'll come with you," said Raven.

"Good," he replied.

"Besides," said Raven, "I'll have to leave the satellite phone locked up in Mr. Rogan's Jeep. I would need to go down there to use it anyway, and I don't want it anywhere around Sissy." She frowned at the briefcase and said. "What's the combination?"

Without looking at the others, Taylor smoothly said, "Step inside and I'll tell you."

When Raven had closed the door behind, Taylor grinned. "It's Melody's last name."

Raven smiled back. "Good choice." Raven keyed in "Hawk," and popped open the case. She set the charger and satellite phone aside, then removed a two-inch-thick stack of papers and checked for staples and paperclips—there were none. She laid them on the table and put the phone and charger back and locked the case again.

Taylor said, "The top two papers you have to sign. They make you full Trustee." She handed the papers to Raven and picked up a Hunters Trust envelope lying next in the stack.

Raven quickly scanned the documents—they were duplicates and simple and direct. Raven asked for a pen and signed them. Taylor countersigned and gave one to Raven and slipped the other into the envelope and sealed it, saying, "I'll deliver it."

Raven looked at Taylor and said, "How did you arrange all of this?" She gestured toward the out-of-doors.

Taylor shrugged a shoulder. "It was a simple matter of making a few calls."

"Simple? Getting a company of Rangers here from a black-ops base to comb the woods? Having Director Kelly tell three BAU agents to drop whatever they were doing, such as trying to catch a serial killer, and come look for my sister instead? Arranging for the CEO of Blackledge Security to personally act as my bodyguard? And all of it overnight? That simple?"

Taylor smiled. "Perhaps you don't completely grasp the power of the Trust, Raven, the power you now fully wield."

"Perhaps I don't," said Raven, "but I still find it remarkable what you have done in an impossibly short time."

"Miss Conway, believe me when I tell you that you now have enormous sway. When your sister is found and this trouble is past, you will need to sit down with George and the partners and me, and we will tell you the extent of what you control."

"Oh, believe me, I will," said Raven, "just as soon as Sissy is found. And speaking of Sissy"—Raven picked up the briefcase—"let's get that mission underway."

As they turned to go, Taylor asked, "By the way, just

how did you know that the Rangers came from a black-ops base?"

"Fort Bradford was decommissioned some six years ago," said Raven, "but this company is stationed there."

"Smart girl," said Taylor, smiling, "a regular Melody Hawk." She laughed, and together they headed out the door.

As they all trooped down toward the lane below, Taylor said, "I'm afraid I'll just get in the way. Is there anything else I can do for you, Miss Conway?"

"Are you leaving?"

"I'm just a fifth wheel around here."

They walked a bit farther, and finally Raven said, "After I plow through that ton of material you brought and have had time to digest it, I'm certain to have a question or a hundred. That's when I'll give you a call."

They parted ways, Taylor heading for the chopper; Garret and Marks and the two agents crossing toward Sergeant Randall and the Rangers and Mills and the men from Benton. Raven and Rogan and Aikens stopped off at the Jeep, where Rogan unlocked the storage space under the rear floorboard, and Raven put the briefcase with phone and charger inside.

While Rogan retrieved flyers, Raven watched as Taylor's chopper lifted off and flew westward over the ridge.

"Oh, hell," said Raven.

"What?" asked Aikens.

"We should have had Taylor's copter join in the search."

"We can probably call her back," said Robert.

Raven glanced at the three Blackhawks and said. "Perhaps three is enough."

Rogan turned around and held up a flyer. "Is this a good likeness?"

Tears sprang into Raven's eyes as Sissy looked out of the page at her.

With a whine of turbines and the *wop-wop-wop* of rotors, the Blackhawks took off.

Up at the edge of the forest, a long, strung-out line of men started into the woods.

Raven and Robert and Nicolas, stood at the command center—the FBI van—where they'd set up a radio link to the choppers and the Rangers on the ground. Deputy Mills' patrol car was parked nearby; Mills sat inside with a Radio Shack walkie-talkie, linked to several of the Benton men.

As one of the Blackhawks passed over the foot of the rise leading up to the forest, it paused and backed up to hover above a small thicket sprouting up in the grassy field. "Captain Garret. Over."

Garret triggered the mike. "Garret here. Over."

"Captain, there's a vehicle in this thicket—a car—but I don't see anyone in it or nearby. Over."

"Stand by," said Garret. He then turned to Raven. "You know anything about this?"

"No, sir."

He called out to Mills. "Deputy. There's a vehicle in that thicket."

"What?" asked Mills, getting out of the patrol car.

"I said there's a vehicle in that thicket."

Mills turned and looked and said, "That one? The

one with the chopper?"

"Yes. Do you know anything about it?"

"No, I don't, but I'll find out." He tossed his walkie-talkie to Robert, then started toward the growth.

"Wait up," called Marks. "We'll go with you." The three agents drew their weapons and hurried after Mills.

Garret keyed the mike and said, "Hawk three, back away thirty, forty meters, but remain on station until the Deputy gives you an okay, then continue your mission. Over."

"Yes, sir." The chopper drifted backwards, then stopped and held station.

They watched as Mills and the agents neared the thicket, and just as they spread out and cautiously entered the small trees, Robert's walkie-talkie squawked and an agitated voice called, "Hey, Ronnie, you there? Come on, Ronnie, you there? This is Charlie."

"It's me, Robert. Ronnie's not here."

"Well, quick, get his ass. We've found a dead body."

"Oh, no, no, no, no, no," cried Raven, "please, God, please, God, no."

She turned to Rogan, and he took her in his arms and drew her close.

8

Aikens keyed the walkie-talkie. "A dead body?"

"Yeah. Some guy. Deader'n hell," said Charlie.

Rogan felt Raven relax in relief, but he still held her close.

She made no move to free herself.

She mumbled into his shirt, "You must think I'm a fracking wimp."

Rogan smiled. "The thought had crossed my mind, but when family is involved . . ."

Oh, God, that's exactly the thing Jake Stone would say. I'm living in one of my books.

She inhaled his scent. *Nice, so nice; he smells faintly of soap, and there's a trace of aftershave and something else—what is it?—I don't know, but nice. Oh, God, what am I doing? I am smelling him and he's smelling me, and I haven't had a shower, and I only took a swipe at my teeth, and—*

Raven practically leapt away.

Rogan smiled. "Practicing a gazelle move? Or was that your impression of a *jeté*?"

In spite of herself, Raven laughed, even as she blushed.

Captain Garret called Sergeant Randall. "Sergeant,

one of the civilians—Charlie—has stumbled across a DB. Find him and stand by for recovery."

"I wouldn't do that if I were you, Captain," said Rogan. "It's a potential crime scene, and the feds are going to want to process it."

"Right," said Garret. He relayed the information to the sergeant, and instead had him cordon off the area. Then he triggered the mike and called the hovering chopper. "Hawk three, set her down and shut her off, and inform the deputy and the FBI that we've discovered a male DB in the woods. Then stand by. I think we might need you to transport it somewhere."

"Yes, sir."

Garret then called Blackhawks one and two and had them reapportion their search areas to cover that of Blackhawk three.

Rogan turned to Raven and Robert. "Both of you might have to take a look at this guy and see if you recognize him."

"But I don't know many people up here," said Raven, turning away from watching the choppers sweep back and forth above Hunters Wood. "Do you think that he might be someone I know who followed me? And what might he have to do with Sissy?"

"I haven't the foggiest, but we need to look."

Shortly, Deputy Mills and Special Agent Marks and Agent Rose came back to the van. Mills was furious. "Goddammit, this is my county and I'm in charge here."

Marks shook his head. "Not in a case of kidnapping."

"But we don't know she's kidnapped. She could just be lost."

"In which case, just as soon as we find her, it will then be your case." As Mills yet fumed, Marks turned to Captain Garret. "Who found him? One of your men?"

Garret shook his head. "One of the civilians, a Charlie, I believe."

Glaring in displaced triumph, Mills took the walkie-talkie back from Robert. "Charlie, this is Deputy Mills. Where are you?"

"In the fuckin' woods, Ronnie. Where else would I be?"

"I mean, exactly where are you?"

"I dunno. Ask the sergeant."

"Well don't let anyone else near that body, you hear?"

"Hell's bells, Ronnie, who would want to go near? I mean the guy is a real bloody mess. Besides, the sergeant took over and has already moved everyone back."

Mills glared at Captain Garret, but swallowed whatever he might have wished to say.

Garret triggered his mike. "Sergeant Randall, send Charlie directly out of the woods. We'll use him as a guide to the DB. Then get everyone else back to searching for Miss Elizabeth Conway. You stay with the DB. —And keep your eyes open."

"Yes, sir."

As they waited for Charlie to appear, Rogan turned to Agent Marks and said, "What did you find in the thicket?"

"A Toyota, a Camry. Registered to a Mary Lou Johnson. Do any of you know someone by that name?"

They each shook their heads.

"We found the keys hidden behind a tire," said Marks. "The key looks like a duplicate, which means the car might have been a planned boost; a lot attendant or valet or mechanic would have access." He looked at Mills. "We'll need to run the plate, as well as the registration." The deputy jerked his head in sullen agreement.

"In the trunk was a break-down case for a rifle. The rifle itself is missing. Had a scope. We also found some .223 ammunition. If I had to guess, I'd say it's an AWC M91BDR."

"That's serious iron," said Rogan.

Captain Garret nodded his agreement and added, "Sniper rifle."

Even as Deputy Mills looked from one to the other, the expression on his face one of surprise, making it apparent that this was news to him, "Hold on," said Rogan. He stepped to his Jeep and opened the compartment under the floorboard and took out two folded up forest-cammoed vests. "Here," he said to Raven. "Put this on."

"What is it?"

"Level four Dragon Skin body armor."

"Good stuff," said Garret.

"Do I really need this?" asked Raven.

"Maybe, maybe not, but there might be more than one sniper out there," said Rogan.

He helped her into the flexible vest, one specifically built for a woman.

"You knew I would need this?"

Rogan shrugged and said, "I believe in the Boy Scout motto." Then he donned a vest himself.

"Why would a sniper be in these woods?" asked Raven. "And does this have anything to do with Sissy?"

"We don't know," said Marks. "Billingsly is partially processing the car, but to do the entire thing, what we need is a team of evidence techs, not only to process the car properly, but also the body in the woods, and Miss Conway's house."

"My house?"

"For evidence that might have been left by someone who took your sister, assuming she was kidnapped."

"Oh. I should have known, since I write about these things."

Agent Rose looked at Mills. "Is there a medical examiner in Benton?"

Mills shook his head. "The closest thing we got is Doc Hanford, and he's just a GP. We'll have to send to the city. Look, I'm going to have to call in Sheriff Winkler, maybe he can bring one. Then you and Winkler can fight it out over whose jurisdiction it is."

"Before you get into a pissing contest," said Rogan, "this isn't State, County, or local land."

"What?" blurted Mills and Marks together.

"It's Hunters Trust land, and outside all of your jurisdictions. And even the Federal Government must tread lightly here."

Now it was Raven who had a startled look of surprise splashed upon her face. Rogan turned to her. "I think you'll find it explained in the papers that Taylor brought."

"With your permission, Miss Conway," said Marks, "the FBI will provide forensics *and* a medical examiner."

"Oh, lord," said Mills, "Sheriff Winkler is gonna have a shit fit. —Oops! Pardon my French, Miss Conway."

"Hey!" echoed a shout.

"There's Charlie," said Robert.

"Let's go," said Agent Rose.

"Wait a moment," said Marks. He turned to Agent Rose and gestured toward the inside of the FBI van. "Grab our satphone and call this in and get forensics here pronto. A medical examiner, too. Make this their highest priority."

"Yes, sir," said Rose.

Marks turned to the others. "Ready?"

Raven turned to Garret. "Captain?"

"I've got to stay here and man the command post," said Garret. He turned to Mills. "Leave the walkie-talkie with me."

Grudgingly, Mills handed over the Radio Shack device.

As they headed cross-slope to where Charlie waited, Aikens said, "Miss Raven, it rained the morning the day you came. But I didn't see any tracks leading into that thicket as we went back and forth to Benton. Did you?"

Raven shook her head. "No, I didn't, Robert."

"Hmm . . ." said Rogan. "That means he went in there before the rain, and whatever grass and weeds that might have been flattened stood back up in the wet."

"Right," said Marks. "We didn't see any tracks either. They had to be washed away.

Rogan looked at Raven. "Who knew you were coming here? Who knew your schedule?"

"Eli, my agent, knew; Elias Traynor, I mean. Um, and I wrote a letter to Sissy, but Robert hadn't delivered it to her yet. Let me see, who else? Oh, George Allenby knew."

Rogan frowned. "Allenby runs the Trust; any number of people there might have known. How about at your literary agency?"

"Well, there's Elias and his brother, Samuel, and their secretary receptionist, Billi Crandall, but I don't think they'd tell just anyone where I would be."

"There were some folks who called you, Miss Raven," said Robert. "Would they have known you were coming here?"

"Well, Dr. Jameson called, but I don't know how he would know I was here. And my cousin, Millicent, which reminds me, I need to call her back. My agent and George Allenby also called, but you already know about them."

As Marks jotted down all the names, Raven asked, "You know, I sound like a broken record, but again I ask: what does this have to do with my sister? More specifically, what would a man carrying a sniper rifle have to do with my sister?"

"Maybe nothing, Miss Conway," said Rogan. "Maybe instead it has to do with you."

"Me? Why would anyone be—? Oh, the Hunters Trust."

"Right. And perhaps that has something to do with your sister as well."

Just then they reached Charlie, and he said, "Follow me."

Into the woods they went, to look at, as Charlie had

put it, a real bloody mess.

9

"Do you know him?"

The distant sound of choppers sweeping back and forth *wop-wopped* on the air.

Raven, verging on sickness, shook her head and turned away. "I don't know for certain, Agent Marks, as mutilated as he is, but I think not."

Marks looked at Aikens. "Same here," said Robert.

The man lay on his back, nothing left of his eyes but empty sockets, where the birds or animals had gotten to him. Half of his face was gone, and something squirmed under his remaining cheek. Blood—long dried and rust brown with age and diluted by the rain two days past— had saturated the dead leaves and ground all about the corpse, and the nauseating stench of decomposition drifted on the air . . . no more, no less than any dead animal lying beside a road somewhere. The man was dressed in black—turtle-neck sweater, pants, and sneakers. Dark streaks of camouflage paint were smeared on what remained of his face and hands.

Rogan said, "He was on a mission."

"What killed him?" asked Raven, not looking.

"Ma'am," said Sergeant Randall, "he has a hole all the way through—from sternum to spine—big enough to shove a ball bat through. I'm pretty sure that's what did him in."

"What kind of a weapon could do that?" asked Mills.

"Bazooka?" suggested Charlie.

Randall snorted.

"Shotgun?" asked Robert. "With a really big slug?"

Rogan nodded. "Maybe. Perhaps a fifty caliber gun."

"Another sniper shot this one?" asked Mills.

"We don't know for certain that this man is a sniper or is the one from the car," said Marks.

Randall said, "Oh, he was probably a sniper, all right."

"And you know this how . . . ?" asked Marks.

The sergeant pointed. "There's a BDR ten meters away."

Raven looked at Rogan. "BDR?"

"Break-down rifle," he explained.

Randall led them to the weapon, a scope-mounted M91, flat-black.

As Marks slipped into a pair of latex gloves, Sergeant Randall recited, "The AWC is built on Remington 700 action in .223 or .308 calibers; it is fully accurized and tuned. The stock is match grade fiberglass, pillar bedded, with a Pachmayr decelerator recoil pad. It has a pistol grip and the fore-end is rough textured. It comes in either flat black or NATO green colors. The barrel is medium weight chrome moly, with a matched chamber and crown. The barrel is client specified in lengths from 16.5" to 20". It has an optional heavy contour barrel in stainless steel, and threaded for suppressor use."

"What?" asked Mills.

The sergeant looked at the deputy and said, "It's a fine gun."

Marks knelt on one knee and lifted the rifle just enough to ease back the bolt and look. "One shot fired: Remington .223; the spent cartridge is still in the chamber." He eased the bolt closed, and lowered the rifle back to the same spot.

"We'll wait for forensics to check this out, but I suspect that the rain took care of all prints."

Raven shook her head. "Not on the cartridge, Agent. If he loaded it himself, the prints should be there.

Rogan looked at her and smiled, and she said, "I write about these things."

Marks nodded and stood and glanced at the corpse. "The medical examiner might be able to tell us what killed him."

Rogan looked at Deputy Mills. "You have any crime-scene tape in your car?"

"Yeah." Then, "—Oh, good idea. I'll get it. I'm gonna radio Sheriff Winkler, too. He'll want to see this."

"Before you go, Deputy," said Marks, "are there any militia around here, local or nearby?"

"No, sir, not that I know of."

"No white-supremists, no anti-government organizations?"

"Nope."

"How about disillusioned vets?" asked Rogan.

"Only Doc Anderson, but I don't think he's disillusioned about anything."

Charlie snorted and said, "He means veterans, Ronny, like from Vietnam or Iraq. Not no animal doctor."

"None of those neither," growled Mills. He looked at Marks. "Is that all?"

Marks nodded, and Mills headed for his patrol car to get the crime-scene tape and alert the sheriff.

Raven looked at Rogan. "I write about mutilated corpses and the odor, but this is terrible."

"We'll go," said Rogan.

"Me, too," said Robert.

As they made their way back through the forest, Raven said, "I think you're right, Mr. Rogan. It does look like that dead man was a sniper on a mission; that is, with the clothing and paint and the rifle, what else could it have been? I can't think of an alternative. Can you?"

"Nope," said Rogan.

"Me neither," said Robert. "I mean, deer hunters round here are serious, but it ain't deer season, and he ain't no deer hunter, not even a poacher."

"Then what mission might he have been on?" asked Raven, knowing one answer but finding it difficult to believe.

Rogan said, "Are you sure you want to hear this?"

"Yes. I might be a fracking wimp, but not when it could involve Sissy."

"All right," said Rogan. "But listen, it's only a hypothesis at the moment."

"I understand," said Raven. "Hypothesize away."

Rogan nodded and said, "Given that the sniper came when he did, I think he might have been planning to set up an ambush in the house. So, his first target might have been your sister."

"First target?" said Robert.

"Yes. And the second might have been you, and Raven his third and prime target."

Aikens frowned. "Me?"

Raven said, "It makes sense, Robert. You are Elizabeth's facilitator, delivering groceries and other things to her and being a general handyman, and had you come before I got here, then you would have been the second victim."

"I see," said Robert. "And you would have been the third."

"Or the second," said Rogan. "Had Raven arrived first, there would be no need to shoot you except on the chance you saw him."

Raven shook her head. "But that leaves the question: how would he know I was on my way to Cathleens Haven?"

"Someone who knew might have inadvertently or deliberately passed the information on until it got to whoever hired him," said Rogan.

"What about this?" said Aikens. "What if Miss Elizabeth was the only target, then what?"

Raven said, "In my novels, it boils down to who would profit." Raven frowned in thought, then said, "If Sissy were the lone target, then the only one I can think of who might be involved is her agent."

"I don't understand," said Aikens. "Isn't she like his golden goose? And if he had her killed . . ."

"Then the price of her paintings would skyrocket," said Rogan, "And whatever he had in stock would be a windfall."

"His entire gallery is filled with her work," said Raven.

"Even so," said Rogan, "Robert is right: she is his golden goose."

"In my case," said Raven, "if the sniper were setting up an ambush to kill me, then I think the one behind it might be someone at the Trust."

"Who would that be?" asked Aikens.

"For the life of me, I don't know. And I won't know until I understand the workings of the Trust itself, and maybe not even then."

As they reached the edge of the forest Raven said, "But still the questions remain: who killed the man in Hunters Wood, what weapon was used, and where is my sister, Elizabeth?"

"I haven't a clue," said Rogan.

"Me neither," said Aikens.

"Crap!" said Raven, "we're still in the dark. —Let's go get some lemonade," and she headed for the house.

10

As Raven, Nicholas, and Robert sat on the veranda and sipped lemonade, a massive helicopter roared its way up the valley.

"Chinook," said Rogan. "A cargo chopper."

"Cargo?" asked Robert.

Rogan nodded. "Probably bringing in gear for the Ranger company."

"Gear?" asked Robert.

"Yeah. If they're going to be here for days, they'll need places to sleep and better food than MREs."

"How long do you think they'll stay?"

"I believe that might be up to Miss Conway," said Nicholas.

They both looked at her, and Raven said, "Me? Not the Army?"

"I believe they'll consider whatever you request," said Rogan.

"Oh, God. I want Sissy found, but the forest is so very large, Mr. Rogan."

"Please, call me Nick. Not even my dad is called 'Mr. Rogan.'"

"Nick," Raven said and smiled at him. "I'm Raven."

Rogan grinned and stuck out his hand. "Pleased to

meet you, Raven."

His grip was firm and lingered, and as he held her hand, "And what is your father called?" Raven asked.

"Nick. Nicholas Rafferty Rogan. Mother Greek, father Irish. He's Nick Senior; I'm Nick Junior."

Reluctantly, Raven released her grip. As their hands slid apart, Raven said, "Isn't it confusing, having two Nicks in the family?"

Rogan laughed. "Only when we are together and someone calls out. That only happens when I go to the Southwest to visit. He's a cop, a detective lieutenant in Homicide."

"You didn't follow in your father's footsteps, then," said Raven.

"No. I went into the service after college. Army. I was a Ranger, just like those guys out there. I served in Iraq and Afghanistan and elsewhere, but had too many misgivings, especially about Iraq. I got out after my second tour and started my own company. It's full of guys just like me."

"Mercenaries?"

Nicholas smiled. "Sometimes. But mostly we take on . . . jobs that require our special skills."

"And what special skill is needed to guard me?"

"The skill to keep you alive, Raven."

His words jolted her, but she took a deep breath and smiled. "My own Secret Service?"

Rogan shook his head. "Better."

The cargo chopper landed, and soldiers jumped out and began unloading gear.

The three watched for long moments, and finally Rogan said, "You know that you're going to have to come to some agreement with Captain Garret and Agent Marks on how long they will stay. There are practical things to consider, Raven. You can't keep them here indefinitely."

"I know," said Raven, sighing.

They fell quiet and watched the Rangers at the Chinook.

Then Raven's heart began pounding and she said, "What about you? I mean, you have a company to run, other missions to take on."

"I have a good exec; my company can take care of itself. For your protection, Raven, I'm in it for the long haul."

A burst of joy blossomed in Raven's chest.

Are you crazy, girl? You just met this man.

Casting about for something to say without falling all over her tongue, and, not trusting herself to speak to Nick and sound like a twit, Raven cleared her throat and turned to Aikens and said, "Robert, something strange happened last night."

Aikens looked at her. "Oh?"

"Yes. I heard something, and I'm not really going nuts, but—"

Oh, God. I didn't want to sound like an idiot, and here I am about to sound like an idiot.

Robert grinned. "I bet I know what happened, Miss Raven. You heard the hunter's horn."

Raven's eyes flew wide in amazement. "You mean other people have heard it?"

Aikens nodded. "Every now and then someone hears it. Them that don't know any better say that's how this forest got its name—Hunters Wood—though you and I know it was Cathleen Hunter the forest was named after."

"Have you heard it?" asked Raven. "The horn?"

Robert shook his head. "No, I never have, but they say it sounds like one of those English horns they use during fox hunts."

"Exactly!" declared Raven. "And the hoof beats were so real, but I didn't see—"

"Hoof beats? What hoof beats?"

"Like horses, and they seemed to run right past and down the slope and across the meadow and up. It was as if ghosts galloped after the stag that was fleeing before them."

"You saw a stag?" asked Aikens.

"I did—a big buck with a huge rack of antlers."

"Now, folks have been catchin' glimpses of bucks like that since I don't know when, but I never heard anyone tell of riders."

Again, something niggled at the edge of Raven's mind, but it was too elusive to grasp.

Rogan frowned. "Were you asleep? Dreaming?"

"I had been asleep, but the horn woke me. I know it's really woo-woo, but the stag, the horn, the hooves, they were real."

Rogan asked, "Robert, do people hunt in there?"

"Not hardly any," said Aikens. "They seem to go in once, but never twice, not even poachers. Some of them wander around, confused-like, and come right back out where they started. It's like they find the forest haunted or hexed. And maybe they're right."

They sat without speaking for a while, watching as the men in the field set up tents. Finally Raven said,

"I'm starved."

Rogan looked at her.

"No breakfast," said Raven.

"Even though it's the lunch hour, Fred whomps up a mean breakfast," said Aikens. "And we can get another bag of cubes for that icebox in there and stock it with eggs and fruit and meat and such."

"Great idea," said Raven. "Let me make myself presentable, and we'll go." She turned to Rogan and asked, "Do I really need to be in this body armor?"

Rogan nodded. "Yep. Any time you're outside the house, until we've made certain the woods and the valley are clear."

"Here you go, honey," said Fred. "Eggs over easy on a bed of pancakes, with sausage links and wheat toast. Just slather on the syrup and dig in." She slapped down three identical plates—one each for Raven, Nick, and Robert.

"Oh, Fred, I can't eat all this," said Raven.

"Sure you can," said Fred. "How else you going to keep up with this man of yours?"

Aikens said, "Fred, he ain't—"

"Sure he is," said Fred. "Don't you see that look in their eyes?"

Rogan grinned and Raven blushed, and, without glancing at him, she dug in.

As they ate, Robert said, "Speakin' of looks in eyes, your sister, Miss Elizabeth, well, this past couple of weeks she was kinda moony."

Raven chewed and swallowed, then asked, "Moony?"

"You know, distracted, sighing, staring out across the meadow, and losing track of the conversation, smiling to herself and sometimes singing to herself, too."

"Good grief, that's the way she acts when she has a new boyfriend," said Raven.

"Could she have gone off with someone?" asked Nick.

"How? I mean, she can't stand cars or anything modern."

"Maybe she ran off with one of the invisible riders," suggested Robert.

"Oh, Robert, that's too weird to contemplate," said Raven.

"Well, maybe so," said Robert, smiling, "but in case you hadn't noticed, Miss Raven, horses ain't cars."

Raven and Nick laughed, and tucked into their meals, and as they ate, the lunch crowd began trickling in. Soon Fred's was humming with business.

Finally, Raven pushed her plate away to join those of Nick and Robert, pancakes, eggs, sausage, and toast all consumed.

Fred reappeared, coffeepot in hand. She smiled at Raven's empty plate. "Good for you, honey, now you can keep up with him, just like I do with my man here." Robert flushed and Fred laughed and replenished all cups and left.

As they savored their coffee, Rogan looked across the table at Raven and said, "It could be your sister didn't leave with a boyfriend. Maybe, instead, the dead man in the woods had an accomplice."

Raven shook her head. "How did he arrive? How did

he leave? There was only one car. —No, wait, you're right, there could have been a second vehicle. I mean, the rain erased all tracks and restored the grass to upright. He might be the one who killed the man in the woods. But why would he do that if he's an accomplice? And where in hell is my sister?"

11

"There's a call I should deal with," said Raven. "Let me make it before we're out of range." She highlighted a message and punched in numbers.

They had just finished grocery shopping and Nick and Robert were loading the bags into Rogan's Jeep.

"Fennway Timber. How might I direct your call?"

Where do they find these perky girls?

"This is Raven Conway. I am returning Millicent Alderton's call."

"One moment, please."

An instant later, another female said, "Ms. Alderton's line."

"This is Raven Conway, I am returnin—"

"Oh, Miss Conway. She's expecting your call. Let me see if she is free."

Within seconds, "Raven!"

"Millicent, you called?"

"How are you, Raven?"

"I'm a bit low, Millicent. Sissy's missing."

"Elizabeth?"

"Yes."

"Oh, my God. What happened?"

"I don't know what happened. All I know is that she

is missing.

"Do you have help?

"There are men searching Hunters Wood for her, but it's not certain that she's even in there."

"This is dreadful, Raven. Is there anything I can do?"

"I don't believe so, Millicent, but thanks for asking."

"Where are you now, Raven?"

"I am in Benton at the moment, though we are just about to leave. I hate to sound brusque, Millicent, but I have to get back to the search, and there's no phone service out there. Anyway, it's your dime. Did you call about your wedding?"

"Oh, you must have gotten the invitation. Good for Allenby. That is, with your travels and all, I didn't know where to send it. I thought of sending you an e-mail invitation, but it is so much nicer to get an actual one. So, I asked him to do it for me. But here I am nattering on with Sissy missing. Why I called can wait."

"No, no, Millicent. There's no phone service out at Cathleens Haven. I do have a satellite phone, but there'd be that obnoxious signal delay to contend with. I'd rather we talked while I'm on my cell."

"All right. I will be quick. Actually, I called for two reasons: the first is because it's been seven years since your mother vanished, and I wished to express my sorrow for that, and, at the same time, my congratulations that you have become or soon will be the full Trustee for Hunters Trust."

"Thank you, Millicent. I had forgotten that Mother disappeared seven years ago. Anyway, I just signed the papers putting me in full control, though I haven't really grasped what that means."

"Well, I'm sorry for your mother, but glad for you."

"Thank you again. But as to your second reason . . . your upcoming marriage?"

"The tenth, Raven, the wedding is on the tenth."

"Love finally found you, then."

"Yes. And he's a wonderful man: Jackson Fenn. He founded Fennway Timber. I plan on keeping my maiden name for business purposes, but Jackson and I are in this together. I don't think he knows about the Trust, but he does know about Hunters Wood. He'd like to log it, but that's impossible, of course."

"Yes it is, Millicent. —Impossible, I mean. But congratulations on your upcoming nuptials. I'll certainly try to make it, but first I have to find Sissy."

"I understand. I hope you find her quickly, and just as quickly come to the wedding. We're going to have a helluva party, and I wouldn't want you to miss it. You see, with George Allenby's help—he has a list of addresses—I've invited all the 'Cathleen Hunter' cousins he knows about. A gathering of the clan, so to speak."

"Ah, nice."

"Anyway, please find Sissy, and then you and she— Oh, wait. Poor Elizabeth, with her affliction she won't be able. But you come, Raven. I remember the times we three spent chasing butterflies in the meadow, and I'd really like you to be at the wedding."

"Thank you, and I will try."

"Take care, Raven, and do find Sissy. I'll keep you both in my prayers."

"Thank you, Millicent. But now I must run."

Raven snapped her cell phone shut on Millicent's

farewell. She sighed. *Sissy has vanished, but life goes on, missing not a beat.*

"Time to go," said Aikens. "Ice is a-melting."

Rogan cranked up the Jeep, and off toward Cathleens Haven they sped.

As they entered the valley, a Blackhawk helicopter flew past them and landed in the field next to the thicket where the abandoned car had been found. As the Blackhawk turbines wound down, three men and two women got out. Four were carrying metal-cased evidence processing kits and all were wearing blue jackets with FBI in large letters across the backs. One of the men was Agent Rose.

Rogan stopped and called out. "Agent Rose, is a medical examiner with you?"

A slight, African-American woman raised her hand.

"We need an evidence tech, too."

Rose said something, and one of the men raised his hand as well.

"Hop in," said Rogan. "One of us will take you to the body."

Aikens slid over to make room, and the woman handed him her case. "Mallory Warbritton," she said as she got in.

The evidence tech said, "Jim Hanford."

"Raven Conway, Robert Aikens, and I'm Nick Rogan," said Nick. "Jim, if I had a running board, that's where you'd ride. But as it is, you'll have to squeeze in. Watch out for the eggs."

Aikens handed the bags of ice to Raven, and she put them in the floor at her feet, then she held a sack of groceries on her lap, Robert holding the other two on his. Hanford and Warbritton sat with their metal tech cases on their laps.

"I'll take you to the dead man," said Aikens, when all had jammed themselves into the Wrangler. "He's up in the woods."

"Is it far?" asked Mallory, her voice carrying a Boston accent, the "far" becoming "fah".

"Nah," said Robert, smiling to himself.

Nick jammed the Jeep into gear, and he drove onward.

Three eight-man tents now sat in the field, and soldiers were erecting another. Some distance away two Rangers were digging. A huge tanker truck sat in the field near the Chinook chopper.

"Good grief," said Raven around her sack of groceries, "it's an invasion for sure, now. But why the truck?"

"For the choppers," said Rogan. "It takes a lot of fuel to run search patterns."

"Oh, right. But why are those men digging in my meadow?"

"Slit trench," said Nick. "Latrine."

"Stupid me. I should have known."

When he came to the line of pickup trucks, Rogan passed around them and drove by two sheriff's cars. He stopped just beyond the FBI van. Captain Garret and another Ranger manned that post.

Garret and the soldier helped unpack the Jeep of its people and contents, and Garret volunteered to help carry groceries. Raven gave him the ice to tote.

They went up the pathway to the house, where

Warbritton and then Hanford used the commode. Then Aikens and the two went out the back and across slope and into the woods, heading for the dead man.

Garret slid the bags of ice into the upper compartment of the box, and Raven and Nick unloaded sacks and put the perishables into the compartment below. Garret said, "Just so you'll know, Miss Conway, my men have penetrated about twelve klicks. So far, nada. They've now swung the line and turned back. Can't have them stumbling around in the dark."

"Rangers stumble around in the dark? Not likely," said Rogan. "Deputy Mills' men, though . . . well, that's an altogether different matter."

"Speaking of the deputy, I saw a second car," said Raven.

Garret laughed. "Yeah, it's Sheriff Winkler. Come all the way from the county seat. He stopped to take a look at the abandoned car, and then drove up and parked and used the walkie-talkie to get Charlie to come and fetch him. He brought a man and a dog team with him, but the dogs, tails tucked way under, wouldn't go in. They're gone now. Back in their truck and away. Charlie and the Sheriff headed into the woods to the DB. I suspect he's in heated discussions with Agent Marks about jurisdiction."

Raven laughed, then said, "Would you like some lemonade, Captain?"

"Yes, ma'am, I surely would."

As Raven poured, she said, "And, Captain, we need to talk about how long you'll be here, and how much you can reasonably accomplish in that time."

"Yes, ma'am, we do need to do that, but first the

lemonade."

In early afternoon, the female FBI evidence technician, who had been at the abandoned car, came up the pathway and found Raven and Nick on the veranda. She flashed her ID and said, "I'm Susan Grayson; are you Raven Conway?"

"I am, and this is Nicholas Rogan of Blackledge Security."

"I'm here to process your house, now, if I might."

"Feel free," said Raven. "Lemonade?"

"That would be splendid. —And oh, by the way, I'll need your prints and Mr. Rogan's, too, as well as anyone who customarily visits, and anyone you know who has been in the house since you arrived."

"My hands are yours," said Raven.

"And I'd like you to point out anything your sister has that I might find her fingerprints on."

Raven stood. "How about a hairbrush and a hand mirror?"

"Perfect.

It was nearly sundown when the search team— Rangers and locals alike—as well as the FBI and sheriff and deputy, brought the body out of the woods on a sent-for litter, along with the rifle and a few bits of collected evidence, sparse though they were. After a short argument with Sheriff Winkler, who wanted the corpse taken to Graham's Funeral Parlor in Benton for the autopsy, they put the body in the back of Robert's pickup, and he and Charlie and Warbritton headed for Blackhawk three to take it to Warbritton's own facilities, where she had the proper equipment for a full postmortem exam.

The remainder of lawmen, along with Raven and Nick and Garret and Sergeant Randall, gathered in the house to review what they knew.

Agent Rose said, "When I went to get the forensic team, I called in the VIN and the plates. The vehicle was stolen five days ago from a woman in Sugar Falls; the plates came from a wrecked car in Mount Holly. The techs dusted for prints, and found a number of them. Warbritton took what we had, and along with the dead man's, she'll get someone to run them through IAFIS."

Marks looked at Billingsly and asked, "Anything to add, Ray?"

"The ammo we found in the trunk is 69 grain, full metal jacket, .223 Remington. There were two boxes, twenty rounds each, one unopened, the other with twelve rounds missing."

"Sixty-nine grains?" asked Garret.

"Heavy load," said Rogan.

Garret nodded and said, "Longer range shots."

Evidence Technician Hanford said, "We found your missing twelve, one of which had been fired. The expended cartridge still in the gun."

"Who was he shooting at?" asked Sheriff Winkler.

Captain Garret said, "You mean who or what."

Sergeant Randall said, "We did a search and didn't turn up a thing he might have killed or even what he might have wounded—no blood spots but his own."

"There's no evidence to know when he fired that round," said Marks.

"Well, if he did," said Randall, "I suspect he missed

whoever or whatever he shot at."

"What killed him?" asked Raven.

Agent Marks sighed. "We don't know. Sergeant Randall was almost right when he said you could shove a ball bat through the hole in the body."

James Hanford said, "I believe Warbritton's first take was that it looked like a one-inch-diameter pole had been jammed all the way through him."

"What the hell kinda weapon is that?" asked Mills.

"I don't know," said Hanford.

"Well, it might be something like a lance or a spear," said Susan Grayson.

"That's gotta be wrong," growled Winkler. "I mean, it ain't like we got a bunch of fuckin' Zulus in this state." The sheriff glanced from Susan to Raven, but didn't apologize.

"Well, whatever it was," said Agent Marks, "by the blood evidence we found and what might have been rain-softened drag marks, before he fell down the dead man was hauled backwards twenty or thirty feet, from where we found the rifle to where he lay."

A momentary quietness fell over the group, and then Raven asked, "Anything else?"

Marks nodded and said to a tech named Armsford, "David, show her what you found in the car."

David snapped open his metal-cased kit and lifted out two plastic evidence bags and passed them to Raven.

Inside each was a five by seven photo with a handwritten name on the back: Elizabeth Ryelle Conway and Raven Caitlin Conway.

"Oh, God," said Raven, paling as she looked at Sissy's face and then her own, "he was after both of us."

12

As darkness fell, Raven lit candles to press back the gloom. She and Rogan were alone in the house, both now out of their body armor. But he had redonned his shoulder harness and the weapon it held. When Raven had looked at it, Nick had said, "Just doing my job, ma'am. Just doing my job." Then he had smiled.

Raven had returned that smile, but she knew that he was deadly serious.

Faint strains of Country and Western music and occasional bursts of laughter drifted up from the Ranger encampment in the meadow.

The pickup trucks were gone, along with the sheriff's cars and the FBI van, all heading for Benton. Blackhawk three had returned, bringing Robert and Charlie back with it, both men bubbling about the chopper ride. Those two had also headed into Benton, aiming for Fred's and beer.

Rogan had pitched his duffel up into the loft, alongside the extra bedding.

Nick had then volunteered to rustle up hamburgers, and now, well armed, he stood at the woodstove, spatula in hand, while four patties sizzled in the copper skillet. Sliced mushrooms sat in a small bowl at hand, ready to sauté.

Raven tore lettuce and chopped radishes and cut green peppers and sliced tomatoes, as she threw together a salad.

A bottle of cabernet sat on the table, breathing.

Nick flipped the burgers over, saying, "Medium rare?"

"Yep."

"Mushrooms?"

"Most certainly."

"Onion?"

Oh, lord, I do love onions, but then I also love to inhale and exhale, and I'll fill up the room with my breath. "Are you having onion, Nick?"

"I am. Vadalias."

"Then I will, too."

"Cheese? It's sharp Cheddar."

"No thanks. I like my meat untainted."

Nick laughed. "Untainted except for the mushrooms and onion and bun and mustard, eh?"

Raven smiled and growled, "You know what I mean, you big lug."

Oh, God, where did that come from? Big lug? He's as slim as Michelangelo's David.

Rogan popped the hamburgers onto the platter with the buns and onion slices. Then he dumped the mushrooms into the skillet and stirred them around with the spatula, turning them over once or twice. He shoveled them out and onto the platter and set the skillet aside and announced, "Madam, your dinner is served." He took the burgers to the table.

Raven quickly dribbled the oil and vinegar over the

salad and tossed it a bit more; she then set the bowl and two forks on one corner of the table for them to commonly share

Rogan poured wine into the goblets, and they sat down to eat, Nick saying, "I'm starved."

"Me, too."

As they assembled their burgers, Raven glanced at Nick and smiled. *Oh, but this feels so good. I really need to do it more often.*

Rogan raised his glass, gleams of red in its depths casting back the candlelight. As Raven raised hers in response, Nick said, "To absent friends."

Raven's feeling of wellbeing collapsed, and tears sprang into her eyes.

"Oh, Raven, I didn't mean . . ." Rogan stood and stepped to her and pulled her up out of her chair and embraced her. "I am sorry. With your sister missing, it was thoughtless of me. It's just that from my days in Iraq and Afghanistan, I toast the memory of those who— Well, you know."

Raven leaned into him and said, "Oh, Nick. I don't mean to be such a wimp."

Yet holding her, he shifted slightly and loosed one arm and lifted her chin and wiped the wetness away from her cheeks. For an eternal moment, Raven thought he was going to kiss her. But instead he completely released her but took her by both hands and said, "If there's any way to do so, Raven, we will find your sister. Now, please, sit, and this time you lift your glass and say the toast, and I will join you. But then we'll eat. After all, I know you are starved."

She laughed, and they both sat. And she took up her

wine, as did Nick, and Raven said, "To absent friends."

He smiled. "Raven Conway a wimp? My ass." His dark gaze caught hers of sapphire, and, with a ping, he touched his wineglass to hers and took a sip.

And then they both dug in.

"Oh, this is good," said Raven, around a mouthful of burger.

"Cooked by the very best, using his secret recipe of exotic herbs and spices," said Nick, laughing.

They ate a moment without speaking, alternating bites of salad with that of hamburgers, all of it taken with wine.

Finally, Raven said, "You've told me a bit about your father. What about your mother?

"My mom's Japanese, er, rather of Japanese ancestry. She and Dad met in Hawaii. He was a Green Beret, and she a nurse."

"Vietnam?" asked Raven.

"Yeah. It seems to be the curse of the Rogans to fight in wrongheaded wars. "Maybe not my Granddaddy Rafferty. He fought in the Big One."

"World War Two?"

"Yeah. But getting back to my mom, her name's Hiroko. It about killed Granddaddy Rafferty when my dad brought his new bride home. Rafferty fought in the Pacific, you see."

"I do see," said Raven. "It must have been difficult to reconcile the face of the enemy with that of a friend."

"Exactly so. Anyway, being a US citizen helped a bit, but she won him over when he found she could give as good as she got, just like my Greek grandmother did, before she and Granddaddy passed away."

"Good for your mother," said Raven. "And I'm sorry that your grandparents are gone."

"Only on Dad's side. Mom Hiroko's parents are still alive and still living on their own in Hawaii."

"How splendid."

"So, you see, I'm quite a crossbreed: Greek, Irish, and Japanese. And if I ever get married and have a child, I'll pass my mutt blood on to that poor kid."

He's not married.

Rogan replenished Raven's glass and then his own. "How about you, Raven. What's your ancestry?"

"Now that, I don't know," she replied.

Rogan looked at her, an unspoken question on his lips.

"I just found out that Sissy and I do not have the same father. One of us might actually be a Conway, the other not. But which is which, I couldn't say."

"You do have the same mother, right?"

"Yes, but not the same dad."

Raven took a sip of her wine. "I was two when Sissy was born. It was not long after that— Oh, my God."

"What?"

"My presumed father, Kevin Conway, took his own life within a year after Elizabeth was born. And the fact that Sissy and I have different fathers . . ."

"You think it has something to do with his death."

"Yes. I'm going to have to speak with Grandmother Meredith if I am to discover anything. That is, if I can get anything out of her. She's not always lucid."

"I'm sorry," said Nick.

"Me, too."

Nicholas turned the talk to his days in college, and

Raven joined in with her own, and they laughed over the pranks Nick had pulled, and over the crushes that Raven had had on various professors.

The time flew by, and the candle burned down, until finally Raven said, "Nick, this is the best evening I've had in I don't know how long. But I do need to get some sleep, having spent the last two in the throes of worry. I need to take a shower, and then it's me for bed."

"Shower?"

"There's a waterfall up slope a bit."

Rogan smiled. "You know I'm going to have to guard you out there."

"I do."

"I'll do my best to be a gentleman," said Nick. "Not peek, I mean. It'll be the toughest test I've ever had to face."

Raven laughed.

"And you know I need a shower as well," Nick added, his smile lighting up his face.

Raven's heart began to race.

With moonlight and shadow revealing and concealing her lithe form as she moved, Raven stepped into the fall long enough to get wet, and then jumped out and soaped up. She moved back in to rinse off.

Smith and Wesson in hand, Rogan sat on a nearby rock, admiring the view. But his gaze also swept the line of the forest and the slope back down to the house. He was clothed in just a towel wrapped about his waist.

Somewhat surprised at her own boldness at having him watching, Raven didn't dare look at where Rogan sat, afraid she would find him looking at her, while at the same time afraid she would not. She soaped up once more and again plunged into the fall to rinse. Finally, she stepped out and took up her towel, and, with her back to Nick, she dried off. She wrapped the towel about herself, then turned to Rogan and said, "Your turn."

Nick walked to her and handed her the Smith and Wesson M&P .40. "Do you know how to use this?"

"I do." She hefted the weapon and then inclined her head toward the cascade and said, "Your turn."

Without word he dropped his towel.

Raven glanced away. Clearly he was aroused. Her own nipples sprang to hardness.

Nick moved to the fall and stepped in. "Gaah! This is cold."

His arousal vanished.

Raven's did not.

She had difficulty in looking anywhere but at him, with his broad shoulders and the chiseled planes of his chest, and his well-defined abs. Slender, while at the same time exuding power, he did have the body of a swimmer, or runner, she couldn't decide which. Moonlight and shadow clothed his body, just as it had hers. As he stepped out from under the fall again, at that moment it hit her: ninja. That's the kind of body Rogan had. Or at least, that's how she imagined ninjas might look. Ninjas and Nicholas: Mercenaries, Inc.

Oh, God, maybe I dreamed that up because he has a Japanese mother. I don't care. He is simply delicious.

Finally, Nick rinsed away the soap a last time, and he picked up his towel and dried off. He wrapped the cloth about his waist, and then took the gun from Raven.

~

Raven lay in her bed, her thoughts whirling: of Nick in the loft, of Sissy, of mother, of Grandmother Meredith, of whose child she might be, of whose child Sissy might be, of her dad putting a pistol in his mouth, of the search and of Hunters Trust, and again of Nick in the loft.

Is he thinking of me, I wonder. Sissy, where are you? Mother, why did you have to vanish? His body is fantastic. I've got to see Grandmother Meredith; oh let her be lucid when I do. Hunters Trust: I have to look at those papers. Six more days to find Sissy. Daddy, if you were my daddy, they say you shot yourself. Did you? Oh, Sissy, Robert says you were moony. Did you have a sweetheart? Run off with him? If so, where are you now, and how did you get there? Are you in the arms of a lover, Sissy, or instead in the hands of a monster? What has the FBI found out about the sniper? Sheriff Winkler is right, there're no Zulus in this state. Nicholas seems gentle enough, even though he's a ninja. God, what a beautiful body. Come on, Raven, you've known him for less than a day, and that means you don't really know him. Raven, Raven, you'll never get any rest this way.

Long she lay and tried to sleep, repeatedly punching up her pillow and rolling over, rope webbing creaking beneath the feathered mattress, her thoughts a tumbling chaos. Finally she gave up and crawled from her bed. She padded barefoot into the hall and the great room beyond. She climbed up the ladder and into the loft. Nick was awake, and he raised the cover to let her slip in beside him.

He held her quietly for a long while, and then his mouth sought hers, and her mouth his.

They made love, or maybe lust, or perhaps both. Whatever it was, it was wild, savage the first time, fulfilling some primal need, but it was sweet and gentle the second, and perhaps this was the promise of love.

Raven easily fell asleep, even as Nick stroked her hair and whispered to her. What he said, she hadn't a clue.

13

Raven awakened to the pop and sizzle and smell of bacon frying. She inched on her stomach to the edge of the loft and peered over. Nick stood at the stove, eggs at hand, bread buttered and ready to be fried as toast, and the coffee had just begun to perk. He was dressed in jockeys and gun.

She slipped into her panties and quietly climbed down. He had his back to her as she tiptoed across the plank flooring, and just before she reached him, without turning Nick said, "With my super-keen hearing, I have tracked you all the way from the loft to where you now stand, and I must warn you I have lightning fast reactions; one step closer and I'll do *this!*" And he spun and grabbed her and pulled her to him, and kissed her softly, chopping her *Eeee!* off midshriek.

When he released her she said, "Oh, God, Nick, I haven't brushed my teeth and I have morning breath and—"

This time his kiss stopped her midprotest.

She pushed away and, laughing, fled to the tub room, to find his shaving gear on the counter next to her kit and his toothbrush sitting upright in the glass alongside hers and Sissy's. The sight of her sister's articles cut into Raven's joy, and she felt guilty that she had had such a wonderful night when Elizabeth was perhaps in dire straits.

Oh, Sissy, if you ran off with a lover, why didn't you take your toothbrush? Did you have a spare? Even if you did, would you leave toothpaste behind . . . and your shampoo?

Raven quickly brushed her teeth and washed, and combed her hair.

"How do you like your eggs?" shouted Rogan.

"Over medium, if you please," she shouted back.

Quickly she dressed—clean panties, bra, jeans, a Coldplay tee shirt, and her ever faithful Skechers.

When she reached the kitchen, Rogan was dishing up the eggs. Barefooted and with no shirt, he was now wearing jeans and gun.

Just as they sat down to eat, someone hammered on the door. With his pistol in hand but held down at his side, Rogan answered the knock.

On the veranda stood Deputy Mills and Agents Marks, Rose, and Billingsly.

"If you want breakfast, gentlemen," said Rogan, stepping aside and gesturing them in, "you'll have to cook it yourself."

None of the agents seemed to note that Rogan was half-dressed, but Deputy Mills looked from Nick to Raven and smirked.

Raven offered, "Coffee?"

"No, thanks," said Marks. "We ate in town. But, please, go ahead."

"We intend to," said Rogan, and then added, "I presume you're here to tell us what you've found out about our sniper. Drag up chairs."

In spite of being turned down for coffee, Raven got four cups and poured, emptying the percolator. Raven dumped the old grounds and added the new along with water and set the pot back on the stove. She carried the cups to the table, and set out sugar and Cremora. The agents took theirs black, but Mills loaded up with several spoons of sugar and two of the cream substitute.

When Raven returned to the table and dug into her breakfast, Rogan looked at Marks. "The sniper?"

Special Agent Marks said, "The name he called himself is Gregor Minchinko. Russian. He was fingerprinted by Homeland Security when he entered the country on a six-month visitor's visa three years ago."

"Three years?" asked Rogan, sopping up yolk with his fried toast.

"We're fairly certain that he became part of the Brighton Beach mob."

"The Russians," said Raven. "Brooklyn."

Agent Rose cocked an eyebrow at her.

"I write about these things," she said, then asked, "Do you have Interpol looking into this Minchinko?"

"As a matter of fact we do," said Marks. "But if the he's not in their system, well, that'll be a dead end."

"Asking Moscow, that'll be a dead end, too," said Rogan.

"Oh, God," said Raven, "I just realized, I mean—" She paused and took a deep breath and then asked, "Who would hire a Russian mob hit man to kill Sissy and me?"

"We don't know," said Marks, "but we've contacted New York, and they are trying to run it down. At the moment we have no one on the inside; chances are slim that we'll find out anything in a timely manner."

Mills looked from Rogan to Marks and said, "For anyone to hire a Russian hit man, that's heavy duty, right? I mean, to come all the way from New York City to here, well, it seems to me that that's heavy duty, what with airplane tickets and all."

"It is," said Rogan.

"What killed him? Minchinko, I mean," said Raven.

Marks shrugged. "Warbritton estimates he'd been dead four days when we found him. She also reports that the wound is a through and through. Whatever it was, it entered the chest and smack out through the spine, snapping it in two. On a fragment of vertebra at one of the ends of the broken spine, she found minute traces of ash wood and verdigris."

"Verdigris?" asked Mills.

"Copper oxide," said Raven. "—Oh, my God. Perhaps we do have Zulus living in the woods."

Confusion spread over Mills' face. "What?"

"Ash wood and verdigris, Deputy," said Rogan. "He might have been killed by a spear."

"Pfah!" scoffed Mills, sneering, but quickly changed his aspect when he saw the others nodding with Raven's and Nick's assessment.

"Has your sister ever handled a spear, Miss Conway?"

"Only as a child, but that was a pretend spear—just a stick. No, no spear, but Sissy did become an excellent hand with bow and arrow. She competed in college. Unlike me, guns frightened her."

"You can use a gun?"

"I knew I would need to know how to handle them, when I decided to write thrillers. So I took up the sport. Not that I'm a gun nut, but I score well with both pistol and rifle. I own a Glock nineteen, but it's not with me."

"Then I would advise you to get it and keep it at hand until we apprehend whoever is behind this," said Marks.

Raven shook her head. "I can't keep a gun in this house because of Sissy's medical condition. In fact, with that much modern technology sitting in the meadow below, even if Sissy were nearby, I think she would become quite ill if we did not quickly clear it away. She can deal with a car or two cars as long as they are kept down in the lane, but with helicopters and a tanker truck and pickups and a van and a Jeep, and all the electronics, well, I think it might be too much for her."

"Miss Conway is right about that," said Mills. "I mean, her sister wouldn't even let me come up to the house. Told me to stay away."

"All right," said Marks, "we'll get out of here as soon as we can, but until we find out who is behind this and where your sister is, I'm afraid we're stuck."

"No, you're not," said Raven. "What I mean is, Deputy Mills is right: there is no need for you to be here at Cathleens Haven. You can just as well do your jobs back at your field office, or wherever you were before you came here. And if ridding the valley of all this gear will bring Sissy back, then I want to get it the hell out of here."

"We can't leave you vulnerable, Miss Conway," said Agent Rose.

"I have Blackledge Security to safeguard me," said

Raven.

"And I have men to keep her safe twenty-four seven," said Nick.

"So do we, Miss Conway," said Marks, "but that's your choice. Still, we offer protective custody until we apprehend those who would do you harm."

"And just how long will that take?" asked Raven, adding, "I think the answer is that you don't know."

"You're right: we don't know. Regardless, you're right. We can continue to work the case from our field office. If nothing turns up today, we'll go. But you need to remain in contact with us, in case something breaks. I would add this: even though it appears that Minchinko was here on a mission to harm you and your sister, we're not certain that the disappearance of your sister has anything at all to do with him."

Raven said, "I understand, Agent Marks. Minchinko might have been a dreadful coincidence. Other things could be at work here. There is a possibility—perhaps remote—that Sissy went away willingly, though if she did, she left her toothbrush and toothpaste and shampoo behind. Not that she didn't have replacements or couldn't get them elsewhere."

"And you know this how?"

"Robert Aikens said my sister had been acting 'moony' lately, and when he described what he meant to me, it is exactly like Sissy would behave if she had a new beau or lover.

Mills snorted. "That ain't much to go on."

"It's all I have, Deputy," snapped Raven.

Mills pushed out his hands. "Oh, I didn't mean nothin' by that, Miss Conway."

"She might have fled in fear," said Rogan.

Raven looked at Nick.

Nick reached out and took her hand. "With a dead Russian assassin in the woods, we don't know just what went on here."

Assassin.

Outside, helicopter turbines began to whine as the choppers started up.

There came another tap at the door. It was Robert, carrying a thermos and a sack lunch from Fred's. "Miss Raven, Captain Garret wants you to know he has started the search, in the—how did he put it?—in the second sector. The boys from town are with him, but tomorrow they won't be, it being Monday and all, and they have to get back to their regular jobs. Besides"—Robert uncapped his thermos and filled it with coffee—"they're spooked, this being Hunters Wood . . . that and the fact a deader was found in there on the very first day." Robert blew across his cup and took a sip, then said, "And I'm sorry, but last night at Fred's I let it slip that you'd heard the hunter's horn, and that spooked 'em even more."

"Horn?" asked Marks. "What horn?"

"It's a legend about Hunters Wood," said Raven. "I was awakened by the call of what sounded like a foxhound horn. I heard running horses, too."

"Were you dreaming?"

"I don't believe so."

Deputy Mills took a deep breath and blew it out and said, "The hunter has been haunting these woods for hundreds of years, since back in Indian times. They wouldn't go in there. —The Indians, I mean."

"Has anyone ever seen this hunter?"

"Uh-uh, but if they did, they were either too scared or didn't live to tell of it."

"Maybe the deader saw the hunter," said Robert. "Maybe that's who killed him."

Marks shook his head. "If anyone is in these woods—hunter or not—I think Captain Garret's choppers will spot whoever it might be, especially if he has horses."

Another knock came on the door. It was Garret.

God, this is becoming Grand Central.

Raven stood and poured the captain a cup from the freshly brewed pot.

Garret thanked her and leaned against the counter next to Aikens.

As Raven returned to the table, Marks looked from her to Garret. "I understand you two have come to an agreement."

Garret nodded. "We have. We will search for six more days, counting today. If my company of Rangers hasn't found Miss Conway's sister by then, we will call it off."

Raven's heart sank, and she took a sip of her coffee to disguise the fact that she was suddenly on the verge of tears.

Garret continued: "The men are now moving into sector two, and, at thirteen hundred hours and some ten to twelve klicks in, Sergeant Randall will shift the line over and sweep back through a different area from the one searched going out. Our intent is for those on foot to cover the woods more or less in the vicinity where Miss Elizabeth Conway is most likely to be found: as we did yesterday, today we'll search to the east; then move round northeast, then north, and northwest, reconning the head of the valley; and finally search the woods across the meadow westerly. Even so, in seven days, counting yesterday, my men on foot will have covered just a fraction of Hunters Wood. My choppers, though, will have swept the entire forest."

"Them woods are mighty thick," said Robert, "and hard to see down into from the air. I mean, yesterday, when me and Charlie helped take that deader into the city, I looked down at the woods, and it was hard to see the ground below."

"It's the best we can do," said Garret.

"It will have to do, Captain," said Raven. "I cannot ask for more. Besides, as soon as we clear the valley of all the equipment, perhaps Sissy will reappear."

"You can't count on that," said Billingsly.

"I know, Agent, I know."

Captain Garret slugged down the last of his coffee and said, "Gentlemen, let's clear out." Then he turned to Raven and added, "Miss Conway, we'll be down at the command center should you need anything."

"All I need, Captain, is my sister."

When the agents and the deputy and the captain had gone, Raven and Nick washed and dried the dishes and silverware, and Robert put them away.

As Raven handed Nick another dish to dry, she said, "What do you know about electricity, Nick?"

"What do you mean? Wiring a house? Designing a power station? Putting batteries in a flashlight?"

Raven laughed. "No, it's this: Robert and I have a hypothesis. We think there might be something about electricity that makes Sissy ill."

Nick handed Robert the dried plate and took another from Raven. "Ah, in a medical sense, eh? Like the claim that living under high voltage lines causes cancer? Or that using cell phones can cause brain tumors?"

"Yep."

"Look, I'm no scientist, but I did pick up dribs and drabs of knowledge here and there: some in college, some in the Rangers—defusing IEDs and time bombs—some in just general reading. As to the medical claims, I think those are based in part on the fact that electrons flowing through a wire causes a magnetic field to form around the wire—and an electric field, too—and some people think these fields are the culprit, especially if it's AC, where they switch back and forth."

"Well, that ain't normal, is it?" said Robert. "I mean, if electricity makes its own magnetic field, what does it do the Earth's natural one?"

"It interferes," said Nick. "A strong enough field causes compasses to deviate."

"Like a lodestone brought near one, eh?"

"That, or a man-made magnet, or plain old iron or steel, or a strong radio or TV signal.

"What else interferes with the Earth's field?" asked Raven.

"Lightning does it. Oh, and a big magnetic flare on the sun, where the solar wind causes beautiful northern lights and knocks out all sorts of technology, sometimes causing power failures and city-wide or even worse blackouts."

Raven handed Nick the washed skillet, its copper clean and gleaming. Raven said, "And so, if our hypothesis is right, the modern world is full of things—cars, cell phones, TVs, computers, whatever—things that cause their own magnetic field or deviations in Earth's natural one."

"Yes, but I rather doubt it's at the root of your sister's affliction. After all, your sister is not a bird."

"What does that have to do with—?"

"They say that some birds navigate by the earth's magnetic field, and that deviations cause their internal compasses to go awry."

"No, Sissy is not a bird, but her DNA is changing," said Raven. "That might make her more sensitive to such things." Nick handed Robert the dried skillet.

Frowning, Robert looked at it and then around the room. "Mister Rogan, did you say that iron interferes with the Earth's magnetic field?"

"Iron, steel: yes."

Robert's eyes flew wide in revelation. "So *that's* why Miss Elizabeth has me take staples out of things and throw away paperclips and such. She told me she can't bear to touch them. That's why there ain't no iron in this whole house. There's brass, copper, bronze, silver, but there ain't even a speck of iron."

14

"Oh, God, if Sissy can't deal with disturbances in the Earth's natural magnetism, no wonder she can't stand being in a car—it's loaded with iron and steel and electronics. And forget about her living in an apartment in a steel-framed skyscraper, with cable TV, electrical wiring, phones, computers. Why, the very air must be sloshing with magnetic fields."

Robert looked down at his rope belt and said, "Force of habit."

"What?" asked Rogan.

"Miss Elizabeth asked me to please take off my belt with its big buckle before coming up to the house. And I always did. It must be made of iron."

Raven looked around the room. "It seems I've always known there's never been iron or steel in this place." Raven glanced at Robert and added, "Not even in the tool shed."

As Nick cocked an eyebrow, Robert nodded and said, "Axes, hammers, buckets, the rest, they all look like something out of the Bronze Age: just brass and copper and tin and bronze. No iron whatsoever."

"Nor anywhere else on this land," said Raven. "It's one reason Sissy came here to live."

Nick looked at Raven and asked, "You knew Elizabeth is sensitive to iron?"

"Yes, but not to the extent it seems she is," said Raven.

"Well, then," said Rogan, "you're probably right that it's the magnetic—rather than the electric—disturbance that's causing her sensitivity."

"How so?"

"Well, iron alone doesn't radiate an electric field, but it does distort the Earth's magnetic one."

"Would changes in DNA cause this?"

"Taylor briefed me on the fact that Dr. Jameson was treating Elizabeth for a mysterious DNA problem, one that kept her away from modern technology. But she said nothing about Elizabeth's DNA changing."

"Well, it is," said Raven. "But Jameson isn't 'treating' her at all. He is simply monitoring the fact that her DNA is continuing to evolve."

"Tell me about this evolution."

Quickly, Raven summed up what Jameson had said about the accelerating mitochondrial drift and the slower change in the primary DNA. "He has no idea why."

"Has he known of Elizabeth's sensitivity to iron?"

"He's the one who first told me," said Raven. "But he said nothing about electricity. And if the disturbance in the Earth's magnetic field is at the root of Sissy's problem, then that's why we couldn't bring technological devices in here either. I always thought it was because of the iron or steel in their structure but not that it might be the electricity flowing through them as well."

"What about you, Raven? Have you been tested?"

"Yes. My DNA seems stable. But, then, Sissy's was stable too, until about three years past."

"And the rest of your family? Mother? Father?"

"I don't know about Mom; she disappeared seven years ago. Her plane was never found. We think she went down somewhere over the Great Lakes. A search was launched, but nothing came of it. By the terms of the Trust, seven years had to pass before she could be declared legally dead."

"And your dad?"

"Well, as I told you, Jameson said that Elizabeth and I do not have the same father. So, I'm not certain that Kevin Conway was my dad . . . or even Sissy's, for that matter. And I know nothing at all about his DNA."

Quietness fell among them, but finally Raven burst out, "Who or what the hell is she becoming?"

Robert looked at her. "What do you mean, Miss Raven?"

"If her DNA is changing," said Raven, "She must be evolving into someone or something else."

"Don't let that slip to a fundamentalist," said Nicholas, trying to lighten the mood. "They don't believe in evolution."

Raven briefly smiled

"And there's never been iron or steel in here before?" asked Rogan.

"Just inadvertently—like my purse with its keys and cell phone and pens and lipstick and compact I thoughtlessly managed to bring into the house when I first got here."

"Well, there's my gun and shaving gear, too," said Rogan.

"And all that stuff the FBI brought in here," added Robert. "Mills, too. And Sheriff Winkler."

"If Sissy shows up," said Raven, "we'll have to get it all out and keep it out."

Rogan nodded and said, "That'll make it a bit harder for me to protect you, but I have ways around it."

Raven sighed. "This place has been iron-free ever since I can remember . . . perhaps even from the very beginning, way back when Cathleens Haven was first built. Maybe there were others like Sissy. Maybe it's an inherited trait." Raven glanced at the document pile resting on a table at the fireplace end of the room. "Maybe there's something in there that might be a clue. But whether or not there is, still I need to talk with Grandmother Meredith. She might shed some light on this place and on Sissy's disappearance."

"Well, then, let's start reading," said Nicholas.

Robert said, "Me, I'm no good at paperwork. I'll go down to Captain Garret and, if anything comes up, I'll fetch you."

"Good grief," said Raven. "Look at this." She spread six Xerox color copies of ornate documents out on the dining table, where she and Nick had moved the pile to go through it.

Rogan frowned at them. "Spanish, French, English, and what are these three?"

"Two of them are written in Latin," said Raven. "Norge might mean Norway, but it's written in Latin. And that one is definitely Latin. The third one might also be written in that tongue, but the words are completely unfamiliar, as if the speaker was transliterating some other language into a Latinate form." Raven pronounced several of the words. *"Chean thal de. Tír na nÓg.* Hmm . . . Sounds somewhat Irish—Gaelic—to me. Anyway, all of them have a wax seal or ornate marking by the signatures. I think we are looking at four separate king's grants, along with one from the Pope, and one from who knows who. But the dates . . . these four are all dated in the 1490s, and the Irish and Norwegian ones are dated in what I think are in the reigns of particular kings; I haven't a clue as to when these might have been, though I think they are extremely old. Maybe before Columbus's time. Perhaps dating back to the Roman Empire."

"Can you read any of them?"

"The English one, certainly. It's signed by Henry VII, 1496. The French one is signed by Charles VIII, in the same year, 1496. The Spanish one, Ferdinand of Aragorn in 1496, too. Pope Alexander VI, also in 1496. Someone named Håkon Eiriksson signed this one in the second year of his reign, whenever that might be. As to the Gaelic one, I haven't a clue as to when that might have been."

"Wait a minute," said Rogan. He began shuffling through papers. "I think I saw a note about an Irish king. I set it aside for later reading— Here it is. Eógan Bél, King of Connacht, Eire." Rogan flipped a page and read: "The first known European discoverer of America, St. Brendan the Navigator, set sail from the province of Connacht, Ireland, in the early part of the sixth century. The king of Connacht, Eógan Bél, signed a king's grant to *Bean Sealgaire*—Lady Hunter—for Hunters Wood, 542 A.D. for the sum of three golden torques, one for each of his then living daughters."

"What?" blurted Raven. "A Lady Hunter laid claim to Hunters Wood in 542 A.D.?"

Rogan looked at her. "That's what it says."

"Holy crap." Raven picked up the copy of the king's grant. "Yes, here's Eógan Bél's mark."

She then looked from the Irish document to the others. "Let me see, from 542 to 1496, that's just short of a thousand years." She picked up the one signed by Henry VII and quickly skimmed through it. "Most of these words are spelled ye olden way. But nearly a thousand years after the Irish king's grant, Henry also deeded to a Lady Hunter, for loyal services rendered, all rights to Hunters Wood." Raven flipped to the next page. "This shows the back of the grant, and there is a description of the land, using lakes and hills and other similar landmarks, and something I take to be a journey measured in days from someplace on the coast." She looked up at Rogan. "What the frack? I mean, England hadn't even laid claim to anything in America in 1496, and yet here we have an English king's grant. And who in hell would be in this part of America at that time? Just Indians, as far as we know. But it seems Lady Hunter knew all about these woods, and yet America was completely unexplored by anyone from Europe in those days."

"I can't disagree with that, Raven," said Nick.

Raven dropped the copy of the English grant and said, "Let me look at these others."

From what Raven could glean from the written languages, the other grants were similar, gold being the medium of exchange, except for the English one.

"What we are saying," said Nick, "is all of these grants were signed and sealed way before America had been explored."

"It looks as if someone was covering his bets," said Raven. "I mean, Irish, Norwegian, English, Spanish, French, the Pope: anyone who could plant a flag on this continent and claim it, be it Brendan the Navigator for Ireland, Leif Eriksson for Norway—I assume that's how Norway could make a claim, sometime around 1000 A.D.—or Columbus for Spain, and subsequently by the French and English, and even the Pope for the Holy Roman Empire."

Rogan puzzled over the documents. "Look here, Raven. Are these the names of those who were awarded the grants? *Dame Chasseuse, Dama Cazadora, Domina Venatrix.* I don't pretend to know some of these words, but I think that 'Dame,' 'Dama,' and 'Domina' all mean 'Lady,' and I happen to know that Cazadora is a female hunter."

"Well, my French and Latin are rusty," said Raven, "but I think that 'Chasseuse' and 'Venatrix" both mean 'Hunter' as well."

"How about the Norwegian one?"

Raven skimmed the copy. "Here is who obtained the grant, and the name seems to be written both in Latin and Norwegian: Domina Venatrix, and Dame *Jeger*, which also must mean Lady Hunter."

"I'll be damned," said Nick. "Here we have someone who, over a span of a thousand years, got six different king's grants for the same piece of land in a totally unmapped continent. Just who is this Lady Hunter, anyhow?"

Raven looked at Nicholas and said, "Surely 'Lady Hunter' is a title, right? I mean, it can't actually be the same woman, can it?"

15

"I don't see how it could be the same woman," said Nick. "You're right: it's probably a title handed down from mother to daughter."

"Oh, good grief," said Raven. "I just realized if that's true, then I am now Lady Hunter."

Rogan cocked an eyebrow at her.

"When I asked George Allenby as to why Hunters Wood was scrambled on Google maps, among other things he said something along the lines that the Wood would always remain private from the public, excepting the women of the lineage of Cathleen Hunter. If Cathleen is a descendent of Lady Hunter, then so am I, for I am a woman in the lineage."

"It's matrilineal? —The Trust, I mean."

"Yes." Raven began searching through the Xeroxed pages. "Allenby also said something about a private Presidential Executive Order Seventeen."

"Something old or new?"

"Apparently it has been passed from President to President," said Raven.

They divided the stack in two and began searching, and after a while, Rogan said, "This might be it. It's signed by George Washington.

"Really?"

"Really," said Nick, handing the copy of the two page document to her.

Quickly she skimmed it. "This is like the kings' grants, Nick. But this one is marked 'private,' and he asks that his successors honor it. It goes on to describe a woodland, and President Washington set it aside as a federal grant to—guess who?—and if you say Lady Cathleen Hunter, you would be right. Well, unlike the previous Lady Hunter, at least we have a first name for this one. It seems she paid in gold ingots, which went to help fund the government. The letter is dated Saturday, May 16, 1789." She looked up at Rogan. "When was he in office?"

Nick shrugged. "I dunno. Somewhere around that time."

"Oh, wait," said Raven. "Here it is. He says this is his seventeenth day in office. Perhaps that's why it's called Executive Order Seventeen."

"Dammit!" said Rogan. "Another mystery to add to the others. Once again we have a grant for a piece of land that was yet to appear on any map. I think the only folks we know of who were even in this territory at that time were probably French trappers and Native Americans."

Raven sighed and set the copy aside and said, "This isn't helping to find Sissy."

Rogan nodded and said, "Look, part of what I am going to say, might sound harsh, but we have to consider the possibilities, and—"

"Sissy is not dead," declared Raven, tears forming. "She can't be. She just can't be. I would know, wouldn't

I?"

Rogan took her hand. "Perhaps you would."

With her free hand, Raven wiped the wetness from her cheeks. "Still, Nick, you are right. We do have to take into account that she might not be alive. What were you going to say?"

"I was going to lay out possibilities and see how we might help."

Raven took a deep breath and said, "Go on."

"All right. I look at it this way: from worst case to best, Elizabeth is either dead, injured, lost, captive, simply away on her own, or off with a lover. And, she's either on Trust land or not. If she is in Hunters Wood, then dead, injured, lost, or a captive, the Rangers are likely to come across her, either on foot, or spot her by chopper. We can leave it to them to conduct the search. If she is not in Hunters Wood, and if we get no further information, then the FBI and other law enforcement agencies are our best bet to discover where she might be.

"If she didn't leave voluntarily, then we have no idea where someone might have taken her. But she might have gone on her own, or with someone, maybe a lover. Who would Elizabeth have fallen in love with out here?"

"I don't know. She didn't write anything about a new boyfriend. Instead her letters were about her paintings and the forest and its peace and solitude, and nature's bounty. She was becoming a regular Thoreau."

"Well, then, where would she go, and how?"

"It wouldn't be any place modern, so it would have to be an iron-free, electricity-free rural setting, and the only place nearby is right here—Hunters Wood. As to how she would travel: she could walk, go by any conveyance without iron or electricity, such as a very old fashioned carriage. There are no nearby rivers, so that lets out canoes and rafts and boats. She could go by horseback, as long as the tack had no steel or iron. But Sissy didn't have a horse, yet she could have gone with someone who did."

Nick nodded, but remained silent.

Raven frowned. "Remember, Robert said that she might have gone off with one of the invisible riders. At the time I thought that would be too weird, but now . . ."

"Raven, I don't doubt that you heard sounds of a horn and running horses, but when it comes to being invisible, I know of no science that could make that be true."

"Well, I know what I heard," said Raven, "and what I saw, and what I didn't see."

"I do not doubt that. But let me ask, is there anyone at all living within Hunters Wood?"

"Not that I know of . . . though . . ."—the thought that had repeatedly been niggling at the edge of Raven's mind finally came to her—"Wait. My Grandmother Meredith used to tell Sissy and me stories, and one of them had to do with the hidden people of the forest. She used to say that they could only be seen if you were one of them or if they chose to be seen by you. I think it's a fairy tale she made up, but then again it could be a story about people who really do live in there, not necessarily invisible people, but those who are very reclusive."

Raven stood and said, "And that leads to something we *can* do, Nick; we can go to Grandmother Meredith and try to find out what she knows. Not only about the so-called hidden people, but about my father, Kevin

Conway, and about my mother and who might have been her lover, and either Sissy's father or mine."

"Where is your grandmother?" asked Rogan.

"In a suburb of the city at a place called Shady Rest. We can get there in an hour."

"The city is a hundred miles away, Raven."

"I have a Porsche. —Oh, wait. Jack Miller has it. Broken control arm."

"We'll take my Jeep, and you will wear your body armor. After all, I am pledged to keep you safe. Besides, now that I've found you, I don't ever want to lose you."

"I'm not someone to be babied, Nick."

Rogan took her hands and pulled her to him and enfolded her in his embrace. "Did I say you were? No, Raven, you are someone to be cherished, and if you'll let me, I'll be the one to do that."

Oh, God, it feels so good to be held.

She lifted her face to him in invitation, and they hungrily kissed. And Rogan said, "If we don't go now, I—"

Raven laughed and pulled away and said, "Your Jeep."

"And your body armor," said Nick.

They paused long enough to tell Robert and Captain Garret where they were headed, and then Rogan slipped the Wrangler into gear, and down the lane they sped.

They paused in Benton and, as Raven gassed up the Jeep, Rogan made a phone call. He filled in Jack Sloan, his exec, and then said, "Have Danny Mack and Johnny Redwing fly our chopper to Cathleens Haven. The directions on how to get here are on my desk."

"I'll just Google it," said Sloan.

"I tried. It's blocked."

Sloan whistled. "Big time, eh?"

"Yep. Something to do with Hunters Trust."

"Okay. What else do you need?"

"Four Cloak nines, a couple of Sauer snipes, that brass double-barrel you said we had no use for, and three Sig 556's, plenty of ammo for all, and night-vision gear."

Sloan whistled. "You want any grenades? C4? I mean, it sounds like you are preparing for a war, Nick."

"With Russian snipers involved, Jack, we just might be. But, hey, no C4 or grenades."

"You sure three are enough to guard that lady?"

"As long as we're out in the sticks, unless they send an army of their own, Danny, Johnny, and I will be enough. Oh, and right now, I don't think whoever is behind this will try anything. We have a Ranger company in the meadow below the house at night."

"Anyone we know?"

"Not me. Captain Garret is their C.O."

"Raleigh Garret?"

"Yeah. You know him?"

"Not personally, but I know of him. He's the one who got those bastards in Ramadi."

"The one who led the Red Nine raid?"

"Yeah."

"Fine job, that."

"Yeah. See if you can recruit him, Nick."

"Maybe so. Okay, Jack, we're on our way."

"Right. Sloan out."

Raven looked at Nick and said, "You actually have

someone named Johnny Redwing in your company?"

"Yeah. An Oklahoma Cherokee. He can smell trouble a mile away."

"What a perfect name. I'll have to put him in one of my books."

"Like Hillerman's Joe Leaphorn or Jim Chee?"

"Yeah, but Johnny Redwing will be even better."

As they pulled out of Benton, Raven called the Shady Rest care facility and made arrangements to see Meredith. And they headed southward, aiming for the distant Interstate some forty miles out of town.

Raven leaned back and let the wind blow her hair into what she hoped was not an uncombable tangle, and Nick turned on the radio and managed to find an AM station playing something other than Country and Western, and they listened to eighties rock—Journey, Palantir, Escape, Pat Shannon, and others.

Apple and peach orchards came and went alongside the three-lane rolling-hills highway, one that would soon be loaded with fruit pickers and haulers. Large white farmhouses sat back from the road, some with kids hanging on fences and watching for cars to come flowing by—as if that was their main entertainment. Some dogs ran the extent of the yards, barking at the red Jeep.

How pastoral. How different from far-distant Seattle, my home away from Cathleens Haven.

Some twenty miles south of Benton, Nick said, "There's a car that's been following us for some time now. And even though this is the best way to the Interstate and it might be just another someone going somewhere, be ready for anything."

Raven leaned so that she could see the vehicle in the right-hand mirror—a white four-door of some sort.

They came to a section of the road where there were no farmhouses in sight, and the highway was clear of all traffic except for the sedan and the Jeep. The car behind began to accelerate. Nick pulled his M&P .40 from his shoulder rig and laid it in the seat at his leg.

Again Nick said, "Be ready."

Raven didn't exactly know what he meant by "Be ready," but if it were Jake Stone in one of her books, he meant for Melody to be ready to duck.

Still the car drew onward.

Would Melody do that? Duck? Come on, Raven, you're no Melody Hawk.

Now the car swung out to pass. There was a white-haired woman in the passenger seat, and a young man driving.

"Looks like a local," said Raven—

—And then she saw the gun.

16

As if by reflex, Raven snatched up the M&P .40 and smoothly chambered a round—the one already in the barrel flying wide—and, as the car pulled even with the left rear of the Jeep, she twisted around in spite of her body armor and her seatbelt and fired two shots behind Rogan and across at the white-haired lady, the man with the gun. The sedan swerved, and Raven fired three more rounds. The gunman jerked and fell into the driver, and the car veered sharply leftward, nearly out of control. The driver shoved at the man, finally heaving him off and into the passenger side door, and the white wig went flying out the window. The driver then floored it, and the vehicle leaped forward and away. Nick slammed on the brakes, even as Raven clicked loose her seat belt and lurched to her feet and grabbed the top of the windshield frame to steady herself and screamed, "Take this, motherfrackers! Take this!" while she snapped off six more rounds at the fleeing car; the rear window shattered, but the car sped onward.

Sitting still in the middle of the road, Nick turned off the radio, shutting out Pat Benatar's "Hit Me with Your Best Shot" midsong. Then he looked up at Raven and gritted, "That's not what I meant when I said 'be ready.'"

Breathing hard, her heart hammering in her chest as if it were trying to escape, and with her windblown hair framing her face, Raven looked down at Nick and, in her best Melody Hawk imitation, said, "No shit, GI. But he was going to shoot."

"God, you're beautiful," said Nick.

She got control of her breathing, then handed the gun back to him. Suddenly she felt weak-kneed and on the verge of tears, and she collapsed back into her seat. With trembling hands she covered her face and mumbled, "Did you get a plate number?"

"No."

"Me, neither."

She didn't know whether to laugh or cry, so she managed to giggle while sobbing.

Nick unsnapped his seatbelt and reached over and pulled her to him as far as he could. As he held her she sniffled and said, "I wish they made cars the way they used to. This damn console is in the way." Then she burst out in laughter, and so did Nick.

Just as suddenly, Raven's laughter chopped off. "Oh, Nick, I might have just killed a man."

"Maybe, maybe not, but it was in self defense."

"Oh, God."

Some while later, Rogan released Raven, and she slid fully into her seat and looped on her safety belt and clicked it shut.

Rogan softly said, "They, whoever they are, they are still after you, Raven."

"I know," she said meekly.

Rogan shifted the Wrangler into reverse and began backing up. "They must have found out their guy is dead."

Raven nodded and, with her voice strengthening, she said, "It's not like that's a secret in Benton. I suspect the whole town was abuzz with the news shortly after Deputy Mills got back." Raven smiled, adding, "Likely it's in their weekly rag. They might have, in fact, run a special edition: Russian Assassin Dead. One Murder Committed; Another Avoided."

"This is serious business," said Rogan, still backing.

"I know, Nick. I know. Gallows humor, that's all. And where in the hell are you going?"

"To get this," said Nick, stopping the Jeep and throwing it into neutral and pulling on the parking brake. He stepped out of the Wrangler and picked up the white wig the would-be shooter had worn. Rogan looked at the underside. "A label: Gashouse Costumes, 3220 East Green."

"Is that in the city?"

Nick got back in and punched the address into the Wrangler's nav system. "It is. But no business is listed there."

"Maybe the nav data base is outdated," said Raven.

"Regardless," said Nick, "we'll stop in and see if we can get a line on whoever rented or bought it."

"Let's hope they used a credit card," said Raven.

Nick handed her the wig and said, "Pop it into the glove compartment. And while you're at it"—he unholstered his M&P and handed it to her—"reload this. There's ammo in there as well."

Raven removed a box of .40 caliber cartridges and

slipped the wig in after glancing at the label. She took the pistol from Rogan and pressed the magazine catch, and dropped out the clip.

Rogan then released the brake and shifted into gear, and as he drove, Raven clicked ammo into the clip, replacing ten of the eleven she had fired. "You want the one left in the chamber?"

"Yep."

Raven fished around the floor, and found the cartridge she had ejected when she had first grabbed the gun. She blew on it and inspected the casing, then pressed it into the clip. Now fully reloaded—fifteen in the magazine and one in the barrel ready to fire—she slipped the clip into the weapon, and handed it back to Rogan. As she put the ammo box into the glove compartment and snapped it shut, "Just one left," she said.

"More in the cargo area under the rear floorboard," said Rogan, reholstering the M&P .40.

They rode a mile or so without speaking, and then Rogan said, "That was good shooting back there."

"Lots of time on the range," said Raven.

"Range time doesn't necessarily translate into good shooting under pressure."

"Mmm . . ." said Raven, then after a while said, "Melody Hawk would have gotten them both."

"Your alter ego?" asked Nick.

"She is, when I'm writing," said Raven. "Though now and then I'm also Jake Stone."

"Tell me about them," said Nick.

They were still talking about Melody and Jake when

they reached the Shady Rest care facility, and by this time Raven was laughing along with Nick. Rogan pulled into the parking lot.

As they got out, Nick said, "Let me make a call."

He got the number for the sheriff's substation in Benton and punched it in, and after a short conversation relating the particulars, he clicked shut his cell phone.

"Smart move," said Raven, as they walked to the front entrance, realizing that by reporting the incident to Mills, who would then relay it to Sheriff Winkler, who would report it to the city authorities, she and Nick would avoid being hassled by anyone until they returned the Cathleens Haven. In the meantime, the locals here and elsewhere would be checking hospitals for a gunshot victim.

After signing in, they were escorted to a small private conference room, and moments later, an attendant wheeled in white-haired eighty-nine-year-old Meredith Lucas.

Raven hugged her and said, "Hi, Grandmother."

Meredith glanced first at the door, where the attendant had gone, then around the room as if seeking something or someone, her gaze skipping over Rogan. Finally she looked at Raven and asked, "Do I know you?"

17

"I'm Raven, Grandmother Meredith, Raven Conway."

"No, you're not. Raven Conway is ten, and you look to me to be more than ten."

"I've grown up, Grandmother."

Meredith Lucas turned her face away, her jaw set stubbornly.

Raven looked at Nick in despair.

"You have to try, Raven," he softly said.

Raven took a deep breath and slowly let it out. She eased herself to the floor at Meredith's feet. "Grandmother, tell me again about the hidden people in the woods."

Meredith turned her face down toward Raven. "Oh, child, where have you been, and where is Sissy? Have you two been up in the forest again?"

"Looking for mushrooms, Grandmother."

"Is it that time of year?"

"Yes, Grandmother."

"And where is Avi?"

"Mom is probably with Sissy, Grandmother."

Meredith looked at Nick and flicked the back of an age-spotted hand at him as if shooing away a fly. She said, "You need to find Avi, Kevin. Else you're going to lose her again."

"I'll look in a minute," said Nick. "But I want to hear the story, too. Tell us about the forest."

Meredith put a trembling hand to her mouth, and peered left and right, a haunted look in her faded blue eyes. "I went in once and came back with one, but Avi went in twice and came back with two."

"Mushrooms, Grandmother?"

"Oh, no, child. Avi and you and your sister."

Raven glanced up at Nick, but he shrugged.

"I don't understand, Grandmother."

"Don't worry, Raven, Avi will explain it in eleven more years."

Before Raven could ask her what she meant, Meredith said, "She loves them, you know."

"Loves what, Grandmother? Mushrooms?"

"Both of them, dark and light."

Meredith then leaned down and whispered, "I think he knows." Then she sat up and said, "Don't worry, Kevin, I'm sure she'll be right back. Even though you don't feel comfortable, still you should go look."

"In a moment, Grandmother Meredith," said Nick.

Suddenly, the old woman jerked in startlement, and her breath came in swift gasps, panic filled her face. "Where is this? This isn't Cathleens Haven. Where have you taken me, Avi?" She began to weep.

Raven reached up and clasped one of Meredith's hands in her own. "Shh . . . Shh . . ." she soothed, stroking her grandmother's worn fingers. "Everything is all right. Everything is all right."

Gradually, Meredith settled down and finally looked at Raven and smiled. "Hello, child. Where is your sister?"

"Picking mushrooms, Grandmother."

"Well, then, she'll miss the story."

Raven nodded and said, "It's one of our favorites, and you can tell it again and again, and it will be like new every time."

Meredith grinned and said, "A strange and perilous people dwell in the Deep Dark Woods, dangerous to those who would do harm. They are not like us here at Cathleens Haven. Instead they are mysterious and secretive, and we cannot see them unless they wish to be seen. They came over the sea long ago, and the great Chief Motaskah, Chief White Bear, gave them these woods in exchange for magical arrows. The Indians quit the forest, for it had become a 'Ghost Wood,' a 'Forest where Spirits Wail and Thunder.'

"The hidden people live in the Deep Dark Forest and settle their debts with gold. Even when Roosevelt took away the gold from everyone, still they paid with ingots—the kings, the queens, even the Presidents. Not the Indians, though; those they paid with arrows instead, and silken bowstrings and wax. Beware, all ye who would do harm to those of Hunters Wood, for the dwellers within will make you pay with blood rather than with ingots of gold."

Meredith's eyes began to droop. "I'm tired, now, child. I need—"

"Oh, please wait, Grandmother. Tell me about my father."

Meredith leaned down and whispered, "Not with Kevin here."

Raven whispered back, "Is Kevin my father? Is he

Sissy's father?"

"Oh, no, child. Neither of you are his."

"Then who is my father? And who is Sissy's?"

Meredith glanced left and right, as if looking for eavesdroppers. She motioned Raven closer and murmured a word. Then Meredith smiled and straightened up and leaned back in her wheelchair and closed her eyes and began to snore softly.

Raven frowned in puzzlement, and Nick stood and held out a hand to her and helped her to her feet.

"What did your grandmother say?" asked Nick.

"She said that Kevin Conway was neither my father nor Sissy's."

"Did you ask her who each of your fathers might have been?"

Raven looked down at this frail old woman who once had been vigorous and witty, but who now had fallen into ruin. "I did, but the answer she gave simply doesn't make any sense."

"What doesn't make any sense?"

Raven shrugged and turned to Nick and said, "I'm certain Grandmother said, 'She.'"

18

As they walked toward the Jeep, Rogan shook his head and said, "'She'? Your grandmother said, 'She'?"

"That's right: 'She.'"

"Maybe instead she said Shea, as in Shea Stadium, not that I'm saying that your mother conceived either you or your sister there."

Raven smiled, but shook her head. "S. H. E. That's what she said, not Shea."

Rogan sighed. "I'm sorry, but you know your grandmother is addled. I mean, how can a woman be your father?"

"Perhaps by parthenogenesis."

"What?"

"Parthenogenesis. It's a kind of reproduction in which an unfertilized egg develops into a new individual, always a female."

"No dad involved?"

Raven shook her head and said, "No dad whatsoever. I think it occurs occasionally in sharks, and in insects and crustaceans and arachnids."

"You, my dear are no spider," said Nick, "even though you have me in your web."

Raven laughed, then said, "Grandmother is addled,

all right, but the tale she told is the one I remember her telling Sissy and me when I was ten and Sissy eight."

Rogan snapped his fingers. "Ah, that's it, then."

"That's what then?"

"One thing your grandmother said, was that Avi would explain it in eleven more years. Avi is your mother, right?"

"Yes. Her name is, was, Avelaine, but Grandmother always called her Avi."

"Well, then, when your grandmother said what she said, you were ten in her eyes, and eleven more years would make you—"

"—Twenty-one," said Raven. "But Mother disappeared before she could tell me whatever secrets she held, and Grandmother Meredith had already lost it by then."

"Alzheimer's?"

"No. She had a series of small strokes that resulted in irreversible dementia. My mother put her in this care facility some eight, nine years ago, and she's been here ever since."

When they reached the Jeep, Rogan flipped on the key, and when the nav system lit up, he punched in an address. "Here's the way to Gashouse Costumes."

"Damn," exclaimed Raven. "The wig. I had forgotten all about it."

When they reached 3224 East Green, they found a vacant lot in between a gas station and a Taco Bell.

"This is 3224?"

Raven glanced at the map and then at the adjacent addresses. She nodded and gestured: "There's 3210 and 3230. So this is where it should be." Then she looked across the street and said, "There's a La-Z-Boy store. Let's ask there."

When they entered the store, they were met by an obsequious salesman, who directed them to the manager when he found out what they wanted. Ms. Harkness, a federal-gold-blond matron, frowned at the fact that Raven was wearing a strange vest, but quickly passed it off and nodded at their question and said, "Oh, yes. It was there. Terrible tragedy, that. It was the middle of three stores." She led them to the wide storefront window. "Let me see, from left to right they were"—she pointed slightly leftward—"Kendra's Candles. Oh it smelled so lovely in there, with its scented oils and beautiful candles—beeswax, you see. Kendra wanted only the best. She made them herself." Ms. Harkness then moved her aim toward the center of the lot. "And then Gashouse Costumes came next; wonderful outfits; Halloween was George's time of the year. People flocked to his store. He was so nice." Ms. Harkness then shifted her point to the right. "And the third store was . . . was . . . oh, it's dancing on the tip of my tongue . . . okay, yes, Brady's Art Supplies, with paints of all kinds, and canvasses and brushes, and a studio in back for teaching. I'm not an artist, but if I had been, his was the place where I would have gone."

"What happened?" asked Raven.

"Oh, dear. Three years ago it all burned to the ground. And when they finally got the fire out, that's when they found George Harris. Turns out he'd been shot. Murdered. Probably a robbery gone bad. He stayed open late, you see, but the others did not, except when there was an art class in session. That night, though, there was not. Anyway, whoever did it tried to cover it up by setting the place on fire. And what with the art store on one side—with its oils and sketch pads and the like—and the candle shop on the other—with its waxes and scented oils and such—is it any wonder that everything went up in a huge ball of flame?"

"Did they find the killer?" asked Rogan.

"Oh, no. Never did. But I know he will get his due, if not in this life, then in the next."

Raven looked at Nick and raised an eyebrow, and Rogan said, "Thank you, Ms. Harkness."

She smiled and said, "Are you certain that I can't interest you in some of our sofas, our recliners. We have a wonderful sale going on right now, and a young couple like you, just starting out, as it were, well, I am sure I can make it worth your while."

Nick took Raven's hand in his own and said, "How could you tell, Ms. Harkness."

"Why, just by the looks on your faces and all. Anyone could see that you are incredibly in love"—Ms. Harkness giggled—"and I think you two need at least a love seat."

"No doubt you are right," said Rogan, nodding and smiling. "And we will keep you in mind."

Hand in hand, they exited, and when they reached the Jeep, each seemed reluctant to let go, and Nick pulled Raven to him and kissed her.

"She's right, you know," said Nick, looking down into Raven's face.

"Who?" Her question, though but a single word, seemed breathless.

"Ms. Harkness."

Even as she smiled in agreement, Raven's thoughts clamored: *Come on, girl. You've known this man, this mercenary, this soldier of fortune for—what?—two days. Is that all? He arrived on Saturday and this is Sunday. And already you two are madly in love? Oh, crap, I slept with him the very first night, and it wasn't even a second date. Slow down, girl. Slow down. But, oh, how I don't want to.*

Raven glanced over at the La-Z-Boy store, and, at the front window, Ms. Harkness smiled and waved.

Raven stepped free of Nick and waved back. They climbed into the Jeep, and Ms. Harkness was still waving as they drove away.

As they headed for the freeway, Raven looked at Nick in profile, and her heart skipped a beat, or at least that's how she thought of it. Grudgingly, she turned her thoughts to the business at hand. "We need to turn the wig over to Agent Marks. Maybe the FBI can get some DNA from it and use CODIS to identify not only the one who tried to shoot us, but perhaps also the killer of George Harris."

Rogan nodded. "Better Agent Marks than Deputy Mills, I would think." Nick glanced at his watch. "Lunchtime, Raven. And me, I'm starved."

They stopped near the Interstate on-ramp at Uncle Bob's Home Cooking, whose sign promised "Come in and have a seat, and, Bob's your uncle, we'll feed you good eats."

As Rogan ate his Uncle Bob's famous hot-roast-beef sandwich, and Raven her Uncle Bob's famous flame-grilled sirloin burger, Nick said, "Eight or nine years ago your mother put your grandmother in Shady Rest, right?"

Raven nodded and said, "She wanted to make certain that Grandmother was well taken care of."

"There might have been another reason as well," said Nick.

"And that would be . . . ?"

"It might indicate that Avelaine was planning on disappearing, and so she put your Grandmother Meredith in good hands first, and then your mother vanished."

With her burger halfway to her mouth, Raven said, "What?"

19

"I said, your mother might have planned—"

"I know what you said, Nick. I was just surprised, that's all."

"The timing might merely be coincidental," said Rogan.

"Her plane was never found," said Raven. "If her disappearance was planned, a Learjet is a bit hard to keep concealed. I mean, someone somewhere would stumble across it, even if it were in something like a warehouse, barn, or hangar."

"Perhaps. But it might not be difficult to disguise— different tail number, paint job, and the like—or to get rid of." Rogan took a bite of his gravy-covered mashed potatoes.

"Get rid of? How? Dismantle it? Cut it into pieces? Sell it to a drug lord?"

Rogan swallowed and took a sip of coffee, then said, "If I were going to do it with my company jet, I'd set the autopilot to fly out to sea, and bail long before then. And when it ran out of fuel . . ." Rogan made a diving motion with his fork.

Raven nodded, then said, "Costly, though."

Rogan smiled. "I can afford it, and so could your

mother, given Hunters Trust."

"There would be wreckage."

Rogan said, "It might never be seen. Sometimes it's harder to find a downed plane than you would think. In a good number of cases, it's years later that the wreck is discovered. And at sea, the chances are even slimmer."

"Still," said Raven, "all indications were that she went down somewhere over the Great Lakes, which is quite far from the ocean."

"I would need to look at her flight plan. Was she alone?"

"Yes. In spite of having both a pilot and a copilot on the payroll, she took off without them."

"As she would have were she planning to vanish."

"But, why would she do so, and why then?"

"I haven't a clue as to why, but as to the when: were you and your sister in college when she vanished?"

"I was a sophomore in the journalism school at the University of Missouri, and Sissy had just begun studying at the New York School of Art."

"So, you didn't have any money worries and were both somewhat secure, somewhat independent?"

"Less than you might think," said Raven, "but I suppose so. Still, Mother's disappearance came as a great blow."

"She left no message behind?"

Raven put her half-eaten hamburger aside and shook her head. "No."

"Oh, Raven," said Nick, "I didn't mean to spoil your appetite."

"It's all right. I wasn't that hungry."

As Nick continued with his roast beef and potatoes,

Raven, picking half-heartedly at her fries, said, "So, we have these questions before us: If Mother went down with her airplane, where did it happen? If she did not go down in her airplane, where did she go, and why, and how?"

"I'll have Jack look into it," said Nick.

"Jack Sloan? Your exec?"

"Yeah."

Rogan finished the last of his beef and mashed potatoes, and on the way to the Jeep, he said, "What did Grandmother Meredith mean when she said she went in once and came back with one, and Avi went in twice and came back with two?"

"Oh, my," said Raven. "I just now get it. She meant babies."

"Babies?"

"Yes. As a young woman, Meredith went somewhere—maybe into a clinic or even the forest— and came out with Avelaine. Mother went in and came out with me, and then she went in again and came out with Sissy."

"What did she do, just find you lying under a mushroom?"

Raven laughed. "No, no. I think grandmother meant that she got pregnant once, and my mother twice. I know our medical records show that we were cared for from onset of pregnancy through term and for some time after by reputable pediatricians—mine in Seattle, Elizabeth's in Portland, Maine. But that still doesn't tell me just who is my father, or who Sissy's is, either."

As they got into the Jeep, Rogan said, "You are dark and Elizabeth is fair, so when Meredith said Avi loved both the dark and the light, I think she was speaking of your father being dark and Sissy's being light. You and Sissy might take after them."

"My father might have been a dark-haired recluse who lived in the forest? Sissy's father a light-haired one?"

"I haven't the foggiest," said Rogan, starting the Jeep. "But it seems your Grandmother Meredith believes it to be true."

For miles along the freeway, Raven sat quietly pondering, and finally she said, "I think you're right, Nick. —About Grandmother Meredith believing my mother loved two different men. I mean, Doctor Jameson told me that Sissy and I didn't have the same father, and Sissy is the fair-haired child, while I am the dark-haired one. *Sister Light, Sister Dark*; there's a book by that name. I never read it, but I know of it. Regardless, I find it hard to believe that both Grandmother and Mother each mated with some recluse or other living in Hunters Wood."

Nick nodded and said, "Remember, your grandmother is quite addled."

They swung off the freeway at the Benton exit, and headed north. Some miles later they passed a road worker leaning against his shovel, his county pickup truck on the shoulder, its yellow light flashing. He turned and watched as the Jeep went by.

"I think he was nursing that shovel," said Raven.

Nick laughed and said, "Your tax dollars at work," and on northward he drove.

A short while later, a sheriff's car went screaming

southward, its light bar flashing.

"Was that Mills?" asked Rogan.

"It didn't look like him."

Rogan nodded, but made no comment.

"Maybe they're after the shooter's car," said Raven.

"I think it's long gone."

"You're right. Probably not."

"You shot someone?" asked Agent Marks, looking at the white wig.

"Yep," said Raven. "It war him or us'n, Sheeriff, 'n' he drawed fust."

"This is not something to make jokes about, Miss Conway."

Raven shook her head and tears welled. "I know, Agent Marks, but if I don't make light of it, I'll cry."

"Remember, Raven, he might just be wounded," said Rogan.

Marks read the underside label and said, "And you think this wig might be related to another crime? A murder?"

"Yes."

"Well, then, I'll need a full report." He looked at Rogan and added, "And your gun."

Rogan looked at Captain Garret. "You got a spare I can use till tomorrow?"

Without a word, Garret unholstered his M9 Beretta and handed it to Rogan.

Rogan gave his M&P .40 to Marks.

Marks said to Raven, "Is it all right if we take the report up in the house?"

Raven looked at Captain Garret. "Is there no word of

Sissy?"

"None. And my men are on the sweep back this way."

Raven turned to Marks. "Then the house will be fine."

Raven watched as Agent Marks headed for the path and down. "I'm a bit wrung out by all of his questions."

"I think you mean interrogation," said Rogan. "But that's the FBI for you: great on detail, less so on action."

Raven smiled. "Well, at least he didn't waterboard me, and he and Curly and Larry are going back to the field office to take up their part of the investigation."

Rogan nearly snarfed his lemonade. "Mo, Curly, and Larry? Oh, that's funny."

Raven giggled. "Huey, Dewey, and Louie?"

"Mickey, Donald, and Goofy?"

They were still laughing when the FBI van pulled away.

"I hope they find something about Sissy's— No, wait. Maybe I shouldn't hope that, because if Sissy is somewhere out in the modern world, she's suffering."

"Even so, we need them looking, Raven."

"I know."

"And we need them investigating the Russian connection and the attempt on your life, Raven."

"You just had to remind me, didn't you?"

"It's my job," said Rogan.

"Well, reminder or not," said Raven, "I think you and I and Robert need to go to Fred's and have a fine meal and some wine, and put the cares of this day behind us."

"Raven, by going to Fred's, you make yourself more vulnerable to another attempt."

"Do you really think there's still another assassin out there waiting for me to show my face in public? Don't answer that. Instead"—with her arms outspread, she slowly turned a full three sixty—"I am wearing the latest fashion—forest-cammoed body armor."

Rogan said, "It doesn't protect you from a head shot."

"I'll duck,"

As they stopped in front of Fred's, Rogan called Jack Sloan and gave him the sketchy particulars of Avelaine Conway's disappearance, suggesting that it might have been planned by her. "Look into it, Jack. See what you can find: motive and means and destination if deliberate, or sabotage or accident if not, and, in any case, where the plane might be now."

In Fred's, Rogan insisted upon a table where there were no nearby windows, no line of sight from the outside on Raven.

In spite of the obvious protective-custody moves, soon Raven and Nick and Robert and Fred were all laughing and enjoying a garden salad and an excellent Chianti while waiting for their order to arrive: tenderloin tips in a spicy ragout to be served on a bed of ribbon pasta, fresh-baked French bread, and a side order of cantaloupe balls garnished with bleu cheese, all to be followed by a serving of German chocolate cake, and a glasses of Madera port.

Even though most of the dinner crowd was still present, Fred had abandoned her hostess post and had joined Robert and Raven and Nick for dinner. Fred and Robert told tales of growing up in the fruit belt, of stealing apples with apples all around, of migrant follies, and of how they came to be a couple, Fred supplying most of that detail with Robert shyly keeping mum but for a word here and there.

The main course arrived, and as they ate, Fred said to Raven, "I'm a great fan of yours, of Jake and Melody, and I want to know how they met. It's not like it's in any of your books so far."

Raven laughed and said, "I wrote of their first meeting when I was thirteen, I think. It's quite mushy and full of people jumping out of the bushes at Melody."

"I'll bet she kicked butt," said Fred.

"Oh, no. She was always saved by Jake. It wasn't until I took up martial arts that Melody became proficient in saving herself, and Jake at times, too."

"Then you must be a regular Melody Hawk," said Fred. She turned her blue gaze upon Rogan. "And that must make you Jake Stone."

"I'm afraid I don't know Jake," said Nick.

"You haven't read Raven's books?"

Rogan smiled at Raven and said, "Not yet."

"For shame!" declared Fred.

"What do you read, Nick?" asked Raven.

"Lots of tech manuals."

"How about something not work related."

"Well, you're going to think this is silly."

"No, no. Go ahead."

"I like Robert E. Howard's work."

"You like Conan, the Barbarian?" asked Raven.

"Among other things by Howard. But Conan, well,

the Ranger Company I was in thought of him as a sort of patron saint. No talk; all action."

"I *love* Conan," said Raven.

"Never heard of him," said Fred. "Is there anything else you read I might know of?"

"Westerns."

"Louis L'Amour?" asked Robert.

"Yup."

"Now, them Sackett Brothers, they are the very best."

Rogan nodded.

Nancy, their server, brought out the German chocolate cake, and the bottle of port, along with small wine glasses, and Fred sliced and served and poured.

Raven raised her glass and looked at Nick. The others followed her lead. "To absent friends," she said, "and to those present as well."

"Hear, hear," said Fred, and she downed her glass entirely and poured herself another.

"Mmm. . ." moaned Raven over a forkful of cake, "this is to die for."

Through the front door stormed Deputy Mills. He looked around and spotted the room Raven and Nick were in, and bulled over to their table. The diners at the other tables grew quiet. Mills looked down at Nick and Raven and said, "I've been saddled with a lot of paperwork on account of you two."

"Oh?" said Nick.

"Yeah, and I just want you to know we found your dead shooter lying in a ditch alongside the road."

Rogan looked around at the crowd of people hanging on Mills' every word. Then he stared steely-eyed at

Mills and said, "And now, everyone knows."

"He was dead?" asked Raven.

Mills nodded. "One in the neck, one in the head. You shot him dead, Miss Conway."

Raven dropped her fork with a clatter and tears filled her eyes. She turned to Rogan and said, "I killed him, Nick. I killed him. I killed a human being."

Rogan stood her up and put his arm about her and escorted her to the Jeep.

Rogan tucked her in her bed and turned to go, but she softly said, "Don't."

He turned back.

"I can't be alone with this," she said.

Without undressing, Rogan laid down beside her and took her in his arms.

20

Raven awoke to kitchen sounds and the aroma of coffee and the scent of something she couldn't quite put her finger on. She slipped out of bed and padded to the tub room and relieved herself, then did a quick wash-up. As she brushed her teeth, helicopter turbines began whining in the distance. *The third day has begun. Four days left.* She combed her hair to the far-away sound of the stentorian voice of Sergeant Randall shouting unintelligible commands. *Please, God, let them find Sissy.* She hurried back to the bedroom, and moments later she was dressed and standing at the stove end of the great room and watching Rogan expertly pitch a pancake onto a teetering pile. He had three separate skillets on the stove, and he dropped a final large dollop of batter into the just-emptied one.

"You ought to marry me, sleepyhead," said Nick, not looking at her, concentrating instead on flipping a hotcake over.

A thrill shot through Raven. *Marry him? Is he serious? Oh, I hope so. You what? You hope so? Are you an idiot? You want to leap without looking? But I've looked, and I like what I see and feel when I'm around him. Come on, Raven, which part of you is doing the talking? Head? Heart? Or your nether parts? My heart, I think. My heart. Though my nether parts are thrilled, too.*

Rogan tossed the pancake up out of the pan and expertly caught it on the way down. "I can cook, you see, and quite adroitly, I add."

Raven laughed and said, "Which, of course, leads to eternal bliss?"

Rogan turned and grinned, and just as suddenly sobered. "Raven, I came here to help find your sister, and instead I lost my heart." And he reached for her. She willingly stepped into his arms.

After a moment, he said, "Oops!" and spun about to rescue one of the pancakes.

Somewhat breathlessly, and feeling guilty for being so happy even though Sissy was missing, Raven set the table.

"How many for you?" asked Nick.

"How many do you have?"

"I dunno . . . thirty?"

"Feeding an army, are we?"

"I suppose I did get carried away. But you see, after yesterday—"

Someone rapped on the door.

"Tol' ya," said Nick. "Watch the pancakes, babycakes, please."

"Babycakes?"

"What can I do to make up for that?" asked Rogan. "Dig in my toe? Tug on my forelock?"

"I'll think of something," said Raven, laughing.

Beretta in hand, Rogan answered the knock.

At the door stood a man with three shoulder-slung

rifles, four pistols in rigs, and a carrying case in each hand. Behind him stood another man bearing two scoped rifles with bipod mounts; a backpack loosely dangled from one shoulder, and a monstrous shotgun was slung across his back.

"Johnny, Danny."

"Step aside, O glorious leader," said the man in the back, "this shit is heav— Oh, your pardon, miss. I didn't see you there."

"What smells so good?" said the first man, leading the other inward.

"Your breakfast," said Raven, dishing up the last of the pancakes and fetching two more place settings. "Coffee, anyone?"

"Jawohl!" said the smaller of the two, as they moved to the fireplace end and set down the gear.

When they stepped back to the table, Rogan said, "Raven Conway, these are two of my less couth associates: Johnny Redwing and Danny McCoy, but everyone calls him Danny Mack. Gentlemen, the lady we are here to protect, Raven Conway."

Raven stuck out her hand and each man in turn took it, Johnny first, whose grip was soft, as if he were afraid of hurting her. He stood a lanky six one. He had long black hair to his shoulders, and his wide-set eyes were so dark as to be black. His high cheekbones and broad forehead and the reddish-tan hue of his face and hands bespoke of his Cherokee ancestry.

Danny, on the other hand, stood five nine and had curly red hair and blue-grey eyes and a square jaw and a mischievous grin, all of which silently shouted Erin go Bragh. And he did not shake her hand, but instead, grinning, lifted it to his lips and kissed her fingers.

As he let loose, Danny said, "Well, now, you're not what I expected of a writer, Miss Conway."

"Call me Raven, please. And just what did you expect?"

"Someone stick-thin and tall, or someone rather roundish and short. And what Johnny and I find instead is a babe."

Raven laughed and Rogan grinned and said, "See, I told you they were somewhat uncouth." Then Rogan gestured at the table and said, "Let's eat."

Soon they were digging in, and Raven said, "Long flight?"

"Nah," said Danny. "A few hops and we're here."

Johnny turned to Nick and said, "We arranged for a fuel truck to come, just in case. It'll park at a farm just outside Benton."

"Good thinking," said Nick.

"Why park it in Benton?" asked Raven.

"Don't want a bomb sitting in the valley below," said Johnny.

"And Benton is close enough that we won't waste a lot of fuel going back and forth to gas up the Bell 430," added Danny.

Johnny turned to Nick. "And speaking of bombs, the Rangers have a tanker down there."

"Yeah, but who's gonna try to light that one up?" said Danny. "I mean, it's in the middle of some bad-ass dudes."

"RPG?" said Johnny. "It would only take one."

"I think the tanker far enough away," said Nick. "Not only is it well guarded, it's beyond their camp."

Johnny shrugged and shoveled more pancakes onto his plate. After a moment he said, "Nick, you want us to make a FLIR run tonight?"

"Yeah."

"FLIR?" asked Raven.

"Forward-looking, infra-red radar," said Nick. "Our chopper is equipped with it; those of the Rangers are not."

"It'll pick up hot bodies," said Danny, waggling his eyebrows and wiggling an imaginary cigar. "You know, like people, deer, horses, and babes."

Raven laughed and Nick said, "We'll use it to make certain that there are no snipers in the forest or the meadow."

"And Sissy?"

"If Elizabeth is out there and lost," said Nick. "FLIR will find her eventually."

"What about the 'hidden people?'" asked Raven.

"What?" said Johnny, a forkful of dripping hotcake halfway to his mouth.

"It's a legend," said Nick.

"A story my Grandmother Meredith used to tell us when we were children," said Raven.

"But there could be some recluses living in the forest," said Nick.

"If so, Raven," said Danny, "FLIR will light them up."

They spent a moment eating without speaking, and then Johnny asked, "I see you have a Beretta in your M&P .40 rig, Nick. Pretty good fit, but not snug. Where's your S&W?"

"FBI's got it," said Rogan. "The M9 is Captain

Garret's."

Danny said, "Garret? The one who led the Red Nine raid in Ramadi?"

"That's him."

"Good man," said Danny.

"It still doesn't explain why your S&W is with the FBI," said Johnny

"We shot a thug yesterday."

"Somebody after Raven?" asked Danny.

"Yeah. On the road south out of Benton."

"Good for you, boss," said Johnny.

"Actually, it wasn't me."

"I shot him," said Raven. "Nick was driving."

Quickly, Rogan filled in the details for Johnny and Danny. When Nick finished, Danny gave a soft whistle, and then cocked an eyebrow at Raven and said, "One in the head and one in the neck. Nice. Especially from a moving car."

"I don't much feel like slapping high-fives for doing it," said Raven, glumly.

"You had no choice," said Johnny and Nick almost together.

Danny grinned and said, "You two ought to hook pinkies, even though it's not the manly thing to do."

Raven laughed.

Amid jokes and jabs they finally finished breakfast—thirty pancakes demolished, the syrup bottle drained, two pots of coffee consumed—and, while Danny and Johnny washed and dried dishes and Nick put them away, Raven explained about Sissy's sensitivity to iron and electricity and electronics. "And if

Sissy shows up," said Raven, inclining her head toward the gear, "we'll have to get all the iron and electronics out of here."

"That's why you wanted that damn brass shotgun, huh, Nick?" asked Danny.

"Yep."

"And the Cloaks," said Johnny. "Oh-ah, and *four* of them. One for Raven, too, I gather."

"Yep. But if you brought extra M&P .40s, I'd rather we start out with them."

"Oh, boss, you doubt our efficiency?" said Danny. He turned to Johnny Redwing and said, "I'm hurt. How about you?"

"Crushed," said Johnny.

"Why would I need a cloak?" asked Raven.

Danny laughed, and Johnny explained, "It's a nine millimeter pistol. All polymer and ceramic. No metal at all—no iron, no steel—though it will fire regular nine millimeter ammo, though after a hundred rounds or so the barrel needs replacing."

"Unless we use the polymer bullets," said Johnny. "We brought a bunch, Nick, just in case we needed to get through a metal detector."

"I get it," said Raven. "It's called a Cloak after Star Trek, because it doesn't show up on metal detectors."

Danny turned to Nick and said, "Smart lady you got there, O glorious leader."

Is it that obvious that Nick and I are . . . what? Are what, Raven? Lovers? Or are we just going to be a few one-night stands? Friends with benefits? No, I believe Nick, and I believe my own heart: it's more than that. Perhaps way more.

"I asked her to marry me," said Nick. "Based on my adroit cooking skills. I do breakfasts quite well."

"He's a mean griller, too," said Danny.

"And he'll do a fine job of feeding you in the jungle," said Johnny. "I mean, when it comes to sniffing out bugs and lizards and snakes and worms in the slime, there's no one better. His leech-finding skills are particularly good, but you'll have to pick them off his backside."

"You've found yourself a winner here, Raven," said Danny, and for once he seemed quite sober. But then he grinned and added, "Of course, I'm so very much better, if you're thinking of dumping this mook." His voice took on a lilting brogue as he said, "After all, me colleen, 'tis that I'm Irish, don't y' see."

"A knucklehead mick, you mean," said Johnny.

"Keepum mouth shut, Tonto," said Danny, "else I makum you a good Indian."

Raven's laughter joined theirs.

They fitted Raven with a shoulder harness, and after changing the grips from medium to small—like Danny's—they slipped an S&W M&P .40 into the holster. Two extra magazines were affixed to the rig. "All in all, Ms. Shooter," said Danny, "you have forty-six rounds."

"One already in the barrel," said Raven.

"I told you she was a smart lady, Nick," said Danny. Then he said in a stage whisper, "Raven, you ought to take him up on his breakfast proposal. I mean, I think you and he are meant to be together . . . perhaps even-steven if it comes to ever having to shoot it out."

Nick said, "Did I mention, she's a martial artist, too?"

"Oh, St. Patrick, 'tis a match made in heaven."

Raven laughed. *I am so glad these nitwits came.*

They inventoried the arsenal: in addition to the items that Rogan had originally requested—night vision gear; four Cloak nines, a couple of Sauer sniper rifles along with day and night scopes to equip them; the brass double-barrel eight gauge shotgun, each barrel nearly with a one-inch bore; three Sig 556 automatic rifles; and plenty of ammo for all—Johnny and Danny had brought three extra S&W M&P .40s, recon com gear, binoculars, combat knives, a couple of sniper ghillie suits, fatigues cammoed for forest combat, boots, socks, gloves, tee shirts, a pair of satellite phones, four small Maglight flashlights, miscellaneous replacement parts, and the tools needed for upkeep and maintenance for all.

"That's it," said Johnny. "—No, wait, we brought the chopper, too."

"And a refueling truck should be somewhere in Benton by now," added Danny.

"Anything we're missing, I figure we can get in Benton or fly to the city for it," said Johnny.

"But, pizza, however, will need to be delivered," said Danny.

"Thank you, Captain," said Nick as he handed over the Beretta.

"I see you are well armed again, Rogan," said Garret. Then he looked at Raven and said, "You, too. Smart move."

"I hope I never have to use it," said Raven.

"So do I," said Garret, noting how Johnny Redwing and Danny Mack kept their gazes continuously scanning across the meadow and the tree lines.

Nick handed Garret one of the Blackledge business cards. "Captain, if you ever think of bailing from the Rangers—"

"I think not," said Garret.

"But if you ever do," said Rogan, "we could use someone of your caliber. I mean, your action at Ramadi is a classic; I understand they're teaching it in Ranger School, now. Regardless, my private number is on the back, along with my exec's."

"Blackledge, huh?" said Garret, looking at the card. "I've heard of you. Mostly ex-Rangers and -Seals."

"Special ops, too," said Rogan. "We're worldwide."

"Well, if I ever, I'll give you a call."

"Good enough," said Rogan. "By the way, we're making a grocery and ice run into Benton, is there anything we can bring you?"

"See if you can find some Jones pure cane cream soda," said Garret. "Sergeant Randall promised me his firstborn if I could get him some."

Danny glanced at Garret and said, "Sergeant 'Too Tall' Randall?"

"Yep."

"Tell him the real McCoy says hi."

"You're Danny McCoy?"

"Uh-huh. But my friends call me Danny Mack. Consider yourself included."

"I believe Sergeant Randall said that if he ever saw you again, he would break your neck."

"He's a sore loser," said Danny, never taking his

gaze away from scanning the surround.

"Says you cheated."

"I did," said Danny, grinning. "He never at all suspected I gave him one doctored round. My score was perfect. He shot 997. I sent him e-mail six months after I shipped out."

In Benton Groceries, as Raven stood looking at feminine supplies, she overheard Johnny's soft voice in the next aisle over. "Boss, our company rule is to remain objective. Not get emotionally involved. That way, we do a better job. But with you and Raven, well . . ."

Rogan replied, "In Italy they speak of something they call *'il colpo di fulmine'*—translation, 'the thunderbolt.' What it really means is: for every man there is one woman who is their thunderbolt; and it strikes straight to the heart, giving the man no choice in the matter. The first time I saw Raven . . ."

As they moved beyond hearing, Raven's knees went weak. *Oh, God, oh God, I am Nicholas Rogan's thunderbolt, and he is mine.*

When they returned from Benton, followed by Robert in his pickup—carrying most of the groceries— they brought seven six-packs of Jones pure cane cream soda with them. "I bought out the store," said Danny. "They're for Randall and you and your men. And I'd appreciate it if you would give the sarge this." He handed Garret an envelope addressed to Randall. At Danny's urging, Garret looked at the card inside: Underneath the smiling green frog on the front it said, "Kiss me, I'm Irish." Inside, Danny had written a note.

"Dear Sergeant Too Tall, Sorry for your piss-poor score. Here's some soda to make up for it. Oh, by the bye, I peed in one of the bottles. See if you can tell which one." It was signed, "RMcC."

Garret laughed. "Real McCoy?"

"Yep."

As the sun disappeared down behind the western ridge, and as Danny and Johnny were preparing to make a nighttime FLIR run, Sergeant Randall strode through the gathering shadows to the Bell 430 and bellowed, "McCoy, prepare for your doom."

"You talkin' to me? You talkin' to me?" said Danny, cockily strutting out to meet Randall.

Randall grabbed him up in a bear hug and swung him around and then dropped him, saying, "You're still a piece of shit, McCoy."

"It takes one to know one," said Danny.

They clasped hands, and Randall grinned and said, "I'm sorry I ever saved your sorry-ass life."

"My life? Oh, no, boyo, 'twas the other way round, to my everlastin' regret."

"Irish pipsqueak."

"Enormous English oaf."

"Beer later?"

"When Johnny Redwing and I finish this FLIR run," said Danny. He looked at Rogan and said, "If it's all right with you, boss."

"How could I deny anyone the privilege of getting to see the sergeant break your scrawny neck."

Randall roared, and Danny giggled.

Johnny emerged from the chopper and said, "All set

for a hop to Benton to gas up and start the run." Then he looked up at Randall and said, "You must be Sergeant Too Tall."

Danny grinned and said, "Johnny, this is the idiot I was telling you about. Idiot, this is Johnny Redwing."

Randall clasped Johnny's hand and then looked at Raven. "Is it all right if we sit on your porch and drink beer and tell lies?"

Raven smiled broadly. "Sergeant Too Tall, I would welcome it."

Rogan grinned, but then sobered and said, "Let's do a com check."

"Roger that."

"You're busy," said Randall, "and so am I. When your chopper lands, we'll have that beer."

Raven and Nick both wore headsets and listened in as the helicopter made fruitless pass after pass, with Johnny chanting above the whine of the turbine and the sound of the rotor.

"I recognize that," said Raven.

"Recognize what?"

"Johnny Redwing's 'heya, heya-yas.' I'm fairly certain it's a song—or part of a song—from the voices of the first nations: Indian women singing and chanting."

"What's the song called?"

"'Starwalker.' The version I have is by Buffy Sainte-Marie. It's beautiful. I suppose it's no surprise Johnny knows it."

"With Johnny, it's more than simply singing a song," said Rogan.

"Oh?"

"Yeah," said Nick. "Y'see, when he chants he gets these premonitions. I don't know how he does it, but that's why I said that he smells trouble a mile away. I mean, he goes into his Cherokee thing, and *voila!* a gut feeling comes to him. It's as if he gets these, um, vibrations."

Raven laughed.

"What?"

"I am amused by your turn of phrase, and the different motifs involved."

"How so?"

"'Cherokee thing,' that form is African-American. '*Voila*' is of course French. 'Gut feeling' is more or less American Red Neck. And 'vibrations' is New Age woo-woo."

"Damn," said Nick. "You, my dear, seem to have an English major's mind. You ought to cash in on it. Become a writer, or something."

Raven's laugh was interrupted by Danny.

"Boss?"

"Yeah, Danny. What's up?"

"Johnny is veering off the pattern."

"Let him run with it."

"Oh, I know that. I just wanted to bring you up to— Hold it! We got something! It looks like a guy and— What the fuck?"

"What is it, Danny?"

"Boss, he just fuckin' disappeared."

21

"He what?" Nick frowned and looked at Raven.

"He just disappeared, boss," said Danny. "We had a guy on FLIR, and as we approached to pop on the lights, he just vanished. First he was there, then he wasn't."

"Maybe he dropped into a hole."

"No, boss, there ain't no hole here we can see."

"Camouflaged? Got a lid? A spider hole?"

"Maybe, but I really don't think so."

Johnny said, "I don't see any big enough clearings nearby, boss, no place I can set the chopper down."

"How far in are you?"

"Ten klicks at most," said Johnny.

"Garret's men should have already covered that area," said Raven.

"Maybe," said Rogan. "But they weren't looking for an escape hatch."

"Ah. Yes."

"What do you want us to do, boss?" asked Danny.

"Get the GPS coordinates, and FLIR sweep the area. If nothing turns up, we'll make a ground search tomorrow."

"Roger that."

Raven and Nick listened to turbine whine and rotor

wop and Johnny Redwing chanting again.

Raven sighed and shook her head, and Nick looked at her and said, "What?"

"Hidden people," said Raven.

Primarily because Johnny Redwing called Nick and said that there would be nothing more tonight, Rogan scrubbed the FLIR runs after one more sector had been searched.

When Danny and Johnny asked where they could clean up, Raven pointed the way to the uphill shower. And when they returned, Danny said, "Nothing like a bracing splash, eh?"

Johnny's face fell into a stoic mien and he grunted and said, "White boy need learn Cherokee way—not scream so much."

"This coming from a redskin who stuck in a toe and squealed like a little girl."

"Was a war whoop," retorted Johnny.

Laughing and taking verbal jabs at one another, they dressed and grabbed a six-pack from the ice box and headed for the front veranda to wait for Sergeant Randall to arrive to share a beer or two and to talk over old times and tell lies.

"When you finally give up, you can bunk in the loft," said Raven. "Me, I'm for a shower and bed."

"I'll have to guard you," said Nick.

"No, me, me," said Danny, repeatedly jabbing a hand in the air, as if volunteering in an elementary-school classroom.

"I'm a fine lookout," said Johnny, crossing his arms and raising his chin, as if looking off into the noble distance. "It's in my blood."

Raven laughed and pulled Nick up out of his chair and they headed for the tub room and the waterfall beyond.

When they returned to the house, they heard Sergeant Randall's roaring laughter coming from the veranda.

"Are you sure you don't want to join them?" asked Raven.

Nick took her in his arms and said, "I'm right where I want to be."

Raven raised her lips to meet his, and after a long moment, she pulled him into her bedroom.

Early the next morning, as Nick, Johnny, Danny, and Raven were preparing to head into the forest, Deputy Mills came calling, a manila folder in hand.

"We identified that shooter of yours."

"Who was he?" asked Raven.

Mills flipped open the file. Inside was a mug shot and a fairly thick dossier, a long record of a criminal past. Mills handed her the picture. "Recognize him?"

Raven looked at the image and shook her head. "Who was he?" She passed the picture on to Rogan, who glanced at it and passed it on.

"Some guy from Chicago—Jimmy Phelps. Had a rap sheet a mile long—mostly petty stuff—though he did spend time in Joliet for beating an old guy half to death. They transferred him to Statesville after a prison-yard fight. He got out after serving eight of his fifteen— prison time, you know. That was in 2003. Since then, he's been a suspect in two murders, but he had rock-solid alibis. They think he's part of the South Side mob. Anyway, that's your shooter, Miss Conway. You took care of a bad'n.'"

Raven sighed, and Robert Aikens said, "Remember, Miss Raven, you didn't have any choice."

"Any news on his accomplice?" asked Rogan.

"Nah."

"How about the car?"

Mills shook his head. "Long gone somewhere."

Robert handed the mug shot back to the deputy and asked, "Have you heard anything from the FBI?"

"Those bastards—beggin' your pardon, ma'am— they took jurisdiction in both cases. Winkler is mad as all hell."

"Ronnie," said Robert, "be that as it may, what I'd really like to know is whether or not they have any news of Miss Elizabeth."

"Nah! They've checked with all the hospitals and women's shelters and such a hundred miles hereabout, and Miss Elizabeth Conway isn't in any of them."

"I knew she wouldn't be there," said Raven.

"But they had to check, Miss Raven," said Robert.

"Is there anything else, Deputy?" asked Rogan.

"Nah. That's all. Any news from here?"

"Not so far," said Rogan. "You can check with Captain Garret."

"Already did," said Mills.

"Well, then, if there's nothing else . . ." said Raven.

Realizing he was being dismissed, Deputy Mills snatched up the file and picture, and Nick said, "I'd like a copy of that."

"Here," said Mills, shoving it at Rogan. "It's an extra

anyway."

As soon as he was gone, Nick looked at Robert and said, "Would you like another chopper ride?"

Aiken's face lit up. "I surely would."

"What's the plan?" asked Raven.

"Danny will fly us in, and then Johnny and I will rappel down from the chopper to the place where the FLIR showed up a man."

"You saw someone in there?" asked Robert, wonder in his gaze.

"For a moment," said Danny. "But then he vanished."

"Well, I should think so," said Robert. "I mean, these are the Ghost Woods. It was probably a spirit."

Danny looked at Raven and shrugged as if waiting for a denial, but instead she asked, "How will you get out?"

"Walk," said Johnny. "It's only ten klicks."

"Well, I'm going, too," said Raven.

Rogan shook his head. "I don't think so. It might not be safe."

"On the other hand," said Raven, "safe or not, if Sissy is there, then I'm the only one she will trust. And for that to happen, I have to be on the ground with you."

Nick frowned, but before he could say anything, Raven patted the M&P .40 in her rig and said, "Besides, I have my Betsy with me."

"Betsy?" said Robert.

Raven grinned and nodded and said, "Named after a woman I heard about, a woman who had, um, 'pep.'"

Robert flushed, but said, "She sure did. And if you want to name a gun after her, well, she was a pistol, too."

"I detect there's a story worth telling here," said Danny, looking at Robert, "and maybe I'll trade you one of mine for it one day."

Nick looked at Raven, and she said, "I'm going."

"Lord save me from this strong-willed woman," said Rogan.

"Do you really want to be saved from her?" asked Johnny.

Nick laughed and said, "Not really."

"I didn't think so," said Danny, "what with all that creaking of ropes coming from the bedroom last night."

Now it was Raven who blushed. *I knew that bed was a dead giveaway.*

Johnny grinned and said, "Ropes, Nick? What's next: whips and chains?"

Raven laughed and said, "Let's get the hell out of here before I die of awkwardness."

"Okay, boss," Danny called above the turbine and rotor, "the GPS says this is the spot, and, from what I can tell, it looks like it, too."

Rogan slid open the door and they leaned over to see. In the morning light a very small clearing sat below. The trees were too close for the chopper to land.

Rogan, Raven, and Johnny slipped on their com gear and checked it once again. Each of them, including Danny and Robert, gave a thumbs up.

Johnny deployed the line and shouldered a Sig 556 automatic rifle and went first. When he was on the ground, Rogan clipped Raven's rappel brake to the line and said, "You've done this before, right."

"A few times," said Raven, "when I was researching one of my books. But it's been a while, so, just in case, why don't you review how it's done."

Rogan smiled and quickly explained the operation, and then Raven eased out. She released the brake and went a lot faster than she planned, screaming "Oh-shit-oh-shit-oh-shit-" all the way down, managing at last to slow herself just before Johnny caught her.

Rogan came down as fast or faster than Raven had, but he was in control.

They fastened their rappelling gear to the line, and Robert pulled it all up and in. Danny then gained altitude and side-slipped off to the west some distance and hovered.

Using line-of-sight markers—trees, brush, saplings—they began a careful search of the area. After a while, Rogan called Johnny over to him. "Does that look like a footprint?"

Johnny knelt and touched the soil. "Might be. If so, he was headed that way."

As Nick and Johnny slowly went that direction, Raven looked to see what it was that might be a footprint. *What the hell are they seeing that I'm not? Oh, wait. This little indention? Doesn't look like a footprint to me. But then, what do I know? I'm no Cherokee.*

"Here's one," said Nick.

"And another one," said Johnny.

Raven followed, trying to keep from stepping where the men were pointing.

"'Nother one," said Johnny and Nick together.

Finally, farther on, Johnny said, "If this here is any

indication, I'd say it's a size eight or nine, very narrow foot—double- or triple-A width—and the wearer weighs about one forty, one fifty. On the other hand, this might be nothing more than a natural mark in the soil."

How in the world could he read all of that from this scuff in the dirt?

After another while, Johnny said, "There aren't any more. That nine triple-A is where it ends."

"Is that where you FLIRed the person when he disappeared?" asked Nick.

"At that exact spot? I dunno, boss. Could have been. But it definitely was *somewhere* in this clearing."

"Well let's stomp around," said Rogan.

"Stomp?" asked Raven.

"Looking for a trapdoor to a spider hole, a lid to a foxhole or tunnel," Nick explained. "Also look for something that seems out of place."

They kept it up for long minutes, working in a spiral outwards. Finally, Nick said, "That's it. Nothing here."

"How else could a person vanish?" asked Raven. "I mean, if not a hidden burrow, then how? What would make him invisible to infra-red? I mean, did he make a sudden move?"

"No," said Johnny. "He simply blinked out. Otherwise, he could have ducked behind a tree, but then we would have followed him there. He could have cooled way down, but then he would be a dark silhouette. He could have stepped in front of something hotter, but then we would have seen the hotter thing. He could have been a ghost and returned to the spirit realm, but would a ghost show up on IR?"

"How about some—I don't know—some thermal

twist in the wind?" asked Raven.

"Nah," said Johnny. "This was a guy."

Raven looked at Rogan, but he turned up his hands in a "Who knows" gesture.

Raven sighed. "Well, then, that said, maybe he really was one of Grandmother Meredith's hidden people."

22

Rogan looked at the helicopter hovering a distance up and to the west. "Danny."

"Yeah, boss."

"You might as well fly the chopper back."

"You sure you don't want to shinny up a rope. It's better than walking."

"Nah. I want to see this forest up close and personal, and a ten klick stroll ought to be enough for me to get a feel for it."

"You mean for Johnny to get a feel, don't you, boss?"

"Yeah. That, too." Rogan looked at Johnny Redwing. "In fact, that especially."

Robert Aikens said, "Miss Raven, you could climb the rope and ride back with us."

"No, thank you, Robert," said Raven. "I need the exercise."

Danny said, "I'll keep the com hot, just in case. Oh, and if we see any wide-enough clearings on the way, we can always land in one and wait for you."

"I don't think you should do that," said Johnny. "These woods wouldn't like it."

Both Nick and Raven looked at the Cherokee man,

and Rogan said, "One of your hunches?"

Johnny shrugged noncommittally but said, "Yeah." He slapped the stock of his Sig 556. "These are not at all cared for, and the chopper would be worse."

Raven touched the butt of her M&P .40. *The barrel is steel. We're bringing iron into the forest.* She glanced up at the chopper. *Lots of iron in that, too ... and electronics. And we are wearing com gear. I think Johnny might be right.*

"Go on, Danny," said Rogan. "We'll see you at the house in three hours or so."

"You got it, boss."

The Bell 430 veered off and away.

Nick took a compass reading, but Johnny was already heading westward. Nick and Raven followed.

With the chopper now but a distant sound and fading, the voice of the forest returned: birds stirred in the trees, insects whined and buzzed, and small animals rustled through the undergrowth. It was quiet enough to hear nearby water trickling over stones and a soothing breeze whispering among the leaves. In spite of those hushed murmurs, stillness seemed to occupy the woodland, as if it were lying in wait for something to occur.

As she had done as a child, Raven marveled at the girths of old hoary oaks, their broad limbs reaching out. Soft moss, bearing tiny pink blossoms, nestled among gnarled roots. Tall elms and maples shared their space with saplings. Knee-high grass and holly shrubs vied for the sunlight that filtered through. The land itself was soft and gentle, undulant with low hills. Occasionally, an outcrop of stone jutted up, but none proved to be an obstacle in their hike.

Whenever they came to a stream or a tiny pool, Johnny Redwing would stoop and touch a drop of water to his tongue. "It's clean, boss. Pure as the world was meant to be."

As they moved on, Raven suddenly realized that Johnny Redwing at times seemed to be whispering, or even subvocalizing, a chant.

After an hour or so, they stopped for a brief rest and a sip from their canteens.

Johnny looked at Raven. "Same water, eh?"

Raven nodded. "It's why the house is built where it is. The water flows year around, even in the deepest freeze."

"You live in paradise, Raven."

"Actually, I live in Seattle."

"Oh. Too bad, for this might be Eden."

Raven smiled, and Johnny added, "I mean, look around. Other than your cabin, this forest has never been touched by civilization. It's as if it's the way the world was meant to be—healthy and hale, pure and clean. Why even the elm and ash trees have never been touched by blight: neither Dutch Elm or Ash disease. Some might call it a miracle, but were I to ask my ancestors, they would say the spirits protect this land."

"And what do you say?" asked Raven.

"Who am I to question my ancestors?" said Johnny, grinning.

Raven laughed, and the forest took in her joy.

Johnny then turned to Rogan and said, "You know, boss, I've often said that we really ought to get one of those rescue winch rigs for the chopper. But even if we had one, I wouldn't have wanted to miss this stroll, though it is the third time we've had to walk out of woods."

Rogan smiled and said, "The last time we were in a forest somewhat like this one, you said you wanted to run naked through the woods."

"Still do, boss, still do. Only that woodland was a just a shadow of this one, and in here I'm having even more trouble resisting the urge to just rip off my clothes and run"—Johnny pointed back into the forest—"thataway."

Amid Raven's laughter, Rogan said, "Well, before it overcomes you, let's move on."

They took up the hike once more, but after a mile or so, as in days past Raven again sensed hidden eyes upon her.

"Nick," she softly said, "I think someone or something is watching us."

Rogan said, "Johnny?"

"She's right," replied Johnny. "They've been tracking us since we stopped back there. I don't know how they are doing it, but they are."

"Hostile?"

Johnny shook his head. "I only catch a slight hint of that. I think it might be because of our guns. But that's it."

"The hidden people?" asked Raven.

"That's as good a guess as any," said Johnny.

They both looked at Rogan, and he shrugged and said, "Let's keep going."

Just before noon, they emerged from the forest uphill from the log house.

"Nice job, Johnny," said Rogan.

Johnny went to his Tonto voice and said, "Um, Cherokee more better than white man compass." Then he laughed and added, "It was just dumb luck, Raven. I mean, I have some Cherokee relatives who can't find their way across a room."

Raven laughed, and as she did, Danny's voice crackled through her com earpiece:

"Where are you, boss?"

"Just behind the house," replied Nick.

"Raven, you on com?"

"Yes, I am, Danny."

"I'm down with Captain Garret. I hate to tell you this, but the Rangers have to pull out."

23

"I am sorry, Miss Conway," said Captain Garret, "but we're a rapid response team, and we've been given the order to bug out."

In the meadow, men struck tents, GIs refueled choppers, Rangers shoveled dirt into the latrine trench, others loaded gear onto the Blackhawks and the Chinook.

"I understand," said Raven, softly. "I just wish . . ."

"So do I," said Garret. Then he looked at Rogan and said, "At least you have your unit with FLIR."

Rogan nodded. "We do."

Raven said, "I don't suppose you can tell us where you are going, and when or if you might be back."

"No I can't," said the captain.

"Black ops," said Raven.

Garret did not reply.

Johnny Redwing said, "Maybe it's for the best, Raven. I mean, the spirit of this forest is unsettled, what with gun-toting men tramping among the trees."

Garret cocked an eyebrow at Johnny, but Danny said, "Let it go, Captain; it's a Cherokee thing."

"Captain!" bellowed Sergeant Randall. He held high a com gear handset and pointed a finger toward the sky.

196 / Dennis L. McKiernan

Garret took Raven by the hand and said, "I wish you luck in finding your sister."

"Thank you, Captain."

Garret turned to Rogan and stuck out his hand. Nick gripped it and said, "Remember, Captain, we will always have a place waiting for you at Blackledge."

"I have your card," said Garret. "And thanks."

Danny and Johnny grinned and snapped a salute, and Robert followed their example. The captain smiled and returned the gesture, then spun on his heel and strode toward Randall and the summons of someone higher up.

As she watched Raleigh Garret walk away, Raven asked, "Robert, do you know what sectors are left to be searched?"

"Yes, Miss Raven, I do."

"Do you think you could round up some high school kids to take up the hunt?"

Robert grinned. "Those that aren't working summer jobs. It'll be something for them to do."

"It'll be like herding cats," said Danny.

"Maybe so," said Raven, "but it's better than doing nothing at all."

"And what'll we do if a kid gets lost?" asked Johnny.

"We'll put Boy Scouts with compasses in charge of navigation," said Robert.

Johnny groaned at that suggestion, but said, "Maybe we can run it like a Cherokee kids' deer hunt."

"Deer hunt?" asked Raven.

"Yeah. When I was a child, occasionally a bunch of us would grab our bows and arrows and get together and go after deer."

"Poaching, I'll bet," said Danny.

Johnny grinned and nodded and said, "By white-man rules, yeah; by Cherokee rules, not so. Anyway, we did it by advancing in a fairly strung out but straight line through the woods. And to do that, each of us kept track of the kid on his left and the one on his right. So, Raven, if we use high school kids, then if we make each kid responsible for the one on his left and the one on his right, and if they can keep a reasonably straight line, and if one of us takes charge of walking them in and back, then we should be okay."

"Yeah, and if any get lost, we have FLIR," said Danny.

"I don't much care for using teens, but if the gains outweigh the risks . . ." said Rogan.

"Let's think it over while having a beer," said Danny. "But first, let me say good-bye to Too Tall, and then I'll catch up."

Both Johnny and Danny headed into the stir of Rangers, and Raven and Nick and Robert moved toward the path up to the house, with Robert saying, "I don't think you'll get anyone to come. I mean, most of those kids have tried Hunters Wood, and something spooks them, each and every one."

"What if we pay them?"

"I don't know, Miss Raven. I can try, but I don't hold out much hope."

As they entered the house Raven looked toward the gear that Johnny and Danny had brought, Raven said, "I need to call George Allenby."

"Be my guest," said Nick, fetching one of the satellite phones from among the pile and handing it to her.

Raven punched in numbers, and when she got through to Allenby, she said, "The Rangers are gone, George."

Allenby sighed. "I know. General Manville sends his regrets, but something came up in Columbia."

"South America?"

"Yes. A special force is needed sub rosa to extract one of our envoys down there, and—"

"I don't have to know any more, George."

"All right."

"George, can you arrange a line of credit for me at the bank in Benton?"

"Of course. How much do you need, one or two hundred?"

"More than that, George."

"All right, a half million, a million, what? I doubt that small bank has a great deal on hand, but we—"

"Wait a minute, George. I think we are on different pages. I need something like twenty-five thousand."

"Oh, just twenty-five? I thought it might be one or two hundred."

Twenty-five? One or two hundred? He's talking in thousands and I'm thinking in ones.

"All right, Raven. I'll have someone do that right away."

"Don't you want to know what it's for?"

"No need," said Allenby.

"I'm going to tell you anyway. It's to pay searchers to look for Sissy."

"Oh, my. I understand. Though it's a shame that you can't rustle up enough volunteers."

"I know, but everyone around here is afraid of

Hunters Wood."

"It's always been that way, Raven . . . from Indian times to now."

"I want to use Robert Aikens as my agent in this, George."

"Good man, Robert," said Allenby. "Been loyal to the family for more years than I can remember. His father before him, too."

"Then I suppose," said Raven, "it runs in his family, and for that I am glad."

"Raven we already have a Hunters Trust account that Robert has access to. I'll just transfer twenty-five thousand into that account, if it's all right with you."

"That's even better, George."

"I'll also put you on the account," said Allenby.

"Thank you," said Raven.

"What do you think of Blackledge, Raven? Is Nick treating you right?"

Oh God, is he ever.

"Yes. There are two of his associates here, too."

"Well, then, you ought to be well safeguarded. And by the way, Director Kelly called me and spoke of an attempt made on your life. Fine shooting on your part, I might add. Kelly also filled me in on some Russian fellow found dead in Hunters Wood. I've got people in New York looking into it. We're trying to keep you safe, Raven. But you yourself have to take care. No more riding about in an open-top Jeep, please."

"George, I'm wearing body armor. Besides, have I no privacy?"

"Of course you do, but then again not. You are after all the Trustee, and we want you out of harm's way. I can send a bullet-proof car."

"No, George, no bullet-proof car. Blackledge is doing quite well, thank you."

"I know they are," said Allenby. "—Oh, Raven, would you mind checking in with me every day? I feel with these attempts going on I'd rather know that you are—"

"—Still alive?" interjected Raven.

"Well, I wouldn't put it that way, but, yes, still alive."

"All right, George, I'll call you every day and let you know that I am still breathing."

"Good," said Allenby. "Now if that's all, I'll get that transfer set up, with Robert Aikens as your agent."

"Thank you, George. Bye-bye."

Raven turned to Robert and said, "Would you go into Benton and offer a hundred dollars a day for each person who joins the search?"

"How many do you need, Miss Raven?"

"As many as you can get."

Rogan said, "We'll need at least thirty people. Any less and the sweep will not be effective."

"And if I can't get thirty?"

"Then up the wages," said Raven.

In midafternoon, Raven and Nick stood on the veranda and watched as the Ranger Company lifted off in their Blackhawks and the Chinook, and the fuel truck pulled away. It seemed eerily still when the thrum of the choppers and the clatter of the diesel faded to silence.

Danny and Johnny trudged up from the Blackledge copter, where they had rigged Raven's laptop to record

FLIR runs. "I've got it on a repeating five minute loop," said Danny. "It writes over the previous five minutes. If we catch anything, I can dump that record into a separate file, and we can then review it and hope we can discover just how these recluses manage to vanish."

With the laptop recording, Johnny and Danny made three FLIR runs that evening and night, but although they detected large and small game—a number of deer, a badger, two bobcats, a pack of wolves, and a bear—they spotted no humans, no "hidden" people.

It was nearly midnight as Raven and the others sat at the table and stared at the display.

"All right," said Danny, tapping the touchpad on Raven's laptop. "Here's the last five minutes of our final run."

The screen filled with a multicolored glow. "The hotter it is, the closer to red," said Danny. "The closer to blue, the colder. You can see that most of the forest is in the cooler ranges, with something like that stream there rather cold, compared to the trees. —And right there, see, a herd of mostly yellowish deer."

"That's amazing," said Raven at the end of the run, looking first at Danny and then Nick. "Truly amazing."

Nick smiled at her enthusiasm and reached out and took her hand.

The next morning, a caravan of cars and trucks and vans arrived. High-schoolers piled out, and several adult women, and an older man leading a Boy Scout troop. All of the people were dressed for hiking and equipped with backpacks bearing first aid kits and water bottles and sack lunches. Some had hiking poles in hand. A few had walkie-talkies. Several had compasses. One or two had GPS units. Some carried horns and others had whistles. Nearly all had flashlights in their packs, "Just in case," said one of the mothers.

Altogether, there were forty-two searchers.

Robert was in charge.

Raven strapped on her vest, and along with Nick and Johnny and Danny, she went down to meet the group.

They gathered around her.

"I just want to thank all of you for coming," she said, raising her voice to be heard. "I know that some of you might be a bit wary about entering Hunters Wood, but I am told by my revered Cherokee associate"—Raven gestured toward where Johnny Redwing stood, trying his best to look noble—"that the woodland will permit you in this emergency to travel unmolested. I will be here, waiting for word, should you find my sister." She turned to Aikens. "Robert."

Robert reminded them of his earlier instructions that morning—about keeping track of the person on their right and left, about what to do if they found something, or needed help—then he had them form up, more or less distributing those with the walkie-talkies along the line. He handed a walkie-talkie to Raven. And then gave the order to start.

As they raggedly moved away, "Your 'revered Cherokee associate'?" Johnny murmured to Raven.

Danny snickered.

"I had to tell them something to keep them from being too spooked by Hunters Wood," said Raven.

Johnny watched as the ragged procession seemed to

collide with the tree line, and then be gently absorbed by the forest. He nodded to Danny and said, "Herding cats."

Around ten in the morning, Nils Anderson, a junior at Benton High and the first string right guard for the Benton Badgers, carried Lori Karlson out from the woods. The waiflike blond had a sprained ankle, and her husky boyfriend had come to the rescue.

"Does this mean we won't get paid?" asked Lori. "I could really use the money for a new skirt and sweater for school, and Nils—"

"Don't worry about that, Lori," said Raven, inspecting the Ace bandage and the ice-pack she had wrapped around Lori's swollen right ankle. "In fact, because you were injured, and because Nils is now officially a hero, I'll tell Mr. Aikens to kick in a little extra." She turned to Danny and said, "Will you please run these two into Benton? Lori needs to keep ice on this ankle and rest. —Lori, you keep it elevated; it'll reduce the swelling. Oh, and, Danny, fetch a couple more bags of ice for the box here. More might need it."

"Yeah," said Danny. "And I'll get more beer to ice down as well. I mean, we can't let our taste for the brew to swell up and die, can we?"

Raven laughed and Nick tossed Danny the keys to the Jeep, and Nils hoisted Lori up into his arms. He turned to Raven and said, "I'll be back tomorrow, Miss Conway. Give you your money's worth." And down the path they went.

As evening fell, the searchers exited the woods.

Sissy had not been found.

Johnny and Danny took off in the chopper for FLIR runs.

Again, only animals were spotted.

Thursday came and went, and although the ranks of the searchers had swelled to sixty-one, still they had no success in finding Elizabeth Conway, nor did Johnny and Danny spot anything unusual in their FLIR runs.

"God, but I'm frustrated, Nick," said Raven, lying in bed that night in Rogan's embrace. Then quickly she amended, "—Frustrated for not finding Sissy, that is. And I'm irritated with having to wear armor. And I'm tired of feeling guilty for being so happy with you, with me, with us, when she is missing."

"I understand, Raven," said Nick, "but life goes on. We cannot stop the world till a problem is solved, nor can we stop it to prolong a time of splendor."

"Time of splendor?"

"Yeah, like this." Amid a creaking of rope, Nick levered himself up on an elbow and bent down for a kiss.

Friday arrived, and, along with it, sixty-seven searchers.

As before, Raven met with those who had come. "Again, I thank you for being here. Though we haven't yet found my sister, still you have been making good progress. If we don't find her today, then tomorrow, Saturday, will be our last day. By then we will have covered all the places where Elizabeth most likely would be. Let's hope today is the day. God bless you all."

Someone in the crowd called out "Amen!" It was Nils Anderson standing among his teammates. He held out a fist, and the footballers laid hands upon hands upon hands. Then Nils counted, "One, two, three," and all of the boys shouted "Conway!"

And again the search was on.

They did not find Sissy that day.

After refueling, Danny and Johnny began their second FLIR run of the evening. As with the previous flights, Raven could hear Johnny Redwing chanting, his *heya, heya-yas* barely audible above the whine of the turbine and the churn of the rotor.

"Uh-oh, boss," said Danny Mack, "get ready. Johnny's veering off the pattern again."

"Good!" said Raven.

"How's the recording?" asked Nick.

"Clear as a bell, boss."

Moments later: "There they are! Crank 'er up, Johnny!"

The turbine whine increased.

"Dip me in shit," said Danny, "one of 'em's on a horse and—"

"—Aw, fuck! They're gone."

24

They watched as the infrared forest rolled by, then Danny said, "Here's where Johnny veered off course. And now, *there! There they are!* There's the guy on the horse and the guy on the ground and now—Poof!— they're gone. It's like they teleported or something."

"Play it again," said Rogan. "Can you isolate and step frame by frame from the moment just before till the moment just after they vanish?"

"Yeah. Let me just run it to where we first see them."

Danny moved the cursor to the slide, and dragged it back to where the images of someone on a horse and another person on the ground came into view. "All right, now to step it forward." Danny clicked on an icon, and a frame counter appeared. He then advanced the images a frame at a time. "You can see them look toward our chopper, and now, they vanish." Danny shook his head. "Maybe they really do teleport."

"Horse and all?" asked Raven.

"Must be," said Danny.

"Back it up to just a few frames before they vanish," said Nick.

Danny did so and stepped it forward; then repeated.

"All right. I thought so," said Rogan.

"Thought what?" asked Danny.

"Just before they vanish, the man on the horse twitched the reins and the animal started to take a step to the right, just like the man on the ground."

"And this means . . . ?" asked Raven.

"I don't know," said Nick. "But it was at that point they disappeared."

"Well, boss, it's not like a door opened in the hillside and they went in," said Danny.

Johnny shook his head and said, "Here it comes."

"Here what comes?" asked Raven.

"He's going to tell us about the people who live under the hill."

Raven looked at Danny, and he said, "There's many an Irish tale about fairy folk who live under the hill—the *Sidhe*."

"What? Did you say, 'She'?"

"I did."

"But you called them *the* She."

"They *are* the Sidhe."

"Wait a minute. What are we talking about? Women who live underground?"

"No, no. I am talking about the fey folk, the Sidhe."

"How do you spell that?"

"S-i-d-h-e."

"S-i-d-h-e is pronounced S-h-e?"

"Aye, me colleen. 'Tis a fine Gaelic word."

"And these are the fey folk?"

"Yes."

Raven turned to Nick. "*That's* what Grandmother Meredith said, 'Sidhe,' not 'She.'"

25

"Raven, perhaps your grandmother did say Sidhe, but your grandmother is—"

"Dotty," said Raven. "I know, Nick. Regardless, she believes my biological father is one of the Sidhe, and a different one of them fathered Sissy. Recall, Grandmother said she went in once and came back with one, and my mother went in twice and came back with two."

"What are you talking about?" asked Danny,

Quickly, Raven summed up her conversation with Grandmother Meredith.

"Well," said Danny, "we Irish tell tales of mortals and fey falling in love. 'Tam Lin,' for example, though that love story is a bit one-sided. In that one, a queen of the fey simply took advantage."

"Probably depends on who is telling the tale," said Johnny.

Raven frowned. "Meaning . . . ?"

"White-man's heroes are Red Man's villains. As I say, it depends on who is telling the tale."

Rogan glanced at the neatly stacked papers Taylor had brought. "What happened to these Sidhe, Danny?"

"Well, according to lore, Ireland was invaded by the

Milesians, and there was a great battle between them and the *Tuatha Dé Dannan*."

"Tuatha Dé Dannan?" asked Raven.

"That's their true name. Calling them the Sidhe came later."

"Go on," said Raven.

"Anyway, after the Tuatha Dé Dannan lost the battle, under the terms of surrender, they were exiled to live 'under the hill.'"

"Underground?"

"Yes, in fairy mounds, and those mounds were called 'sidhe,' which simply means 'hills,' or 'earthen mounds.' Later, the term 'sidhe' came not only to mean the hills, but also meant those fairy folk who lived within them. Some of the Tuatha Dé Dannan, though, rather than live underground, were said to have sailed over the western sea."

Johnny grunted and said, "And from Ireland, the only sea to the west is the Atlantic, with America on the other side."

"Which agrees with the story Grandmother told," said Raven.

"Well," said Danny, "whether underground or over the sea, they went . . . away. —Oh, crap! They left because of iron. Iron swords, iron spears, iron armor, iron anything, even iron bells ringing. They could not stand it."

"Like Sissy," said Raven, looking at Nick.

"But not like you," said Johnny.

"Maybe I didn't inherit that trait."

"Mmm. . ." said Johnny, nodding.

Raven turned to Danny. "When did they sail over the

western sea?"

Danny shrugged and said, "I don't know. But I do know that the Milesians brought iron weapons to Ireland sometime around the second or first century B.C. That must be why the Sidhe lost."

"If we are to believe legends," said Raven, "there were fairy folk in existence in King Arthur's time."

"That would be around five hundred A.D.," said Nick.

"Probably those who lived in the mounds," said Danny.

Raven gestured toward the documents. "In there is a copy of a paper telling that the king of Connacht, Eógan Bél, signed a king's grant to Bean Sealgaire—Lady Hunter—for Hunters Wood in 542 A.D. for the sum of three golden torques, one for each of his then living daughters. It could have been because St. Brendan the Navigator had reached America, and those fey folk who had sailed over the western sea feared another invasion by Milesians bearing iron. And so they struck a bargain with the king of Connacht."

"So, they came to America sometime between the second or first century B.C. and 500 A.D.," said Danny.

Raven nodded. "And Grandmother Meredith told us a story, where the people of the forest came from over the sea long ago and Chief White Bear gave them Hunters Wood in exchange for magic arrows.

"Oh, Nick, what if everything she told us is true?"

"This is getting weird," said Johnny.

Danny looked at Johnny. "Faith and begorra, do I believe what I'm hearing? You, Johnny Redwing, Cherokee to the core, you are saying that something is getting *weird*? I think it must be snowing in the infernal region."

Johnny said, "People who disappear in a blink? People who might be your Irish fairy folk? You don't think that's weird?"

"Yes, but—"

"Case closed," said Johnny.

Danny took a sip of his beer and then said, "The old stories say the *Sidhe* could make themselves invisible, vanish in the blink of an eye."

"Anything else?" asked Raven.

"They are incredibly beautiful," said Danny.

She's been getting lovelier by the day. "Oh, my God," said Raven. "The changes in her DNA: Sissy was—is—becoming one of them."

"Raven," said Nick, "the only way we'll ever know the truth is to talk to one of these people of the forest. Until then, this is all speculation."

"You're right, Nick, but all the facts seem to fit. I'm positive that Grandmother Meredith must have said '*Sidhe*' and not 'She.'"

"Leave it to the Irish to muck up words," said Johnny.

"Oh? Like Cherokee is any better? *Ki'lo*, meaning 'someone' instead of being a measure of weight."

"Actually, you Irish mick, it's a measure of mass."

"Mass, my ass—"

"In fact," Raven interjected, "kilo really means one thousand . . . kilometer is a thousand meters, kilogram is a thousand grams, and so on. There are lots of cross-cultural homonyms, sound-alikes that have completely different meanings, depending on the language."

"You heard the lady," said Johnny. "Now shut up and drink your beer."

"Is that beer, as in the nectar of the gods, or bier, as a platform on which the dead lie, or . . ."

Johnny and Danny were still arguing, when Nick and Raven took to their bed.

In spite of being held by Nick, Raven did not sleep well that night.

26

"Maybe like my mother and my grandmother before her—and who knows how many generations back— Sissy might have gone into the forest with a lover and might come back pregnant."

"Raven," said Nick, "you are putting a lot of faith in what your grandmother said, and you know at times she's not lucid."

"Not only that," said Johnny, "you're setting great store in this Irish mick's legends."

"Oh, and I suppose you're one to talk, my tobacco-scattering Cherokee chanter?" said Danny.

"Well, in the case of the Cherokee legends, they just happen to be true," said Johnny.

Then they both broke out laughing.

"Raven," said Nick, "legends or not, stories or not, you are putting a lot of faith in your grandmother's tales."

"I know I am, Nick, but you yourself said that Sissy might have gone off with a lover. And the thought of Sissy being in the forest with a sweetheart came to me in the throes of the night, and I couldn't put it aside. It kept circling and circling, like some sort of vulture."

"Did you actually see a vulture in your mind?" asked

Johnny.

"No."

"Good. Vultures are omens of change, usually baneful."

Danny smiled. "Is that a Cherokee belief?"

Johnny shook his head. "Lakota." Then he added, "But I pay attention."

Danny spread some jam on his toast. "You think she has a lover in the woods?"

"Maybe."

"One of the—what'll we call them?—the hidden people? One of the Sidhe?"

"I don't know whether or not Sissy has a lover in the woods, no matter what we call him," said Raven. "But Robert told me how she seemed to be acting in the days before she disappeared, and what he described is exactly how she behaves when she's in love, or at least when she's infatuated with someone."

Johnny took a sip of his coffee, and then said, "If your sister went for a simple tryst, why hasn't she returned?"

"And why would she go there rather than her lover come here?" added Danny.

On the verge of tears, Raven shook her head. "I don't know."

Rogan reached out and took her hand, just as there sounded a rap at the door.

Gun in his grip, Danny answered it.

It was Robert.

"The word has spread, and I've something like one hundred twenty, one hundred thirty searchers—teens and adults, both—most from town but some from nearby. I think I'm going to need more money in the account"

"How much is left?" asked Rogan.

"Just under eight thousand. I'll need five, six thousand more."

Raven took a deep breath and stood and said, "Let's go down and thank them. Then I'll call Allenby and have him add another ten thousand."

The searchers went up the western slope and over the ridge and onward. Some eight klicks inward, they swung the line and came back, arriving just before sunset.

They did not find Sissy that day, the last one that would have boots on the ground to look for her.

From this point on, it would be up to Danny Mack and Johnny Redwing and FLIR.

As darkness fell, the pickups and cars and vans pulled out, with Robert leading the mob to Benton to cash in their final chits, George Allenby having arranged for the bank to stay open late each day to pay the searchers. And as the vehicles pulled away, Johnny and Danny took off to refuel the chopper and make their first run of the night.

Raven and Nick finished the last of their beef on dark rye sandwiches. The waning half-moon had long since set and only starlight glittered down. Raven stood and said, "I'm going to step inside and light some candles and crank up our com gear."

Nick chugged the last of his lemonade and set the glass down and followed her. Just as she reached the table, Nick wrapped his arms about her from behind.

218 / Dennis L. McKiernan

Then he slipped off her shoulder rig set it to the table, and then slowly began pulling loose the Velcro fasteners on her body armor. Gently, he lifted the vest over her head and laid it beside the gun. His hands then cupped her breasts.

She gave a soft moan and turned in his embrace.

Nick bent down and kissed her, and then whispered, "Mmm . . . spicy mustard. My favorite."

"I love you, Nicholas Rogan, in spite of your evil ways, taking advantage, as you did, of my mustardly mouth."

They kissed again, long and lingering, and Raven pressed herself into an aroused Nick. When they came up for air, they could hear the distant sound of the chopper returning. Rogan said, "Darling, as much as I would love to, we've a mission to attend."

"I know, I know, even though I don't want to," said Raven.

"Later," promised Nick, and he released her, and she reluctantly let him go as well.

As Raven moved toward the fireplace mantel to fetch candles and matches, Rogan clipped on his com earpiece and mike and clicked on the com gear.

"—the fucking line!" shouted Danny. "Nick! Nick! Get on th—!"

"What is it, Danny?"

"FLIR. Five guys! At the house. Guns and—!"

The door crashed open.

The rip of an Uzi stitched the darkness, muzzle flash lighting the room.

27

As gunfire shattered the blackness, at the fireplace Raven momentarily froze, her heart leaping to her throat. By the eruption of flashes from the UZI, she saw Nick fall to the floor. *Oh, God, don't let—* Then Raven dove to the hardwood as the raking stutter swept her way. In a scrabbling crawl, she lunged toward the couch, seeking its marginal safety. And she grabbed for her M&P .40—*Shit-shit-shit! It's on the kitchen table!*

Bam-bam-bam! She heard the roar of Nick's M&P .40—

The UZI fire ripped up and back, and, silhouetted by starlight, the man in the doorway lurched hindward and—

—Turbine whine and rotor whop roared, and bright light blazed—

—fell to the veranda, and another man stepped over him and into the doorway—

—Again, Nick's M&P roared and the man in the doorway stumbled backward, falling over the dead UZI gunner on the veranda and crashed down—

—In the glow from the chopper lights on the end table, light glinted golden—

Raven saw someone step from the hallway, his arm

outstretched toward—

—Raven snatched up the brass double-barrel and—

—*Bam-bam!* The man at the hallway fired two—

—*Kabloom!* In the huge flash of both barrels firing, Raven was knocked backward by the shotgun recoil—

—Outside, gunfire ripped, and through the com gear Danny shouted, his yells unintelligible but for the word "motherfucker"—

—the double-barreled blast hurled the hallway intruder sideways, slamming him into the corner and down —

—Nick rose to one knee, shouting, "Raven, Raven, are you all right?"—

—Raven fumbled for the box of shotgun—

—Another man emerged from the rear of the house and aimed—

—"Hallway, Nick!"—

—Nick fired, and the man lurched backward, his own shot going wide.

Whop-whop-whop-whop . . .

"Boss! Boss! Nick! . . ."

"Raven! Raven!"

"I'm all right. I'm all right."

"Stay where you are. There might be another!"

Her ears ringing, Raven broke open the shotgun and extracted the two spent cartridges and shoved in two fresh ones from the ripped-open box.

"Danny!"

"Four in the house, boss."

"All dead."

"One dead out here."

"That's five," said Johnny.

"FLIR for more," said Nick.

The chopper lifted and sidled about the house, and then ran a spiral pattern outward, Danny keeping up a running commentary.

Nick stood and stepped quickly to the end of the great room where Raven crouched and handed her armor and pistol to her. "Stay down," he said, and he snatched up a flashlight from among the gear. Raven slipped into the vest and gun rig as, quickly, silently, Nick moved to the hallway and vanished.

Moments later, he was back. "All empty. Still, we wait until Danny and Johnny finish their sweep."

It was then Raven began to shake.

In the dawn light, Special Agent Marks surveyed the damage. "Looks like a helluva firefight."

"Little Bighorn," said Johnny. "Only this time Custer won."

Out in the yard at the front of the house, a fifth intruder lay dead—shot by Danny from the chopper. An evidence tech searched the grass with a metal detector, marking where ejected cases lay.

The copter itself now had five bullet holes—three in the sliding door, two in the interior roof—all taken in the exchange of gunfire. An evidence tech worked at digging the bullets out.

Down near the end of the lane, the agents had found an auto rented from Avis, presumably the one the men had come in, and a tech was processing that vehicle as well.

At the house, on the front veranda and inside, two more techs from the CSU took photos and fingerprints and measured and recorded the scene. They retrieved spent cartridges and put them in evidence bags, and dug bullets and buckshot out from the walls and the floor and ceiling.

In the hallway, Medical Examiner Mallory Warbritton knelt by one of the two men who had come through the back of the house, noting the wounds and making comments into a handheld recorder.

The other man, the one with half his head blown off, lay at the corner of the passage and the great room. Agent Marks winced as he looked at him. "What did this?"

"That shotgun," said Johnny, gesturing toward the fireplace end of the room.

Marks looked that direction and his eyes widened in surprise. "Lord, looks like a cannon."

Johnny nodded. "Eight gauge—eight bore, I mean."

"What is it, brass?"

"Yeah. It was an oddity the boss picked up in Africa. The Sudan, I think. It's nearly fifty inches long and heavy as hell. Must weigh twenty, twenty-five pounds. Nick had the shells custom made."

Marks looked from the double-barrel toward the dead intruder. "Helluva blast. Who shot him?"

"Raven."

"Jesus."

Agent Marks sighed and then turned and walked out and around to the south side of the veranda, Johnny trailing after.

Raven, Nick, and Danny sat sipping coffee.

"Another attempt on your life, Miss Conway," said the agent.

Raven nodded without speaking, her cup clutched tightly in two hands as if to keep it from escaping.

"My offer yet stands," said Marks.

Raven looked up at him.

"Protective custody, I mean," added the agent.

Raven shook her head.

"We got that covered," said Danny.

Agent Marks looked at Rogan. "It seems to me it was a close thing."

Rogan nodded and said, "More of my men are on the way."

Marks leaned back against the railing. "And you've seen none of these intruders before?"

Raven shook her head.

"Well, with the Russian in the woods, and the Chicago thug on the road, and now with these five dead ones, it seems someone is determined."

Raven nodded.

A silence fell among them, and moments passed, and a red pickup rounded a curve in the lane and trundled toward the house.

"Betsy," murmured Raven, her first word of the day.

"What?" asked Marks.

"Betsy," repeated Raven. "Robert Aikens calls his truck Betsy. That's him coming now."

A stricken look fell over Robert's already distressed features. "Oh, lord, I brought them with me yesterday."

"You what?" asked Marks.

Robert pointed at the man lying dead near the front steps. "I'm pretty sure that one there was one of the searchers. Said he'd come to Benton to help. —Oh, wait! Not only that, but I handed out a hundred and two chits to all those who came to look for Miss Elizabeth, but only ninety-seven were cashed in. I thought it was just people being charitable, but instead it was these killers trying to get close."

"Well, they got close, all right," said Marks, loud enough to be overheard by Raven and Rogan and Johnny and Danny. "Too close."

Raven took a deep breath and stood and said, "Come on. Let's go to Fred's and get some breakfast."

"What about another attempt?" said Danny. "We need to keep you safe. And I think the boss would rather you not ride in the open-top Jeep."

Raven turned to Danny and said, "We'll take the copter."

Johnny grinned and jumped up and said, "Let's go."

"There's still an agent in the chopper," said Danny.

"He can go to Fred's, too," said Rogan, adding, "I'm flying."

They swung by Robert and took him along and headed down the path.

"I'm going to need your guns," called Agent Marks after them. "Statements, too!"

"Right!" barked Danny over his shoulder, and they all kept walking.

Rogan took the pilot's seat, and he sat Raven in the copilot's chair.

Evidence Tech James Hanford went along for the ride.

As they ate bacon and eggs and toast and pancakes and sausages and drank coffee at Fred's, Deputy Mills came storming in and demanded, "What the hell is going on out there?"

Robert looked at him and asked, "What's got you all riled up, Ronnie."

"What's got me riled up? I'll tell you what's got me riled up." Mills turned and looked at Raven. "I'm riled up 'cause Sheriff Winkler called to tell me the FBI is back out at your place, Miss Conway, and a morgue wagon is coming from the city. That's what's got me riled up. Seems I've got to hear it from my boss off at the county seat rather from anyone here about! I should be the first one to know, not the goddamned last!"

"You have no jurisdiction out there, Ronnie," said Robert. "And neither does Winkler."

"Maybe so. Maybe not. But, dammit, I'm right next door!"

Fred, standing nearby, said, "Ronnie, right there before you sits Miss Raven Conway. I believe you once told her not to get her panties tied in a knot. Well, seems to me it's your panties that are tied in a knot 'stead of hers."

Danny and Johnny broke out in loud guffaws, and Deputy Mills began to splutter. Raven held up her hands in a peace gesture and said, "Calm down, everyone." She looked up at Mills and said, "You're right, Ronnie. I should have called you to explain what was going on. It just didn't occur to me at the time. You see, the FBI has nominal jurisdiction, I'm told, and Nicholas is the one who called them. At the time, I was somewhat upset."

"About what?"

Rogan looked at Deputy Mills and said, "Five thugs tried to assassinate Miss Conway, and we killed them all."

"Five? Five? No shit? —Er, beggin' your pardon, Miss Conway."

Raven looked at him and nodded and said, "Five, Ronnie. Five." Then she added, "No shit."

When they flew back to Cathleens Haven, Agent Marks took all of the weapons that had been fired: Rogan's and Danny's M&P .40s, and the brass shotgun Raven had used.

"Pat and Tracey are bringing more S&Ws," said Rogan. Then he took Raven's M&P .40 and slipped it into his own rig, and he hooked her up with a Cloak 9.

Danny armed himself with a Cloak, and he also took up one of the Sig rifles. "These bastards are determined," he said, checking the Sig magazine.

After Danny and Johnny made another FLIR run to make certain the area was clear of any unknowns, they went out to sit on the north-side veranda, just as Evidence Tech Susan Grayson walked up the path and onto the porch. "They had your and your sister's pictures, Miss Conway, only this time written on the back in addition to both of your names it also said 'Hunters Trust.'"

28

"Damn," said Raven, "I really hate to think that whoever is behind this has something to do with Hunters Trust." She was down on her hands and knees and treating the smears on the hallway floor with Pet Gold. Robert had made a run into Benton for the enzymatic stain remover; among other things, it promised to eliminate blood spots.

Beside her and scrubbing the product into the stain, his strokes following the grain of the wood, Danny nodded. At the front door Rogan scoured cleaner into the blood on the veranda. "Someone at the Trust might be involved. Even so, it could be that this team of killers simply noted the information in passing."

It was late at night. The morgue wagon had come and the bodies had been removed. Agent Marks had taken all of their statements. All evidence had been bagged—spent cartridge casings, shotgun shells, dug out bullets and double-ought buckshot, as well as the weapons that had been used in the firefight, along with blood swabs and bits of skull bone and brain matter. Jack Miller had come with his tow truck and had loaded the killers' Avis rental onto his flatbed, and had headed for the CSU garage in the city.

228 / Dennis L. McKiernan

Agent Marks and his forensic team had gone.

Wearing night-vision gear, Johnny was out away from the house standing guard.

Robert, working on the corner and wall where blood and bone and brain matter had spewed from the shotgun blast, held up a lantern and said, "Appears mine is coming right off."

"We'll see what it looks like in daytime," said Raven.

Robert grunted an assent and then said, "I'll bring some Murphy Oil Soap when I come in the morning. And I'll bring what I'll need—wood putty and the like—to patch up the bullet holes." He glanced overhead at the ceiling, where the UZI had left a track. "And a ladder, too."

Raven sat back on her heels and took a shaky breath.

Without looking at her, Danny said, "It'll get better, Raven."

A moment passed, and Raven took up scrubbing again. Her voice was soft when she said, "I thought Nick had been killed. I saw him fall." She swiped a hand at her brimming eyes.

"Probably diving for the floor," said Danny.

"I know that now, but not then."

Danny nodded and then said, "You saved his life, you know."

Raven did not answer.

Danny looked at her in the lantern light and reached out and touched her shoulder. "Thank you, Raven."

Her eyes glittering with unshed droplets, Raven glanced across at him and smiled. Then tears began to flow, and she put her face in her hands and said, "I'm such a wuss."

"Oh, no, Raven," said Danny, "you are anything but. Without you, this would have been a disaster."

Raven shook her head and said, "Without me, you wouldn't have been here."

"But I'm glad we are," said Danny.

Raven took a deep breath and looked at him. "Me, too."

As a fresh spritzing of the enzymatic cleaner worked on the greatly diminished blood stains, Robert downed the last of his beer and stood up from the kitchen table and said, "Me, I'm outta here and on my way to Fred. But as I said, I'll be back bright and early with the fixin's for the holes, and Murphy Oil Soap for the last of the cleaning."

Rogan held out an opened Negra Modelo to Robert and said, "Would you drop this off to Johnny. He might be a bit thirsty."

"And tell him we did all the hard work," said Danny, "while he lollygagged out there in the dark chanting his Cherokee woo-woo."

"Now, now, Mr. Danny," said Robert, taking the beer in hand, "there's more to this world than meets the eye."

"Yeah, you're right," said Danny, stabbing his thumb over his shoulder in the direction of the forest, "Hunters Wood for one."

Johnny, Danny, and Nick each took a shift standing watch, and at each change of the guard they made a FLIR run. When the morning came, Raven brewed coffee, fried bacon and then toast, and scrambled up a dozen eggs. She looked across the table at Danny and said, "You are right; it does get easier."

Danny nodded and slathered more jam on his toast.

"Nonetheless," said Raven, "I never want to forget, even though they were trying to kill us, they were people."

"Not very good ones," said Johnny. "And besides, you saved Nick."

"Where'd you learn your shotgun skills?" asked Danny.

"Actually, I thought it would be just like a rifle," said Raven, "but it knocked me down."

"You shoot both barrels at once?" asked Johnny.

Raven nodded. "Yeah. It knocked me down, and if it hadn't've been for all that scrubbing yesterday my shoulder would really be sore."

"Girl," said Danny, "no wonder it knocked you down. I mean, an eight bore, and what do you weigh? One ten one twenty?"

Johnny shook his head and said, "You dumb mick. A gentleman should never ask a woman her weight."

"Who said I was a gentleman?" asked Danny. "Point him out and I'll knock him flat."

"Flat? Flat? I seem to recall the last time you tried to do that, it was you seeking stars in the sky, and I had to jump in and . . ."

Raven was laughing when Nick came into the house after making a FLIR run. He looked at Johnny and Danny and nodded his thanks.

That afternoon a second Blackledge chopper set

down in the field next to the first. Two people emerged and began unloading gear. Danny and Johnny went down to help them lug up the equipment.

"Who are they?" asked Raven.

"Patrick Foley, a former navy seal, and Tracey Blaine—she's an ex SWAT sniper, one of the best I've ever seen."

"Tracey's a girl?"

"Yep. A trained martial artist, too."

"Good," said Raven. "Maybe she and I can get in some practice. I feel rusty and out of shape. I mean, I'm not getting in my morning runs, and I miss not going to my dojo once a week."

Nick grinned at her. "You need even more morning exercise?"

Raven laughed and said, "A different kind of workout, Mr. Nicholas Rogan, and thank you very much."

Wiping his hands on a rag, Robert emerged from inside the house. "All done. Holes plugged. Putty drying. Tomorrow I'll sand. Oh, and the Murphy Oil Soap has set the place to looking like new."

"Let me see," said Raven, getting to her feet and following Robert.

The blood stains had vanished from the veranda at the front door and the hallway and wall as well, and Robert pointed out the places where he had wood-puttied the holes. "They're kinda ugly right now, Miss Raven, but when they dry and I sand 'em down they'll look all right."

"I'm sure you'll do a beautiful job, Robert," said Raven. "Now let's go meet the newcomers."

~

His hair somewhere in that indeterminate range between brown and blond, blue-eyed Patrick Foley stood a trim five eight, and had an infectious grin. With her own chestnut hair tied back in a ponytail, Tracey Blaine at petite five four looked like a teenager. She turned her blue-green gaze upon Raven and said, "Why would any man ever want to shoot you? I mean, heck, girl, if I had your looks, they'd be beating down my door to sweep me off my feet."

Pat grinned and said, "Tracey, your door has been wide open, and you've been swept off your feet so many times I— Ow!"

Tracey turned and smiled at Raven and said, "Now, that's what you call 'knocking up a frog on someone's arm.'"

"Looked more like a cobra strike to me," said Raven.

Tracey cocked her head. "You do martial arts?"

Raven nodded. "I was just telling Nick that I need to get to my dojo."

Raven ducked a spin kick and countered with a squatting leg sweep.

"Damn, look at them go at it," said Danny.

With a kip-up, Tracey was back on her feet.

"Looks like Jet Li versus Jackie Chan," said Johnny.

With a blurring flurry of hand and foot strikes and blocks, both women chopped at one another, each pulling their punches but not at all letting up on speed

"No, more like Michelle Yeoh versus Ziyi Zhang," said Danny.

"Who the hell are they?"

"Didn't you ever see *Crouching Tiger, Hidden Dragon?*"

"Oh, those two."

"Yeah."

Danny and Johnny, lemonades in hand, sat on the south-side veranda and spectated as Raven and Tracey went at each other on the grassy side lawn.

Now and again, Danny or Johnny would pick up their binoculars and scan the field and the tree line for intruders.

One of the two Blackledge choppers droned in the distance. Patrick was making yet another FLIR run down the valley and back. Nick was somewhere in the other chopper, the one with Raven's laptop acting as a recorder, as he swept the forest in a new sector.

"Damn, she's good," said Johnny.

"Which one?"

"Raven."

Danny nodded. "Yeah, but so is Tracey."

"I'll drink to that," said Johnny.

He and Danny clinked glasses and took swigs.

The com gear chirped, and Patrick said, "All clear to the highway."

Johnny triggered his mike. "Did you remember to scan the forest on each side?"

"Am I an amateur or what?" Patrick replied sarcastically. "Of course I remembered to—

Danny burst out in raucous laughter. "Look, Johnny, look!"

Johnny glanced up to see Raven and Tracey floundering to their feet in the pond, and then Tracey, knee deep in the water, sloshed in slow motion onto the shore, cursing, "Jesus! Frickin', frickin' cold!"

Laughing, Raven waded back out. Then Tracey began laughing as well.

Arm in arm, they headed to the house.

"Aw, poop!" said Danny. "The girl-fight's over."

Patrick was back from his chopper run, and Danny and Johnny regaled him with descriptions of the fight, evoking images of Chan and Li and Yeoh and Zhang and Bruce Lee and even Chuck Norris, with Danny now and then riffing the theme from the old movie *Mortal Kombat*.

They were still laughing, when Raven and Tracey, drying their hair, stepped back out to the veranda, Raven wearing her armor over her terrycloth robe. They had turned down Danny's offer to guard them while they took their showers. Instead, Raven, armed again with an M&P .40, stood watch as Tracey cursed under the waterfall, and Tracey stood guard as Raven took her turn.

Raven paused in toweling her hair and looked down the two-track. "Deputy Mills?"

A sheriff's car barreled up the lane, and above it flew Nick in the other Blackledge copter as he returned from making a refueling stop.

They all looked, and Danny said, "I wonder what he's coming to bitch about now."

The car slid to a halt, and Mills got out and watched as Rogan settled the chopper down.

"Charles Lawrence," said Mills. "The dumb-ass put in an insurance claim. I mean, like we wouldn't be looking for a white car with a shot-out rear window. Bullet holes, too. And blood in the seat."

"He's a nephew of Jimmy Phelps?" asked Raven, handing back the jpeg photo array to Mills.

"Yeah. Seems he wanted to get out of Mount Holly and go to Chicago and join the South Side mob, just like his uncle."

Mills made a note in his folder that Raven Conway had identified Charles Lawrence as the driver of the white car.

"It was a Ford Taurus, by the way," said Mills.

"How old is he?"

Mills looked at the rap sheet. "Eighteen. Up to trying to kill you, he was mostly into petty crimes."

"Wait a minute," said Nick, "you say this kid was from Mount Holly?"

Mills again looked at the rap sheet. "Yep."

"But isn't Mount Holly where the plates were taken from a junkyard wreck and used on the stolen car that the Russian was driving?"

"By golly, I think you're right." Mills scribbled a quick note.

"There might be a connection here," said Rogan. "What did he have to say?"

"He claims all he knows is that his uncle hired him to drive the car."

"Did the uncle mention the name 'Hunters Trust?'"

"Y'know, I didn't ask. Anyway, even if I had, the FBI is keeping a tight lid on what they tell me . . . tell us, that is. I mean, I've told you everything they told me before they sent me out to see if Miss Conway could ID the driver from their transmitted photo array, which she nicely did."

Nick looked at Raven. "We need to talk with Agent Marks."

Raven stood and said, "Let's go."

Nick glanced at the sun now sinking behind the western ridge and said, "It's late, Raven. How about instead I call Agent Marks and set up a meeting for tomorrow?"

Raven sat back down.

Using a satellite phone, Nick spoke briefly. He clicked it off and said, "All set. Tomorrow, ten a.m."

Raven smiled and said, "Then what say I grab my laundry and we head into town and do the washing and eat at Fred's while the dryer is running?"

Robert said, "I think Fred will let you use her machines. She lives above the restaurant, you know."

"Fred is a she?" asked Tracey.

"I'll tell you about it on the way in," said Robert.

"No Jeep," said Rogan, standing. "Chopper instead."

"Sounds like a plan," said Patrick.

Johnny said, "Hold on. We can't leave this place unguarded. One of us has to stay behind."

Danny groaned and said, "Rock, paper, scissors?"

29

"Charles Lawrence was the young man driving the car. He has a fairly long rap sheet, mostly petty theft in Mount Holly. He's a nephew of Phelps, the shooter in the car. The boy's DNA, along with Phelps', was in the wig. When we showed the wig to the kid and asked him how he got it, he eventually confessed to killing George Harris at Gaslight Costumes and setting the place on fire. Said it was an accident. That Harris caught him trying to steal the wig. Said he shoved the old man and he hit his head. But then we told him we knew he had shot the guy, and he gave it all up."

Raven said, "That was three years ago."

Agent Marks sighed and said, "Yeah. He was fifteen at the time. Just a punk kid."

Rogan took a sip of his coffee, then asked, "What about the five guys who broke into Cathleens Haven?"

"We've identified four of them." Agent Marks picked up a folder and handed it to Nick. Rogan opened it and looked at the pictures inside—mug shots, all but one. He handed the packet to Raven.

Raven winced at the fifth photo.

"Three from New York and one from Chicago," said Marks. "The fifth guy—the one you shot, Miss

Conway—isn't anywhere on our radar, not in IAFIS or CODIS or any other system we have available."

"These guys from New York tied in with the Russian?" asked Nick.

"Not that we know of," said Marks.

"Any connection between the Mount Holly kid and the junkyard plates on the Russian's stolen car?"

"We're looking into that, but so far, all we know is that the plates and the kid were both from Mount Holly."

"Speaking of the Russian," said Raven, "what about Interpol? Do they have anything on him?"

"Nada. Zip. Zero," said Marks. "All we know is that he came into the States as Gregor Minchinko and no one seems to have his fingerprints or DNA on file."

"Do any of these people have anything in common?" asked Raven. "—Other than criminal records, I mean."

"Two of the five are reputed to be freelance hit men . . . killers for hire."

"As was the Russian?"

"We think so."

"Then that's six people altogether who . . ." Raven's voice dwindled.

Nick reached out and took her hand.

Raven turned to him. "It's got to be someone at the Trust. I mean, who else has the money and potential contacts to hire freelance killers?"

"If we can find out who gains," said Rogan, "then we find the one behind it." Nick turned to Raven and said, "Who is next in line of succession? I mean, if you and Elizabeth were eliminated, who would then become trustee?"

"I have no idea," said Raven.

"We can look into that," said Marks. "I have an experienced man on my staff who has run down other genealogies. We just need to know your parents."

"Well, that's a problem," said Raven.

Nick said, "Agent Marks, Hunters Trust is matrilineal. You only need to know the mothers."

"In that case," said Marks, "who is your mother?"

"My mother is Avelaine Conway, nee Lucas," said Raven, "and her mother is Meredith Lucas, nee O'Brian. Our lineage stretches all the way back to Cathleen Hunter, a woman in George Washington's time."

Marks jotted down those names. "We'll follow that up. But if it's someone in the Trust who is trying to have you eliminated, then we also need to follow that line as well. Is there anyone at the Trust you have complete confidence in?"

Raven frowned. "I would have said George Allenby, but he might have the most to gain. I mean, he's been the administrator for seven years, and should I be killed, or if Sissy isn't found, then he would once more have complete control."

Marks asked, "What about Taylor Raines? Could you trust her?"

"I just met her—what?—ten days ago? I know nothing about her."

Nick glanced at Raven and said, "Taylor and I have a minor bit of history, but not enough for me to put full faith in her. But she *is* the troubleshooter for the Trust and as such would have many contacts with people who can, um, solve problems."

"Like paid assassins?" asked Marks.

"Like paid assassins," agreed Nick.

"But what would she gain?" asked Raven.

Nick shrugged. "Perhaps even more power in the running of the Trust."

"Well, no matter what, it won't be easy investigating that empire," said Agent Marks.

"I can do it from inside," said Raven. "After all, I *am* the Trustee."

"Too much risk," said Nick.

Marks nodded his agreement and said, "Miss Conway, you would be even more exposed than you are now. But, listen, you can do this: as Trustee, you can ask that the books be audited."

Raven frowned. "Even with what little knowledge I have, I've come to realize that the Trust is an enormous enterprise, with its fingers in all sorts of pies. Auditing it would be a colossal undertaking."

"Exactly so," said Marks. "And that will give us the opportunity to send several agents in with the auditing firm. If anyone there is trying to kill you to keep you from uncovering a crime—embezzlement, unauthorized loans, shaky stock transactions, or other financial misdeeds—then we are likely to uncover it. Besides, with your permission as Trustee, we can tap the phones and bug the offices."

"Big Brother is watching you," said Raven, glumly.

"You might think so, Miss Conway, but I know of no other way to succeed."

Nick shook his head. "I've worked for Hunters Trust a number of times, and I know that they have a top-notch anti-industrial spy firm make weekly as well as random sweeps for taps and bugs. You can't bug them.

Not even with lasers that pick up audio vibrations on their office windows."

"Well, then," said Marks, "it's back to running an audit."

Raven sighed and looked at Nick, who said, "It's your decision to make, Raven."

"But I have no experience in hiring auditors."

"What you need," said Marks, "is what is known as a forensic auditor, one who is especially trained to pick up on illegal financial moves and follow the money trail. If you'd like, I can arrange for a team to do it. That way, we can insert our own investigators. I'll need a couple of weeks, if not a month, to set things up."

She turned to Marks and said, "All right."

On the way back to the airport, Raven fished out her cell phone and punched in Allenby's number.

"Hello, Raven. Are you all right?"

"Yes, George. I'm fine."

"Well, given the second attempt on your life, perhaps you and Mr. Rogan and his team should consider going somewhere remote, where these ... people cannot get at you. Staying at Cathleens Haven makes you a fixed target."

"Perhaps so, George, but until Sissy is found I'd rather be at a place familiar to her."

Allenby sighed. "As you will, Raven. But I am worried."

"George, I called to see if you had learned anything about the Russian. Nicholas is with me; let me put you on speaker."

"Hello, Mr. Allenby," said Nick.

"Hello, Nicholas. Where are you two? It sounds as if you are in a car."

"We are," said Raven. "Now what can you tell me about the Russian?"

"We have a bit of information, but little on the Brighton Beach connection. Taylor has men working on it, but the Russian mob isn't easy to infiltrate, nor easy to gather much intelligence about. —Only what the media report, and who knows how accurate that might be? Regardless, she has discovered through our Moscow contacts that this Minchenko is an alias of Vassily Akunin, a former agent of the FSB."

"FSB?"

"Successor to the KGB. Still, a secret service as far as Taylor is concerned. In any event, Vassily was drummed out of the FSB, and for a Russian to be drummed out of that organization, well, he must have committed a crime against the State . . . or perhaps against someone high up. I can put Taylor on if you'd like."

"No, George. But you might pass that information on to FBI Agent Marks, or have Taylor call him."

"Ah, yes. I'll do that."

"Thank you, George."

"Is there anything else I can do for you, Raven? Money, perhaps. More guards?"

"Not at the moment, George, but I'll let you know should I need anything."

"I have a remote cabin in the woods where you might find refuge, safety."

"Thank you, but no thanks. Perhaps after Sissy is found."

"As you wish, Raven."

"I have to ring off, George; we've reached our destination."

"Call anytime, Raven. I like hearing from you. Oh, and remember to check in each day as you have been doing so that I know that you are all right."

"I will, George. Good-bye."

"Good-bye, Raven."

Raven clicked her cell phone shut. "Now I'm suspicious of everyone, even George. I think he's really concerned, but he might instead be keeping tabs on me: where I am, who I am with, how many guards I have. Oh, God, am I paranoid or what?"

244 / Dennis L. McKiernan

Rogan smiled and said, "With people shooting at you, I'd say you have every right to be paranoid."

Raven suddenly burst out in laughter, and when Nick looked at her, she said, "I have this vision of a very empathetic psychiatrist who lurks in the shadows where paranoids pass by and follows them at a distance, just to make each one of them feel vindicated in their belief that someone is out to get them."

"A good way to get himself shot," said Rogan, pulling into the car rental lot.

Raven's face grew somber. "Oh, Nick, I just hate to think that someone I've trusted all these years might be at the bottom of these attempts."

"Et tu, Brute?" said Nick.

"Exactly so," said Raven.

"Well, if it is betrayal, then we can hope the next line in the play does not come true," said Nick.

Raven frowned, and then her face lit in enlightenment. "If I have a Brutus, then I am playing the part of a Caesar. And the next line is, 'Then fall, Caesar.'"

Nick nodded and said, "And, my dear Julius, I'll do everything in my power to see that you do not fall."

They turned in their rental car, and, after getting through security—Nick's Cloak 9 easily passing the metal detector without a murmur—they hopped a shuttle to the helipad, and some long moments later they finally got clearance from Control and were airborne and away.

"But I don't want to," said Raven. "Sissy is out there somewhere, and if she is alive, I need to be here when she is found."

Rogan stood looking out of the window at the meadow below. Danny sat at the table at the kitchen end of the room, along with Robert. Tracey was somewhere on patrol outside the house, and Patrick was in one of the choppers making a FLIR run up the valley, checking for intruders. Johnny Redwing was in the other chopper making a FLIR run over another sector of the forest. Raven stood at the sink, washing a cup.

"Miss Raven," said Robert, "Mr. Nick is right. You staying here is just begging whoever is behind it all to come and get you. I mean they know exactly where you are, and that's bad, real bad."

Danny nodded and said, "Might as well paint a big bull's-eye on this place."

With tears in her eyes, Raven reached for the dishtowel and began to dry the cup. Silence descended upon the room. Finally she put the cup away and then turned to face the others. "What is this? A family intervention? Like for some addict? Some junkie of a sort?"

Rogan turned from the window and walked to where she stood. He put his arms around her. She did not resist his embrace.

"My love," he whispered, "I cannot lose you now that I've found you."

Raven tightened her hold on him.

Danny said, "Canoodle all you want, you two, but that doesn't alter the fact that by staying here, Raven brings danger."

Again a quietness fell over the room.

But then suddenly Raven gasped, and she pushed away from Rogan and looked up at him. "Oh, God, what Danny said, it cuts both ways. As long as I am here I am putting all of you in danger as well."

"No matter where we are," said Nick, "we can deal with danger. It's just that we need to reduce the risk to you, Raven. And by going somewhere else, somewhere that whoever is behind these attacks doesn't know about, we will do just that."

Raven again moved into Nick's arms and clasped him and leaned her head against his chest. "But what about Sissy? I cannot just abandon her."

They held one another for long moments, no one speaking. Finally, Raven asked, "How long until the whole of Hunters Wood has been FLIRed?"

Rogan glanced at Danny.

"If we step it up, five, six days; a week at most," said Danny.

"Then in one more week, you can take me wherever you wish."

Danny growled, but Nick said, "All right."

The Blackledge team also stepped up their FLIR-run surveillance of the meadow and adjoining woods, seeking intruders, should any come. Raven was sequestered even more tightly, and, whether indoors or out, she carried a weapon and wore her Pinnacle Armor vest. Patrick had suggested that should someone get close enough, with two or three RPGs they could take out the whole house. But Nick had said that with FLIR, they could keep that from happening. They had discussed having lookouts at the entrance of the valley, but decided that would spread themselves too thin. Deputy Mills could provide no help, and they hesitated to put any of the locals in danger. They had briefly considered bringing more Blackledge forces, but Raven had noted that no matter how many people they had, they simply couldn't cover the perimeter of the entire forest, consequently posting sentries at the way into the valley would be superfluous. And so, making frequent runs with FLIR, coupled with each of them taking turns at guard, would have to be enough. "Besides," Raven had said, grinning, "what can possibly go wrong in just seven days?"

Danny had groaned, but Tracey had burst out in maniacal laughter.

Days passed, and no attacks came, though Nils Anderson and Lori Karlson did drive in one day to be stopped and then eventually pass through the gauntlet. They had come to thank Raven for what she had done to get Lori back on her feet. And they thanked her as well for the bonus she had given them on the day Lori had sprained her ankle.

Sectors of the forest were FLIRed, but neither Sissy nor any "hidden people" were spotted.

Robert came and went, bringing groceries and ice,

and ferrying laundry.

Even though Jack Miller had repaired Raven's Porsche, she made arrangements with him to store the car for an indeterminate time.

Raven reported in to George Allenby every day, and he continued to express concern over her remaining at Cathleens Haven, where just anyone could find her. Raven did not tell him that they would be moving soon.

And the search went on with the FLIR sweeps, and seven days altogether passed.

And no one tried to kill Raven.

At 2 p.m. on Tuesday, twenty days after Raven had first arrived at Cathleens Haven only to find Sissy missing, Johnny came in from the final FLIR run of the last segment of the forest. "That's it," said Johnny. "Every sector has been searched, and, Raven, I'm sorry to say, we didn't find your sister."

Raven sighed. "Then tomorrow we leave."

"Before you go," said Robert, "Fred wants to throw you one last meal."

"Oh, I would like that," said Raven, and she looked at Nick, and he nodded.

"Seven o'clock? Eight?" asked Robert.

"Seven p.m. would be fine," said Raven.

"I'll run in now and tell her," said Robert.

After Robert had gone, Raven said, "I am sorry we didn't tell him where the place is we are going to retreat to."

"The less who know, the better," said Nick. "That way, no one can get it out of him."

"Who would do—? Oh, wait. That's a dumb shit

question. It'd have to be whoever is behind this."

Nick nodded. "Right."

They quietly sat for a moment, and then Raven said, "I keep having this thought that right after we pull stakes, Sissy will reappear, and no one will be here to keep her safe."

Nick reached out and took her hand.

Raven looked at him and said, "It's irrational, I know, but still . . ."

Nick stroked her fingers. "Robert has promised to come every day, and if Elizabeth shows up, he'll call us."

"I'm going to miss you, Raven."

"And I'll miss you too, Frederika Johanna Olsen."

The two women embraced, and Fred, with a tear in her eye, squeezed Raven rib-cracking hard, paying little heed to the gun in its rig and the armored vest Raven wore.

"Tell that Danny good-bye for me. He's a pistol."

"I will, Fred."

It was late at night and the dinner was over, and they all were making ready to get back in the chopper and head to the house. Johnny was carrying a meal for Danny, who had lost at paper, scissors, rock.

A few minutes later they were airborne, Nick flying, Raven at his side, with Tracey, Pat, and Johnny lounging in the seats behind.

A thin crescent moon hung low in the west, and the sky was a spangle of stars.

As they flew up the valley, Rogan flicked on the lights.

Raven frowned. "What are you—? Wait, isn't that Betsy?"

A red Ford pickup truck sat at the foot of the path.

"But we just left Robert back at Fred's," said Johnny, now standing and peering over Nick's shoulder.

"Something's wonky," said Patrick.

Nick flicked on the FLIR, and angled the chopper toward the house.

Johnny studied the screen. "Nobody, boss. Not even Danny, who should be out in the yard."

Rogan sidled around the perimeter of the house.

No one showed up on FLIR.

"He could be inside," said Tracey, taking up one of the Sig rifles.

"I'll make a wider sweep," said Nick.

He backed the chopper out to the center of the meadow and started to make a three sixty.

"Wait, wait!" barked Raven. "What's that?"

Nick zeroed in on the heat signature.

"It's a body. Someone lying down," said Johnny.

"Danny," said Raven. "It could be Danny."

"He's not moving," said Johnny.

"Oh, crap," said Raven, her voice tight with tension.

"Boss, there might be someone in the house."

"I'm going to set us down," said Rogan. "Pat, you stay with Raven and Tracey in the copter till we've cleared the house."

"Frack that," said Raven. "I'm going with you. I've got on the armor, and I'm a good shot. —Besides, I know where the stretcher is, and if that's Danny and he's hurt, or anyone else, for that matter, we're going to need it. And before you say anything, there's no need to

252 / Dennis L. McKiernan

argue. Danny could be bleeding to death."

"Shit, shit," cursed Nick. Then he said, "You'll wait outside till we clear the house. And Tracey will stick to you like glue. Understood?"

"Got it," said Raven.

"What about me, boss?" asked Patrick.

"I want you in the copter on FLIR. And if necessary, we'll need the chopper to make a run to a hospital."

"Right."

Before setting down, Nick swept a three sixty, and then once more sidled completely around the house.

No one showed up.

He maneuvered to the pickup and around. "FLIR shows no one inside," said Johnny.

"I'll set down" said Nick, flipping off the chopper lights. "You and Tracey scope it out."

Tracey slid open the side door, and the moment the wheels touched dirt, she and Johnny were out. They zigzagged in crouching runs toward the truck.

In the feeble moon- and starlight, first Tracey on the left and then Johnny on the right gave an all-clear signal.

Nick moved out from the pilot's seat, and Patrick took his place. Then Raven and Nick exited, and moments later Patrick was airborne.

Raven and Tracey approached the house from the north side, while Nick and Johnny came in from the south.

Some distance away from the veranda, Tracey knelt, and Raven followed suit.

Nick and Johnny split, and as Johnny took the front, Nick took the back.

Johnny disappeared inside.

Long moments passed, and every second, Raven, with her heart wildly hammering in her chest, even though it was in her throat, expected gunfire to erupt.

Still more moments passed, but finally Nick stepped out on the veranda and motioned for them to enter.

As Raven stepped to the porch, she whispered, "Did you check the tool shed?"

Nick nodded. "It's clear."

Raven retrieved the aluminum-framed litter from the tub room, where she and Robert had stowed it with the rest of the first-aid gear. At Raven's direction, Tracey shoved gauze and bandages and disinfectant and tape and other such into a sack, and then, pistols in hand, and with a rifle slung across Tracey's back, they stepped out the rear door where Nick and Johnny waited. Johnny was wearing night-vision gear, and Rogan had his com gear headset in place. The four then angled upslope and southward to where someone lay just inside the edge of the forest.

Nick and Johnny had both grabbed up flashlights, but they didn't turn them on.

Swiftly, quietly, and just inside the woods they made their way a hundred yards or so to where—

"It's Danny," hissed Raven, dropping to her knees beside his still form. "He's been shot."

She grabbed up Danny's wrist. "He has a pulse, but it's weak and _hread. We have to get him to a doctor."

Raven then ripped open Danny's shirt, and quickly she applied dressing to the wound high on his chest, and with Nick's help she wrapped a long Ace bandage tightly around Danny's body to apply pressure to slow the bleeding.

They rocked Danny up on his side, and slid the litter under. Then Nick triggered his com gear and said, "Any strangers, Pat?"

"FLIR is all clear, boss. No heat signatures but you guys."

"All right, Pat, we're heading down to the meadow. You and Johnny can fly him to the city where he can get the best aid. Johnny, on the way you keep pressure on the wound; the Ace bandage is not enough."

Rogan then turned to Raven and Tracey. "You two head back well inside the trees to the house. But stay in the tree line up on the slope until I get back. I mean, we don't know where this bastard might be, and I don't want Raven exposed to sniper fire. I mean, crap, he might be buried, though even there he'd have a heat signature. When I return, we'll make a run and get inside the house. And we'll stay there till Pat gets back and makes another FLIR run."

"What about the other copter, boss? You could FLIR with it, or get Raven and Tracey to it and even run away."

"With the bastard who did this nowhere to be found, I don't want to have Raven out in the open any more than necessary, and I think two of us need to stay with her until you and Pat get back."

"Right."

"Okay. Let's go." He triggered the com. "Pat, set her down."

As Patrick slid the chopper over to the base of the long slope, Johnny and Nick hoisted the litter and started down.

Well inside the tree line, Raven and Tracey headed

northward toward the house.

They came to a stop just upslope from the dwelling, and Raven heard the chopper take off.

Tracey looked at Raven and gave her a thumbs up. Raven nodded, and as the chopper moved away to the west, Tracey and Raven crept down toward where the woods came to an end.

As they moved past the outcrop of rock and the waterfall and on toward the tree line, someone stepped out from behind the cascade and, with a coughing *chuff!* Of a suppressor-fitted pistol, shot Tracey in the back.

Even as Tracey tumbled downslope—*chuff!*—a second bullet slammed into Raven and knocked her to her hands and knees, and her M&P .40, lost to her grip, went pinwheeling away.

31

As Raven scrambled for the gun, "Hold still," barked the shooter, a man. "I'm aiming at your head."

Raven stopped, her pistol too far.

"That vest won't save you again," growled the man. "I'm an expert shot, and your skull is not bulletproof."

Raven's heart hammered like that of a caged wild bird.

"Stand up," said the man. "I want to see you."

Slowly Raven rose to her feet, her hands in the air.

Dive to the side? Leap downslope? Run?

"Turn around."

She pivoted to face the man.

In the starlight and the light of the slender moon, Raven could see a stocky man, five eight or nine, who might be in his forties. Raven could almost make out his features, but the moon- and starlight was too dim for her to recognize who he might be, though an ephemeral *something* twitched at the corner of her mind, but it was gone before she could capture it.

"You are a tall one," said the man.

Keep him talking. Nick is on his way.

"What have you done to my sister?"

The man gave a soft chuckle. "Before someone

killed him, I have no doubt my hireling, Minchenko, did away with Elizabeth. But you, Raven Conway . . . you are a hard person to kill."

Hurry, Nick, hurry!

"Why are you doing this?" asked Raven. "Who hired you?"

"Who hired me?" His voice took on a smirking tone. "No one. They say when you want something done right, do it yourself. That's why I am here instead of my surrogates. Good-bye, Miss Conway."

He raised his pistol toward her head, and then lurched forward a step or two. He looked in surprise at the copper point and a bit of a shaft protruding from his chest. And then he collapsed to his knees and toppled face down to the ground.

An arrow jutted up from his back.

Startled, her heart racing, Raven looked into the moon-cast shadows of the forest. Something huge moved her way.

It was a horse.

And on its back—

"Sissy!"

32

Again Raven screamed, "Sissy!" And she ran toward her sister.

Bow in hand, Elizabeth Conway threw a leg over the horse and leapt to the ground. She was dressed somewhat boyishly in soft dark leathers and looked rather like a slender lad, but for her long ash-blond hair shining in the starlight, and her delicate features seemingly aglow in the pale radiance of the low-hanging crescent moon.

The sisters embraced, Raven sobbing in relief and murmuring, "Oh, Sissy, Sissy, I thought, we thought . . ." And the younger sister comforted the older and whispered, "Shh, shh." Through her tears, Raven looked over Sissy's shoulder. She could dimly see a group of riders in the shifting shadows of the forest.

One of them moved forward and said, "Iron is here, Ryelle."

"I know," replied Elizabeth.

"And more is coming," said the rider.

"That, too," said Elizabeth.

Then Elizabeth held Raven at arm's length and said, "You must remove the iron and I will come again."

Elizabeth mounted her horse and said, "Tend your

companion," and she twitched the reins to the right . . . and vanished, as did all the others.

Astonished, stunned at the abrupt disappearance of her sister into thin air, Raven gaped at the space where Sissy had been, but suddenly Elizabeth's last words echoed in her mind: *Tend your companion.*

—Oh my God, Tracey!

Swiping at her tears, Raven turned and stumbled past the corpse of the man and hurried downslope to Tracey's side.

Swiping at her tears, Raven turned and stumbled past the corpse and downslope to Tracey's side.

Even as Raven looked for the wound, Tracey groaned and opened her eyes.

"Don't move," said Raven. "You've been shot."

Tracey grabbed Raven and pulled her down, and rolled over and hissed, "We've got to take cover."

"He's dead," said Raven. "The guy is dead."

"What?"

"He's dead."

"He's dead? Good, but there could be more than one."

"No, he came solo, Tracey. But listen to me: stop thrashing around, you've been shot."

In spite of Raven's words, Tracey struggled to a sitting position. "Shot? Me? I don't think so."

"Dammit, Tracey," barked Raven, "I said—"

"I tell you I'm not shot," interjected Tracey, spreading her arms wide as if to demonstrate she was completely fit.

Out from the dimness, Rogan suddenly appeared and knelt at Raven's side. "What the hell?"

Raven threw her arms about him. "Oh, Nick. The guy is dead. Sissy shot him."

"I didn't hear any gunfire. Why is Tracy on the ground? You found your sister?" Rogan swiftly scanned the surroundings, spotting the dead man upslope.

"Sissy killed him with bow and arrow," said Raven. "Remember, I told you she—"

"Where is she, then?"

"Vanished," said Raven. "But the dead guy shot Tracey. —Rather, he wasn't dead when he shot her, but he did."

"I tell you I'm all right," said Tracey, getting to her feet. She put her hand to the side of her head and winced. "Somebody conked me, though."

"What?" said Raven. And, using Rogan's flashlight, she examined Tracy's skull just above her right ear. A small trickle of blood oozed out. "There's a lump all right, and a bit of blood. Did the bullet bounce off?"

"I always knew you were hardheaded, Tracey," said Rogan, "but this is ridiculous."

"The rifle," said Tracey, unslinging the Sig 556 from her back. "The shot must have hit the forearm or something, and the barrel in turn hammered me." She examined the weapon. "Yeah. Here it is. His bullet slammed into the action. It's destroyed."

"Lucky for you," said Nick.

They moved uphill to where the body lay.

"Where did he come from?" asked Rogan.

"I think he was behind the waterfall," said Raven.

"No wonder we didn't spot him on FLIR," said Rogan. Then he shined the light on the dead man's face. It was streaked with camouflage paint, just as the

Russian's had been. "Who the hell are you?" he muttered. "And why were you after Raven?" Then he added, "Do either of you recognize him?"

"Not me, boss," said Tracey.

Chasing an elusive memory, Raven frowned, trying to dredge up where she might have seen this man's face, but finally she shook her head and said, "It's not anyone I know, and thank heavens for that. I was so afraid it might be someone I trusted. Whoever he is, he's the guy behind it all."

"And you know this how?"

"He first told me that Minchenko was his man, and that the Russian had no doubt eliminated my sister before he himself was killed. He said I was a hard person to kill. When I asked him who hired him, he told me no one. And he said that when you want something done right you have to do it yourself. And he said that's why he was here instead of his surrogates. He raised his gun to shoot me, and that's when Sissy shot him."

Raven threw her arms around Rogan. "Oh, Nick, Sissy is alive. She's alive. She came here with several riders, and they all vanished because of the iron. She's become one of the hidden people, Nick, she's become one of the Sidhe."

Rogan called Agent Marks' private line and informed him of the assassination attempt and the death of the perpetrator.

A short time later, Patrick and Johnny flew back from Mercy Hospital. Nick told them what had happened, and then sent them back to Mercy to keep watch on Danny. At 2 a.m. Patrick called one of the satphones and reported that Danny was still critical, but the doctors thought he'd pull through. Nick asked them to stay in the city.

Agent Marks scratched his head and looked down at the corpse. "We'll run his prints through IAFIS and his DNA through CODIS and maybe discover who he is."

Medical Examiner Mallory Warbritton stood up and deadpanned, "I'm fairly certain the proximate cause of death was an arrow, probably the one sticking out from his back."

Evidence Tech Susan Grayson bagged the slain man's pistol. They would compare the bullet that had been dug out of Danny with one fired from that weapon—a Glock 21 with an MX Minireflex Moderator sound suppressor. A .45 caliber gun, it was the weapon that had shot the bullet that struck the rifle slung on Tracey's back. The impact had sent her tumbling downslope, but it was not the barrel that had hit her in the head; instead it had been a rock along the way, a rock now blood spotted, that had conked her.

Agent Marks turned to Raven and said, "It's damn dangerous being around you, Miss Conway."

"I think it's at an end," said Raven, smiling. Then she added, "Would you transmit a JPEG of this guy to George Allenby? I mean, if it's someone from the Trust, he would know who it is."

Agent Marks frowned. "Miss Conway, are you certain that this man was acting alone?"

"Look, I told you his exact words," said Raven, "and he was gloating, so I believe he was telling the truth. After all, I was a dead woman in his eyes; who would I

264 / Dennis L. McKiernan

tell?"

"He might have merely been taking credit where none was due," said Marks. "And there's always the chance that he is, was, in league with someone at Hunters Trust."

"Even so, I would like you to send his picture to Allenby."

Marks sighed, but nodded. Then he said, "I'll need a statement from your sister."

"I'll see what I can do," said Raven. "But she has a terrible reaction to iron and steel and electricity, and until you all clear out, and until I can get all of this stuff out of the house, she will remain in hiding in the woods."

Again Marks sighed. Finally he said, "Tell you what: I can authorize Susan to stay behind to take the statement, if that's all right with you. Your sister might feel more comfortable with a woman agent than with a man."

"We'll chopper your agent back," said Rogan.

Susan looked up and smiled and said, "Ooo, I've made it all the way to the big time." Then she laughed.

Robert Aikens came walking up behind the house and said, "There's a red Ford pickup down there that looks a lot like Betsy."

"That bastard," said Tracey. "While we were at Fred's, he weaseled his way up to the house by pretending to be Robert. And when he got close enough, he shot Danny. Goddamn him, I think I'll shoot the sonofabitch myself, even though he's already dead."

"Planning like that calls for good observation on his part," said Rogan. "And he somehow knew he could hide from our FLIR by getting in the space behind the waterfall. But the question is: how did he even know about the waterfall? Maybe if we identify who he is, we'll get that answer. Regardless, to get the upper hand he needed to split the party. So he shot Danny and carried him to where we would spot him. He deliberately didn't kill Danny, knowing that we would fly him to a hospital. The bastard figured we would first clear the house, and that would make the house the most likely place we would head for once the chopper with Danny was away. He counted on Raven heading back here while a couple of us got Danny to the chopper. Anyway, he lay in wait for Raven to pass by to ambush her. Even if Raven didn't pass by, he had gotten his odds down to just three people. Slick plan, but it had so very many things that could go wrong, yet he went ahead anyway. I suspect he was desperate. But why, I haven't a clue."

"Wrong or not, desperate or not," said Mallory Warbritton, "you sound as if you admire him."

"Not really. I mean, everything went just frigging perfectly for the sonofabitch, and if it hadn't been for Elizabeth showing up when she did . . ."

Rogan took a deep breath and slowly exhaled, then he and Raven each reached out for the other's hand.

"My God, Sissy, you look incredible, or as Robert puts it, ethereal." Raven paused and then added, "He said you were growing lovelier every day, but you're well beyond being simply lovely."

Had Raven not known better, she would have sworn her sister had just stepped out from a renaissance fair.

Elizabeth was dressed in a bright white gown with narrow gold striping around the neck and sleeves and curving under her breasts. Her long ash-blond hair framed her face and tumbled in a flow down her back to her slender hips. She smiled a dazzling smile, and with a piercing grey gaze, she looked from Nick to Raven. "You have grown lovelier, too, Rave, and I think I see the cause."

It was early afternoon, and Marks and his team had gone, but for Susan Grayson. They had taken the corpse with them. And the house had been cleared of all iron and steel and electronics. Susan had even been given a quill pen and a tin inkpot with which to write down Elizabeth's statement on loose sheets of paper. Susan had shaken her head in wry amusement at having to do so.

Raven, Elizabeth, Rogan, Tracey, and Susan sat at the table. Robert stood out on the veranda. He had broken into tears at seeing his Miss Elizabeth, and he remained out there, blowing his nose and sniffling.

"Ready?" asked Susan.

"Yes."

Susan dipped the quill into the inkpot and scribbled a title and a place-name and date, then asked, "Where have you been these past three weeks?"

"In the forest," said Elizabeth.

Susan dipped and scribbled, and then asked, "With someone?"

"A friend."

"Name?"

"He's not involved."

Susan nodded. "Did you know there was a massive

search going on for you?"

"What has that to do with the fact that I put an arrow through a man who was going to shoot my sister?"

Susan frowned and wrote that answer down. "Why do you think the searchers didn't find you?"

"I suppose they weren't where I was," said Elizabeth.

"It is a vast forest," said Raven.

Susan nodded. "Then it was just a coincidence that you happened to be in the right place at the right time with a bow and arrow?"

"I suppose you could say that," replied Elizabeth.

The questioning continued for another five minutes or so, and finally Susan said, "Please, just tell me in your own words what happened."

"I was in the forest with my bow and arrows and heading toward the house, when I saw a man holding my sister at gunpoint. I overheard him say that my sister was hard to kill, and when he said, 'Good-bye, Raven,' and aimed at her head, well, that's when I shot the arrow."

Susan wrote swiftly, dipping the quill often, and finally she signed the paper, and slid it over for Elizabeth's signature. Susan then looked at Nick and Tracey and said, "I don't quite know the protocol, but would you please be two impartial witnesses?" First Tracey and then Nick took the quill and signed.

"I'm going to run Susan into the city and then check on Danny," said Nick.

"I'm staying with Sissy," said Raven. "I'll see Danny later."

By this time Robert had quit blubbering and had

come into the house. And he said, "You two must have a lot to catch up on, so I'm going to leave you to yourselves, if that'll be safe, I mean."

Raven looked at Nick. Clearly, he was torn.

Elizabeth said, "Go. I *and mine* promise to keep her secure."

Nick looked at her. "And yours?"

Elizabeth nodded. "And mine."

Susan frowned, but said nothing.

Nick nodded, and then pulled Raven up from her chair and kissed her and whispered, "I love you."

Elizabeth smiled, knowingly.

Then Nick turned to the others and said, "Let's go."

Raven and Elizabeth watched them troop down the path and to the helicopter. And as it became airborne and vanished over the western ridge, Elizabeth turned to Raven and took her hand and said, "Come, I have something to show you and someone for you to meet."

And together hand in hand, just as they had done as children, they went through the house and out the back door and up and into the forest.

33

As they went upslope, Elizabeth said, "I am in love, Rave. Truly, sincerely, completely in love."

Raven smiled. "Robert said you had been acting 'moony' of late. What is your lover's name?"

"Anlon."

"Anlon. Does that name have a meaning?"

"Yes, and it fits him perfectly. It's Irish, and it means 'Champion.' Oh, Rave, the first time I saw him, it was like, like—"

"Il colpo di fulmine?" said Raven.

"Exactly!" said Elizabeth. "It was just as if a thunderbolt had struck my heart."

Raven smiled and said, "I have my own thunderbolt."

"Nicholas?"

"Yes."

"I'm so happy for you, Rave."

"Just as I am for you, Sissy."

Elizabeth looked back toward the house. "We've come far enough."

"Far enough for what?"

Elizabeth reached out and said, "Take my hand again."

Raven put her right hand in Elizabeth's left, and Elizabeth said, "It's just like stepping around an unseen corner. Now, come with me."

And she and Raven took a step to the right and they were . . . elsewhere.

The forest about them suddenly seemed brighter, somehow more vibrant, while at the same time more . . . tended, almost as if manicured. It was not the same as Hunters Wood, a less colorful but wilder place.

"Where are we?" said Raven, gazing about in amazement.

"In the distant past they called this Faerie," said Elizabeth. "Hunters Wood is one of the few remaining places with access to it."

"I am stunned," said Raven. "Truly stunned. How do you do that?"

"You have to think of going from here to there and then step that way. Given your heritage, Rave, you should be able to manage it."

Raven cocked an eyebrow of doubt.

Elizabeth smiled at her sister's skepticism, but said, "Come, Anlon awaits."

As they moved inward, Elizabeth said, "You must stay near me, for to do otherwise might bring on dire results."

"Dire results?"

"Do you remember the tales that Grandmother Meredith used to tell us, the ones about a mortal dancing and feasting in Faerie? He would spend a night in revelry, and when he emerged back into the mortal world, all his friends and family and acquaintances had grown old and died. Although but a single night had passed where he was, decades had elapsed back in his own world."

"Are you saying that's what would happen if we were to travel deep into this world?"

Elizabeth nodded. "I am saying that there are places herein where that would truly happen, and I would not have you be a victim of such a calamity."

"Twin paradox," said Raven.

Elizabeth frowned, an unspoken question on her lips.

"Einstein said that if one of a pair of twins took off from Earth and flew at the speed of light to a distant place, and when he got there he made a U-turn and flew back at the speed of light, then when he came back to Earth, he would be nearly the same age as he was when he left, but his twin, the one who stayed here, would have grown old in the interim. And the farther away one travels before making the U-turn, the more time passes back on Earth. It's all part of Einstein's theory of relativity. I don't understand it myself, but, in that example, apparently time can run at different rates, depending on where you are and how fast you are going."

"I don't understand it either," said Elizabeth, "but it is true that the farther one travels into Faerie, the more likely one will stumble upon a place where such time has elapsed when one returns."

Raven stopped stock still. "I don't want to lose Nick."

Elizabeth smiled. "Don't worry. You won't. There is but a minor time-shift here. Besides, we've arrived." They were at the edge of a small clearing in which stood a man.

He was tall and slender and had golden hair, and he was dressed a dark blue tunic trimmed in silver over a white silken shirt. He had on dark blue pants, and soft black boots. A silver belt graced his narrow waist, and an elegant indigo cloak cascaded from his shoulders. He moved with effortless ease as he came to meet them. His features had a symmetry seldom seen. His eyes held the hint of a tilt and were pale green, as of the finest jade, and when he smiled Raven could see his even, white teeth. His shoulder-length hair was held in place by a silver circlet upon his brow. He was perhaps the most handsome man Raven had ever seen.

"Caitlin, pure and innocent," said Anlon, inclining his head to Raven. "Ryelle has told me much about you."

"Pure and innocent?"

"The meaning of your Tuatha Dé Dannan name," said Anlon.

Raven smiled and said, "I'm not certain I fit the criteria."

"It's a variant of Cathleen," said Anlon. "and given that you are the new Bean Sealgaire presiding over Cathleens Haven, I find it most fitting."

Bean Sealgaire? Oh, wait: that's Irish for Lady Hunter.

"Thank you," said Raven. "What about Ryelle's name? What is its Tuatha Dé Dannan meaning."

"'Tis a variant of Rielle," said Anlon, "and has many, many meanings, for every name that ends in 'rielle' lends itself to my love."

"Brielle, Abrielle, Aubrielle, Gabrielle," rattled off Elizabeth. "Apparently I am supposed to take on the characteristics of all those names."

Anlon said, "Let us talk as we walk back toward Cathleens Haven. I would not have you stay overlong herein."

"Please," said Raven.

They chatted as they moved westward, and the farther they went, the darker it became, and when Anlon finally said his farewell, again Elizabeth took Raven's hand, and they stepped back into the mortal world.

Night had fallen, and choppers swept the valley and forest nearby.

"It appears we've upset your Nicholas," said Elizabeth.

"No doubt," said Raven. "After all, it was day when we entered Faerie, and now, in but a short time, it is full night."

"As I said, that's one of the perils of that place." Elizabeth embraced Raven. "I had better let you go."

As they held one another close, Raven said, "Oh, Sissy, I am so very glad you are alive and that you are my sister."

"Having you in my life is a joy, Rave," said Elizabeth. "Had that monster succeeded, my tears would fill that crescent moon and spill over onto the stars."

Releasing their embrace, Raven turned toward the house and Elizabeth toward the forest, and they each went to their beloveds.

A very relieved Nick called the search off, when Raven returned to his arms.

34

"I think Sissy might have become an immortal," said Raven, lying in Nick's embrace.

"Immortal?

"That's what they say of the Sidhe. Besides, Dr. Jameson says that Sissy has incredibly self-repairing mitochondria as well as self-repairing telomeres."

"And these are . . . ?"

"The mitochondria are the engines of the human living cells, and the telomeres are the caps on the ends of the DNA strands, and as long as they are in place, the strands do not unravel. Both of these things promote health and long lives."

"Ah, I see. And this is why Elizabeth is an immortal?"

"That, and I think her DNA changes made her so."

They lay quietly for moments, and then Raven said, "Sissy told me that I was a success and she a failure."

"How so?"

"I can withstand iron; she cannot."

"Ah. Does that mean you and she were some part of a breeding experiment?"

"Nick!"

Rogan laughed. "I'm just teasing you, my dear."

"I know, you big lug." Wincing a bit from the large bruise on her back where the .45 caliber slug had struck her Dragon Skin vest, Raven twisted in Nick's embrace and kissed him, then turned back spoon fashion.

"Sissy was out hunting mushrooms and greens, when the Russian sniper came, and her lover killed him from horseback with a lance, the force of the charge driving the sniper hindwards. So, instead of being dragged ten meters from where he was impaled to where Charlie and the searchers found him, he was shoved there on the shaft of a spear in the hands of a man on a horse in full gallop. The Russian's shot went wild."

Rogan yawned.

"Am I boring you, darling?" asked Raven.

"Not at all, love, but we must sleep sometime. After all, we've been running and shooting and ducking and getting Danny to the hospital and . . ."

"I know. But speaking of Danny, there's one more thing I need to share."

"All right."

"Danny was right about iron and the Sidhe. Anlon said they came to the 'land across the sea' when iron became too pervasive in Ireland. Of course we know they made a deal with Native Americans for this forest, since it is one of the ways between here and, um, Faerie. He said the Indians avoided the 'Ghost Woods,' the 'Woods where Spirits Wail and Thunder.' You see, the wail is their hunting horns, and the thunder is made by their galloping horses, which they brought here in a time when there were no horses at all on this continent. Sissy calls traveling between here and Faerie like stepping around an unseen corner, but I think of it more as stepping through the fabric of space-time, even though I don't know what that is. And the changes in Sissy allow her at will to 'see' across the boundary between this world and that, to 'see' the hidden ones when they are nearby, even though they are in Faerie watching this world. That's how Sissy first saw her lover: she could 'see' him, and she fell in love. Lastly, she said that she was a 'changeling,' because of the alteration of her DNA. —Oh, one more thing: when they were nearby and watching this world as I was searching for Sissy, that's when I felt their eyes on me. And both Johnny and I sensed them watching us, when the three of us hiked through the woods. By the way, that's how they make the woods so spooky to interlopers; they stand very close, but just barely on the other side of the tissue-thin border that separates their world from this one, and people can sense that something is nearly on top of them, like 'knowing' deep in your gut there's a dreadful thing under the bed or a monster in the closet, and it drives people away."

A single soft snore sounded in Raven's ear. Nick had fallen asleep.

Raven freed herself and turned and raised upon one elbow and looked into his face, beautiful in repose.

Oh, how I love you, Nicholas Rafferty Rogan, Jr. You are the light of my life. And even should my own DNA begin to change, nothing will ever change that. I will love you forever, my darling, come what may.

Raven smiled and turned and slipped back into his embrace and into slumber herself.

~

Sometime in the night and on the verge between this

world and that, a horn sounded and horses galloped past.

Tracey, on guard and wearing night-vision goggles, scanned the meadow as the hunt ran by, and she did not see a thing.

Moments later, both Johnny and Patrick stood at her side, and listened as the pursuit ran up the western slope and beyond.

Neither Raven nor Nick awakened.

35

Two days later, Agent Marks appeared. "We've identified the shooter your sister killed."

"Who is he?" asked Raven. "Or rather, who was he?"

"Well the prints on file named him as James Jackson. He was a hired killer—never convicted—who disappeared eighteen years ago. We thought that his mob life had caught up with him and that he would be found in a landfill in the Jersey marshes. But not so. Instead, your George Allenby identified him as Jackson Fenn, the man who was to marry your cousin Millicent."

"What?" Raven looked from Marks to Nick and back. "My cousin Millicent's husband to be? The one who founded Fennway Timber? —Oh, God, the invitation!"

Raven sprang to her feet and shuffled through the pile of Trust papers squirreled away on a corner table. "Here it is." She pulled the wedding announcement from the envelope and looked at the stocky groom-to-be. "And there he is. Damn! Why didn't I recognize him?"

"His face was streaked with camo paint," said Nick.

"Even so, I should have . . ."

"Not really," said Marks.

"What possible motive could he have had?" asked Raven.

"Our genealogical expert discovered—following you and Elizabeth—Millicent Alderton is next in line to become Trustee of Hunters Trust. Also, our contacts out there tell us that Fennway Timber is on the verge of going under. James Jackson, AKA Jackson Fenn, her intended husband also knew she was next in line, and he saw Hunters Trust or Hunters Wood as his salvation."

"But by the terms of the Trust, he couldn't harvest this forest," said Raven, "and Millicent knew that. But are you saying that Millicent herself was part of—?"

"No, no, not Millicent," said Marks. "We don't think *she* was involved in Jackson's scheme. You see, we looked at Jackson's computer, and it was clear that he had researched Hunters Wood, and that led him to the Trust. He discovered Hunters Trust was a major—if not the *only*—client of Allenby, Allenby, and Cartwright, and with the huge law firm that is, well, that meant the Trust was quite considerable. And so, his main motive was to get control of the Trust through Millicent, and if the Trust was not of considerable wealth, well, his fallback was to get control of Hunters Wood. Yes, Millicent knew that the woods were sacrosanct, but Jackson didn't. Further, we don't think Jackson had any idea as to the size of the fortune Millicent would have access to, were she to become the Trustee. Whether or not he did, we think he duped her into the upcoming marriage, and to speed things along he sent his old acquaintances after you. You see, Millicent had asked Allenby to help her find several cousins so that she could invite them to her wedding. When George Allenby found out that you were on your way to visit your sister, and knowing how close you three had been in childhood, he told her where you would be, and she in turn mentioned it to Jackson. That's how he knew where to send the Russian sniper. —Oh, and the unknown man of the five who broke into your house—he's Jackson's little brother, Tommy, AKA Tommy Rot.

Raven cocked an eyebrow. "Tommy Rot?"

"Was a mob enforcer in the garbage hauling business."

"Ah," said Raven.

"Anyway," said Marks, "Tommy had connections to the Russians, and Jackson probably asked Tommy to arrange for the hit. Incidentally, we are fairly certain your cousin, Millicent, was completely unaware of Tommy, or of Jackson's true intentions as she went forward with her upcoming wedding to him."

"Oh, my. Poor Millicent. How appalling." Raven took a deep breath and then let it out

No one spoke for moments, but finally Nick looked at Marks and asked, "Is that it?"

"Yep. —Oh, wait, I brought all your guns back, including that brass cannon of a double-barrel shotgun. No one at the Bureau had ever seen a weapon like that before."

"Then I assume the case is closed," said Nick.

"It is indeed. George Allenby got to Director Kelley, and that sucker of a file is now shut tight."

Raven looked at Nick and said, "Let's go into town. I need to call Allenby, but I especially need to call Millicent, and I don't want to suffer the awful satellite phone delay."

~

On the way into town, Raven said, "We need a suitable cover story to explain Sissy's absence to all those involved in the search."

"How about we tell them the truth . . . but not quite all of it," said Rogan. "We'll embellish it just slightly by saying she simply had taken enough gear and supplies and had fled into the woods to escape the people who had tried to kill her. The whole town knows about the assassination attempts. At least by hiding out with enough camping supplies, staying in the forest for three weeks would seem reasonable and quite mundane. And we can say where she fled was beyond the range of the search. I know it's a rather lame story, but it's mundane enough that people will not blow it out of proportion."

Raven slowly nodded. "The sensation is that people were trying to kill her—me, too—but given that we are involved with the Trust, that's the truth, and one they will easily accept. And, come to think of it, the fact that she fled into the forest is the truth as well."

They rode along in silence for a moment, and then Raven said, "You are a sneaky one, Nicholas Rafferty Rogan." And then she broke out in laughter.

The autumn air was crisp and the foliage of the forest had turned the woodland into a beautiful gold and scarlet and russet thing of wonder. Three months had passed, and Danny was healthy again. Johnny Redwing and Tracey and Pat had returned from South America, and they all sat with Raven and Nick and sipped Negra Modelos in the large gazebo down in the meadow.

The pavilions and metal detectors were long gone,

the wedding having taken place two weeks past. It had been rather private, even though there were nearly a hundred guests, a strange mixture of corporate culture and a rather large gathering of elegant people who seemed to have just stepped out from the Renaissance.

George Allenby and Taylor Raines and several officers of the Trust had attended, along with Sissy's agent, Gray Thompson, and Raven's, the Traynor brothers. Fredericka Johanna Olsen had come with Robert Aikens, along with Jack Miller, who had arrived in Raven's fully repaired Porsche. Agents Marks and Grayson had come, as well as Jack Sloan, Rogan's exec from Blackledge. They had all shedded metal and electronics at the entrance to the valley, where limousines and Mercedes and BMWs shared space with a lone pickup truck named Betsy.

Millicent Alderton, the new CEO of Fennway Timber, had come, her company buoyed up by the insurance settlement from the peculiar death of its founder . . . that and a mysterious infusion of cash from an anonymous benefactor. And she had been welcomed to Cathleens Haven, a place she had visited as a young girl, a place she had once innocently described in full to Jackson Fenn.

Nick's father and mother had come from the Southwest to see their only child wed, the senior Rogan walking with a slight limp, beautiful Hiroko on his arm.

Senior threw a thumb over his shoulder and asked Junior, "What's with the shakedown, my boy? They took my belt and gave me this one. —Oh, and my keys, too."

"And my cell phone," said Mama. "And a few things from my purse."

"That's nothing," said Jack Miller standing nearby and wearing moccasins. "They took my steel-toed shoes. I always—I mean *always*—wear them whenever I go anywhere . . . from the moment I get out of bed till the moment I get back in, showers excepted, of course. I mean, you never know when you're gonna drop a hammer on your foot or an engine block for that matter."

"Do you drop a lot of things?" asked Dad Rogan.

"I've been known to do my share," said Miller, grinning ruefully. "Besides, I have sensitive toes."

Dad Rogan turned to his son and said, "I'd still like to know why the shakedown."

"We have some guests coming who are allergic to iron," explained the junior Rogan.

Hiroko looked up from her tiny four eleven and demanded, "Where is this woman you have rushed off to love?"

"Honey," said the senior Rogan, "he told me upon seeing her the very first time it was all of a nanosecond before he knew she was the one for him. No different from the way we did it, back when I first saw you riding a wave, Surfer Girl."

"Come, I'll introduce you," said Nick, Jr.

"No, no. Mustn't see the bride before the ceremony. Just point and I will find her."

Nick pointed toward the house, and Hiroko headed for the path.

"Come on, Dad," said Junior, "let's go get a flute of Champaign."

Senior grinned. "I thought you'd never ask." And he

threw an arm over his son's shoulder, and toward one of the pavilions they went.

And just before the ceremony, from the forest and on horseback a cavalcade of beautiful riders had ridden down into the meadow, Ryelle and Anlon at their head.

It was then that Johnny Redwing and Danny Mack had finally met Elizabeth, and they were both in unrequited love with her.

George Allenby, as a surrogate father, had given Raven away. Elizabeth Ryelle Conway stood as Raven's maid of honor, and Jack Sloan as Nick's best man.

The ceremony had been lovely.

And because of the confiscation of all things bearing electronics and iron, there had been no pictures or camcorder tapes or disks or cell phone shots of the affair. The only thing that had appeared in any paper— and that one the Benton Weekly *Bugle*—was the simple announcement that Raven Caitlin Conway and Nicholas Rafferty Rogan, Jr., were wed at Cathleens Haven. The Trust had gone to lengths to keep all else from the news—rumors and facts alike.

But now, two weeks later, all the friends, family, and guests were gone, having given their congratulations to the bride and groom, and all that was left as a reminder was the wooden gazebo where the vows had been exchanged, a gazebo held together by pegs.

The structure now served not only as a gathering spot but also as a place to store equipment—guns, satphones, laptops, and the like—in built-in brass-bound chests.

It was late in the day, and twilight covered the land, and stars had begun to appear. And Raven and Nick and Danny, Johnny, Tracey, and Patrick sat in the gazebo and sipped beer and "told each other lies."

They were laughing over Danny's description of the booby trap he had set for Sergeant Too Tall Randall when next he would have opened his duffel bag— something to do with a shaving cream bomb waiting to go off. And as Danny giggled and Johnny snapped a remote salute to Randall, Nick's satphone rang.

Nick picked it up and triggered it on. "Rogan here."

A short phrase murmured in Nick's ear.

"Hi, Jack." Nick looked at the others and mouthed "Jack Sloan."

"I wonder what the exec wants?" asked Patrick.

"Probably to drop us in another fricking swamp," said Tracey.

"Ooo, sounds exciting," said Danny. "Leech soup."

"Ah, you dumb mick," growled Johnny, "everyone knows leeches suck."

Raven was still laughing, when Nick clicked off the phone.

"Saddle up, gang. You too, Raven Caitlin Conway Rogan, we've a mission to fulfill."

"What's up, *boss*," asked Raven, grinning as she got to her feet and glanced at the chopper nearby.

"Well, Raven, Sloan has a lead on your mother, Avelaine. . . ."

"The Game is afoot. Not a word! Into your clothes and come!"

S. Holmes
"The Adventure of the Abby Grange,"
by Arthur Conan Doyle

About the Author

Photo by Silhouette Studios

Dennis L McKiernan lives in Tucson, Arizona, with his wife of 55 years (as of 2012), Martha Lee (MLee).

40478923R00170

Made in the USA
Middletown, DE
27 March 2019